THE LAST STAGE

THE LAST STAGE

BRUCE SCIVALLY

HENRY GRAY HG PUBLISHING

Granada Hills, CA

"Select books for selective readers"

Copyright © 2022 Bruce Scivally
All rights reserved.

No part of this book may be reproduced in any manner whatsoever without written permission except in the case of brief quotations embodied in critical articles and reviews.

For information, contact:info@henrygraypublishing.com

Publisher's Cataloging-in-Publication Data
Names: Scivally, Bruce, 1961-.
Title: The last stage / Bruce Scivally.
Description: Granada Hills, CA : Henry Gray Publishing, 2022. |
Identifiers: LCCN 2022916039 | ISBN 9798986680590 (pbk.) | ISBN 9798986680583 (ebook)
Subjects: LCSH: Earp, Wyatt, 1848-1929 -- Fiction. | Earp, Josephine Sarah Marcus, 1861-1944 -- Fiction. | Holliday, John Henry, 1851-1887 -- Fiction. | Bereavement -- Fiction. | Loss (Psychology) -- Fiction. | Outlaws – Fiction. | Tombstone (Ariz.) – Fiction. | Vidal (Calif.) -- Fiction. | BISAC: FICTION / Action & Adventure. | FICTION / Family Life / Marriage & Divorce. | FICTION / Westerns.
Classification: LCC PS3619.C58 L37 2022 | DDC 813 S38—dc23
LC record available at https://lccn.loc.gov/2022916039

Library of Congress Control Number: 2022916039

Made in the United States of America.

Published by Henry Gray Publishing, P.O. Box 33832,
Granada Hills, California, 91394.

All names, characters, places, events, locales, and incidents in this work are fictitious creatinos from the author's imagination or used in a fictitious manner. No character in this book is a reflection of a particular person, event, or place. The opinions expressed are those of the characters and should not be confused with the author's.

For more information or to join our mailing list, visit HenryGrayPublishing.com.

The author looked across the table to his subject who, like him, concentrated on putting together a puzzle with many irregularly-shaped pieces.

"Wyatt," said the author, "just so you know, I've taken some liberties with your story."

Wyatt's eyes narrowed. "What kind of liberties?"

"Considerable."

For the true stories of Wyatt Earp and his wife, Josephine (Sadie) Earp, please see:

Wyatt Earp: The Life Behind the Legend
    by Casey Tefertiller (Wiley, 1999)

and

Lady at the OK Corral: The True Story of Josephine Marcus Earp
    by Ann Kirschner (Harper Perennial, 2014)

Chapter 1

SUPPOSE

January 12, 1929

   Rain fell.
   The night was dark as pitch. Far in the distance, a hazy light approached. It appeared at first as one white circle, then, as it came closer, it separated into two. They were the headlights of a 1928 Ford Model T, chugging forward through the pounding rain, engine thrumming.
   The car rolled past dark streetlights standing like silent sentinels and stopped at the sidewalk outside a courtyard complex. The driver, Stuart Lake, a 39-year-old war veteran who'd gypsied through a variety of jobs including newspaperman, wrestling promoter, press aide, and finally writer for magazines and movies, stepped out, wearing a rain slicker.
   Up a few steps from the sidewalk were a baker's dozen of small single-story bungalows arranged like a horseshoe, with six on each side facing each other across a central courtyard, and a larger two-story one at the end. Like dandelions, thought Lake—ever since Hollywood became the nation's picture-making capital, these low-cost housing developments were springing up all over.
   With a slight limp, he trotted up a walkway into the courtyard. There were no lights on in any of the homes, other than the glow of candlelight and lanterns. Lake stepped onto the porch of one of the bungalows, shook off the rain, and knocked gently on the door.
   After a moment, he heard footsteps approaching from inside. The door was opened by Josephine "Sadie" Earp, a short, stout woman of 67, her hair dyed jet black. On all of his previous interactions with her, Sadie had come across as tough and severe, but tonight, for the first time,

Lake saw her vulnerability; she was distressed, a hard woman made soft from the prospect of losing her lifelong companion.

"Mr. Lake! Thank God!" she said, dabbing at her red-rimmed eyes with a handkerchief. She held the door open for him. As he entered, he noticed something he hadn't seen on prior visits—a third of the way down from the top of the door, on the right side, was a mezuzah, a narrow decorative box. Lake knew the box contained a rolled-up parchment, upon which was written words affirming belief in one God: Sh'ma Yisrael, meaning "Hear, O Israel," from a prayer that continued "the Lord is our God, the Lord is one." Lake had enough friends in the motion picture business to be aware of Jewish customs, so before stepping across the threshold, he touched the mezuzah with his fingers, then touched his fingers to his lips. He saw the slight flicker of a grateful smile on Sadie's face.

Once inside, Lake wiped his shoes on a doormat and shucked off his rain slicker. Underneath, he wore a casual suit and necktie, dressed for paying respects. Sadie took his slicker and hat and hung them on a peg behind the door.

"Power's been out all afternoon," she said, trying to make small talk to normalize an abnormal situation.

Lake nodded. "Looks like it's off everywhere east of Fairfax."

The dingy room was small and cramped—a kitchen sink and stove in one corner, partially hidden behind a pull curtain, and a tiny bathroom in the opposite corner with a shower/bathtub combo, a wash basin, and a toilet all tightly packed together; the bathroom was the only separate room with a door. Near one wall was a dining table, on top of which was an unfinished puzzle and a Menorah. The Menorah had only a couple of partially-melted candles in it, casting a warm, faint glow.

As he quickly scanned the dim room, Lake saw some mismatched chairs, a small half-bookcase overflowing with books beneath a few weeks' worth of newspapers stacked on top, and a short cabinet supporting a gramophone. On the walls were a handful of family portraits, and a mirror covered by a black cloth.

Against the opposite wall from the dining area was a bed, a few chairs arranged around it. On the small table next to it, a single candle burned, illuminating the frail figure of a tall man supine beneath the covers. A black-coated doctor hovered over him, administering an injection into the frail man's inner elbow.

As Lake approached them, he was immediately struck by the slight, distasteful odor of ammonia noticeable around the bed, emanating from the slender man upon it. Even in the dim candlelight, the man appeared pale, with receding white hair and chevron mustache, lips slightly parted, eyes closed. It was Wyatt Earp, once one of the most feared lawmen of the West, now largely forgotten in an era when pulp magazines and motion pictures made heroes of outlaws like Billy the Kid and Jesse James.

Sadie came over to make introductions, saying, "Dr. Shurtleff, this is Mr. Lake. He's that writer I told you about." Dr. Fred Shurtleff, a clean-shaven, bespectacled man in his fifties, acknowledged Lake with a polite nod as he taped a piece of cotton over the injection site in Wyatt's arm.

"How is he?" asked Lake.

"Hanging on," replied Dr. Shurtleff. "'Bout all I can say."

"He was moaning a few minutes ago, before you got here," said Sadie.

"Expect he's in considerable pain," said Dr. Shurtleff. "The morphine should help." He put the hypodermic needle and bottle back into his doctor's bag.

A little brown-and-white Border Collie mix, Earpie, crawled out from under the bed and sniffed around Lake's shoes. Lake had met Earpie before, so the dog already had Lake's scent and didn't bother to bark. Lake bent down to acknowledge the affable pet, rubbing his head.

Sadie took a seat beside the bed, resuming her vigil. "I'm scared, Mr. Lake," she said. "He hasn't been in his right mind. Sometimes, I hear him jabbering away, talking to Doc Holliday, or Virgil, or Morgan. But no one's here."

Dr. Shurtleff looked at her with sympathy in his eyes. "They do that sometimes," he said. "Like the body's shutting down, but the brain's still active. Hallucinating. Or maybe... I don't know. I sometimes wonder if it has something to do with what people say about your life passing before your eyes when..."

"Don't say it!" snapped Sadie. Then, after a silent moment, she said quietly, "He'll pull through this. He has to." She looked down at her hands, folded in her lap. "He just has to."

Dr. Shurtleff cast a concerned glance at Lake, who moved to the other side of the bed and leaned down to speak into Wyatt's ear, "Wyatt— it's Stuart Lake." To Lake's eyes, Wyatt appeared to be comatose. More

THE LAST STAGE

to soothe Sadie than anything else, Lake added, "Better get up now. I've got a few more questions for you." There was no response from Wyatt, no indication that he could hear Lake, or that he was even aware of anything happening around him.

Lake and Dr. Shurtleff took seats on either side of the bed, joining Sadie in her vigil. In their hearts, both men knew that, despite all Sadie's hopes and prayers, the odds were against Wyatt's recovery, and both also knew that she would be utterly lost without him. They were there to honor Wyatt in his final moments, but more importantly, to give support and comfort to Sadie—as much as she would allow them to—and guide her through this depressingly bleak ordeal.

Earpie jumped up onto the foot of the bed, waddled up beside Wyatt's prone body, and cuddled against his chest. After a moment, there was a slight twitching of the fingers of Wyatt's right hand. He extended his arm enough to touch Earpie's face, and rub the top of the dog's head with his thumb. Earpie licked Wyatt's fingers.

Seeing this, Sadie let out a little gasp, tears in her eyes. She reached out and wrapped her hand around his. His fingers slowly closed over hers.

"You see that?" she asked, astonished and elated. She leaned closer to Wyatt's ear, and said, "Talk to me, Shug. Speak to your Sadie-Belle."

Wyatt remained still for a moment, then his eyes fluttered, half-opened. With a hopeful note in her voice, Sadie said, "Wyatt? Hon?"

Wyatt's eyes held a dreamy, unfocused, faraway look. And when he spoke, it was in a faint but clear voice:

"Suppose...

... suppose..."

His fingers relaxed. His eyes slowly closed.

And his still-active mind descended into a twilight realm...

Chapter 2

HOLLYWOOD

Wyatt felt as though he were spiraling in a black void, weightless, drifting. He heard a woman's voice call his name…

"Wyatt…!"

Was it Sadie? Or a voice from even farther back in his past?

"Wyatt…!"

Aurilla?

And then overlapping it came a man's voice—

"Quiet!"

Suddenly, bright sunlight flooded onto the scene, dispersing the darkness, and Wyatt found himself standing straight as a pine tree on a dusty street between rustic buildings, populated by horses, men in cowboy hats and boots, and women in ankle-length skirts. Was he back in Wichita? Dodge City? Tombstone? No, wait—there were also men milling about in contemporary clothing, clearly not from the 1880s. And at one end of the street was a tripod with a boxy motion picture camera atop it.

He heard the man's voice again—"Quiet on the set! Okay, all my townspeople over here…" It was an assistant director, giving instructions to extras, the people seen milling in the background of movie scenes.

And now Wyatt recognized this place. He was in the San Fernando Valley, Iverson Ranch in Chatsworth, the preferred location for filmmakers looking for dramatic rock formations and remote vistas, a relatively short drive northwest from the studios in Los Angeles. This is where the picture-makers went to film their cowboy sagas. And here he was, standing in front of a weathered dry goods store, with black tarps behind it to hide the fact that it was nothing more than a storefront and two side walls, what the filmmakers called a façade. Inside, it was hollow and empty—like these Western films on which he was sometimes called to consult, a sideline that allowed him to occasionally make a little ready cash. He watched as the film crew arranged the camera and put rocks in the dusty street where the actors would stand—"marks" they called them—to be sure they remained in focus range of the camera.

Somehow, Wyatt had traveled back in time. But not far back—his hands were still wrinkled, and his reflection in the window of one of the fake buildings showed his hair remained snow white and thinning. But his eyes, as ever, were piercingly blue. His 170 pounds were distributed over a lithe, fit, broad-shouldered six-foot frame. Despite the heat, he looked dignified in his Oxford shoes, gray three-piece suit, necktie, and bowler hat. He could have passed for a retired banker.

A tall, dark-haired cowboy with a handsome, angular face came up to him. "You okay, Wyatt?" he asked. It was William S. Hart, one of Wyatt's many Hollywood acquaintances, and one of the most popular actors in the world. Hart had first come to Hollywood in 1907 to reprise the role he'd originated on Broadway in 1899, playing Messala in an adaptation of the best-selling novel, *Ben Hur*. When he eventually settled in Hollywood, Hart switched to cowboy roles and found favor with the cinema-going public as the embodiment of Western chivalry, usually portraying a bad man who found redemption through the love of a good woman.

Seeing the faraway look in Wyatt's eyes, Hart said, "This take you back to the West you remember?"

"Not quite," said Wyatt. "I remember the streets being busier, noisier, and full of a lot more horse shit." Hart smiled. Though a man of patrician tastes himself, he wasn't put off by Wyatt's profane bluntness. He respected the older man, whom he felt had earned the right to speak his mind, however coarse it might be.

The two men watched as director Clifford Smith positioned actors in front of the corral fence. The performers were dressed as legendary gunslingers—Calamity Jane, Bat Masterson, and Doc Holliday. An actor named Bert Lindley was portraying Earp, with dark mustache, round-topped hat, and six-shooters. Wyatt regarded them like they were a bunch of kids play-acting at being grown-ups. He'd known the originals, or at least Bat and Doc, and found these powder-faced facsimiles a poor substitute.

"Bill, we're ready for you," said an assistant director. Hart—who was playing Wild Bill Hickock, though without Wild Bill's bushy mustache and long hair—stepped in front of the other actors.

"Is this where you want me, Cliff?" he asked the director.

Smith glanced over at him. "That's fine, Bill." Smith looked to Wyatt. "How's it look, Mr. Earp?"

Wyatt stepped forward and eyed Lindley up and down. "Shoulders back," he said. "Head high. I never slouch." Lindley stiffened his stance. Wyatt took a cigar from his pocket and stuck it between Lindley's lips. Then he pulled out a box of matches, struck one, and lit the cigar.

"Don't know why they've only got Wyatt Earp in one scene," grumbled Lindley. "They ought to make a whole movie just about you."

Wyatt never knew how to take a compliment from actors. Was Lindley saying this because he truly believed Wyatt's story was worthy of a motion picture, or did he think if there was an entire film devoted to Wyatt, it would mean a starring part for him? What Lindley didn't know is that Wyatt and Hart had been speaking off and on for some time about the possibility of a film, but if it happened, it would star Hart, not this glorified day-player. Wyatt just answered with a slight smile, looking Lindley over. The actor really bore no resemblance to him but, hell, this was the movies, and Wyatt liked getting paid.

"Look mean," he said. "And hook your thumb in your belt, like this."

Lindley did as he was told, mimicking Wyatt's stance. Wyatt nodded his approval, then said to Hart, "You know, I never actually met Calamity Jane or Wild Bill Hickock."

Hart shrugged. "Poetic license."

Poetic lying was more like it, thought Wyatt. He gave Hart a look that signaled he was in on the joke, that he knew he was here to provide authenticity to an inauthentic situation. They'd ask for his opinion, but they weren't about to let it get in the way of telling an entertaining story. More than anything, they just wanted to be able to publicize that Wyatt Earp had given the film his seal of approval. And now he had. He ambled to a row of canvas chairs behind the camera and took a seat.

Smith, standing next to the cameraman, said loudly, "Alright, let's go." Then, eyeing the actors closely, called, "Roll 'em." The cameraman began turning the hand crank on the side of the Bell & Howell in a steady rhythm. Then Smith said, "Aaannnd….. action."

THE LAST STAGE

Wyatt watched from the sidelines as Wild Bill—played by Hart—faced off against the dastardly McQueen—played by a sturdy actor named James Farley. Smith shouted out directions, the actors doing as he commanded.

"Okay, Bill," said the director, "You see McQueen. McQueen looks at all the gunmen. But he's not scared. His hand goes down to his pistol. Now, draw on three—one, two, THREE!"

Both Hart and Farley whipped up their guns—Hart more slowly than his nemesis. The blanks discharged—first Farley's, then Hart's—but Farley was the one who dropped to his knees and plopped over on his side, playing dead. Smith called, "Cut!" Farley stood back up, brushing himself off. Hart came over to Wyatt and said, "Another baddie bites the dust."

Wyatt gave him a rueful look. "Except he was faster on the draw. Should 'a been you sniffing dirt."

"Oh, we'll fix that," said Hart. "Next we'll get a close shot of me whipping up my gun and shooting, and then we'll get a cut of Jim clutching his chest like he's been hit, and when we put 'em together in the editing room, it'll look like I'm faster. Movie magic."

"Ain't that something," chided Wyatt. "All those years I thought I needed to be quick, but all I really needed was movie magic."

~ • ~

The work day ended as the sun set over the rocky hills, changing their color from gray and tan to a pastel orange hue. Crewmen broke down the camera gear, while wranglers loaded the horses into carriers.

Wyatt strode over to a table where the purser was counting out cash to the day players and horse wranglers. When he got to the head of the line, the purser asked, "Name?"

"Wyatt Earp."

The purser counted out a few dollars, and as he handed it over, he said, "I didn't think you were real."

Wyatt took the money and said, "Sometimes I don't think so myself."

After collecting his pay, Wyatt lined up with all the other actors and crew waiting for the trolley bus to come and ferry them back to their cars. Most of the actors were still in costume, standing under an awning jutting from one of the building façades, waiting for the shuttles. Hart waved Wyatt up to the front of the line, where he stood with Smith and Lindley.

Following a little polite small talk, Hart asked Wyatt, "How's your book coming?"

Wyatt gave a little shrug. "Me and Sadie are still working with that reporter, Stuart Lake."

"How'd you settle on him?"

"Well, he'd done a little work for Bat Masterson at the newspaper when he was back east. And after that, he was a publicity man for Teddy Roosevelt's last campaign."

"Pretty accomplished, then," said Hart.

"Yep," said Wyatt. "But mostly, it's 'cause he'd been hit by a truck during the war. I figured if he could survive Bat, and Teddy, and being hit by a truck, then he might be able to survive dealing with Sadie."

Hart laughed, then said, "I'm just glad you finally got a real author and not that man Flood."

Wyatt chortled. John Flood had originally been hired nearly twenty years earlier to be his mining engineer. He was also a fast and accurate typist, and as time went on, became an unpaid secretary for Wyatt and Sadie, keeping track of their accounts. They figured that, given their close association with Flood for all those years, he'd know them well enough to tell their story as they—or at least Sadie—wanted it told. But as Wyatt would learn, just as it took more to be a lawman than being quick on the draw, it took more to be a writer than being quick on the keyboard. The book that Flood produced was a florid, amateurish manuscript, its pace constantly interrupted by the sound effects he'd written into it, such as "Crack! Crack! Crack!" and "ing! ing! ing!" during the gunfights.

Hart had championed the project, even helping to get the manuscript first to *The Saturday Evening Post*, who declined to serialize it in their magazine, and then to one New York publisher after another. When they all turned it down, he went further afield; an editor with Indianapolis-based Bobbs-Merrill Publishing wrote Hart that the story got lost in "the pompous manner of its telling." Eventually, it became clear not only to Hart and Wyatt but also to Sadie, who had delighted in the book, that there was no sense in continuing to beat the bushes when all they were really doing was beating a dead horse.

"Lesson learned," Wyatt said to Hart. "Don't hire your accountant to write your memoirs."

A trolley bus pulled up with placards on each side touting the currently filming William S. Hart extravaganza, with a painting of Hart, six guns held chest-high and ready to blaze, and the words: "COMING SOON: WILLIAM S. HART AS *WILD BILL HICKOCK.*"

"Here we go," said Hart, as the bus rolled to a stop. He stepped up into it and took a seat in front, Wyatt following and sitting next to him. Smith and Lindley took the seat behind them. When the bus was full, the driver began the short haul down to the gas station parking lot where the cast and crew left their cars.

As they jostled along over the rough dirt road, Hart continued, "Just got to get the new book done, Wyatt. Picture companies aren't that interested unless they can say a film's based on a book."

"Reckon as long as you play me it'll be alright," said Wyatt, then—looking back over his shoulder to Lindley—added, "No offense." This was Wyatt's wish, that Hart would portray him in a Hollywood movie. Wyatt had also consulted on films for Tom Mix, but Mix was more of a showman, an expert horseman and crack shot who worked in the traveling Miller Brothers Wild West Show before he rose to fame as the star of simplistic, cartoonish Westerns with clear villains and dashing heroes and lots of derring-do action stunts. Hart's Westerns were more adult, more nuanced—though still a far cry from the reality Wyatt had lived. Turning back to Hart, he said, "I just hope there's enough meat on the bone to make a movie."

"All the things you've done, we ought to have material for three of four pictures," said Hart.

"I appreciate you sticking with it."

"Oh, I promise you, I'm not giving up," Hart replied enthusiastically. "I'll keep hammering away at it until the hot place freezes over."

Wyatt nodded. He didn't give his trust easily, but he felt he could trust Hart.

Taking advantage of the break in conversation, Lindley leaned forward. "Mr. Earp, what was it really like?" he asked.

Wyatt craned his head around to look at Lindley. "What was what like?"

"Tombstone."

Wyatt snorted, "Honestly, Tombstone was rough, but if you want to talk about a place absolutely crawling with claim jumpers, crooked politicians and outright frauds, ain't none hold a candle to Los Angeles."

It wasn't the answer Lindley expected, but it made him and the other men laugh. Wyatt smiled, too—until the bus hit a pothole. Jolted in his seat, he winced, instinctively putting his hand to his side.

The gnawing pain in his gut was growing worse by the day.

Chapter 3

SADIE

Wyatt Earp's 1923 Packard Single Six sedan rolled up and parked on the street outside the housing court. Climbing out of the car, he ambled up the walkway to his bungalow. Before he even stepped up onto the porch, he could hear Earpie barking from inside. As soon as he opened the door, the small dog jumped up to his waist, over and over, eager for attention and yapping excitedly, his tail spinning 'round like a maple seed on a spring breeze.

Wyatt shushed the mutt, petting him and scratching him behind his ears. "Whoa, Earpie," he said. "Settle down, now. You hungry? Where's your ma?"

He strolled farther into the room, looking about. There were dishes piled in the sink, and newspaper pages cast haphazardly to the floor in bunches beside the dining table. A coat was thrown over the couch, and there was a partially-eaten slice of toast topped with jam on the table, beside an open, half-empty grape jam jar.

Wyatt was a tidy man. He didn't like messes. But he knew what all these little signs pointed to, and he figured a mess was brewing. Suspicious and worried, he strode over to the bed. Beside it was an old pair of worn-out, scuffed boots, one upright, the other on its side. He picked the latter one up and turned it upside down. An envelope fell out. This was the envelope that usually held his cash, and which he thought was safely hidden in the boot's toe. Even before he looked he could tell the envelope was empty.

Leaving Earpie behind, and with his ire rising, Wyatt stomped out of the bungalow and marched purposefully down the street. He passed a drug store, a grocery store, and a newsstand with a rack of pulp magazines, most of them featuring Western stories with paintings of cowboys and gunfighters on their covers, and then he entered a corner cafe.

He stepped to the counter, where a too-friendly host, Pete, stood beside a cash register.

"Afternoon, Mr. Earp," said Pete. "Care for a—"

"She here?" asked Wyatt, sternly. Pete's guilty look told Wyatt all he needed to know. "Thought I told you not to let her in."

Pete shrugged, saying, "If you can't handle her, what makes you think I can?"

Wyatt continued past tables where a few diners were seated and went to a door at the back of the room. He gave three short, sharp knocks on a speakeasy grille. A little door behind it opened, revealing a man's eyes.

"Open up, Joe," commanded Wyatt.

"Wyatt, I—"

"Now, 'fore I kick it in."

Joe reluctantly opened the door, and Wyatt stepped inside to find a half-dozen tables, a bar fully stocked with liquor, a bartender, and, at one table in the corner, Sadie, playing poker with three oily-looking gamblers. Ned was in his 20s, a baby-faced kid in a too-big coat. Roberto, a 30-something Mexican, had the build of a bullfighter and the brilliantined hair of a Valentino, while Miller, 50s, looked like a businessman visiting from the Midwest.

Wyatt marched to the table and loomed over Sadie. He could see she was in her cups, eyelids slightly drooping. And she was obviously losing. There were only a couple of dollars in front of her, while in front of the others were much bigger piles of money. His money. Within reach of all of them was a nearly-empty bottle of whiskey, much of which Wyatt surmised had ended up in Sadie, judging from the state of her inebriation in comparison to the men.

Calm but insistent, Wyatt said, "Step away, Sadie."

With a slight slur in her voice, she replied, "Beat it, 'fore you jinxsh me."

"Time to come home."

"When I finish thish hand."

Wyatt took a quick glance at her cards. "It's already finished. You're just too soused to see it."

THE LAST STAGE

Baby-faced Ned snarled, "Butt out, Grandpa. This ain't your business."

Miller, with a stubby cigar in his mouth, gave Ned a sharp look, saying, "Hush, boy! You know who you're speaking to?"

"A fella 'bout to get his head spilt if he don't scram."

Miller cautioned him, "That's Wyatt Earp!"

Ned just shrugged and blurted, "So?" Obviously, he'd never heard of the Old West lawman.

Wyatt bristled. Sadie could see that this might turn very ugly very quickly. Wishing to be spared the embarrassment of any commotion, she touched Wyatt's arm and said quietly, "Don't." Then, throwing down her cards and rising unsteadily, she said, "Uh'm out." She scooped up the couple of dollars that she still had on the table.

Taking hold of her arm, Wyatt guided her toward the door. As they reached it, he gave Joe a disappointed look. And just as they stepped over the threshold, he heard Roberto say, "THE Wyatt Earp? I thought he was dead..."

Wyatt paused, looked back over his shoulder at the gamblers with a glare so sharp it could cut the buttons off their coats. Sadie knew that look. Knew that it usually presaged violence. "Wyatt..." she whispered. Holding his anger in check, he escorted her out.

Once on the sidewalk and headed for home, Wyatt continued to grip Sadie's arm tightly, pulling her along. "How much you lose?" he asked.

Sheepishly, she answered, "Hunnert and fifty."

"How much?!"

"I was up seventy."

"When?"

"An hour, two hours ago."

Wyatt sighed. "When are you gonna learn? Stay at the table too long and you lose everything."

Sadie didn't go off the wagon often, but when she did, she went way off. Wyatt wouldn't have minded that so much, except that the liquor tended to bring out her bitter side, revealing an ugly, mean drunk. And he did his best to keep Sadie's imbibing in check, but he couldn't keep an eye on her every hour of every day, so he'd had to accept that the occasional slip was the price he paid for her companionship.

Wyatt himself was never much of a drinker in his younger days—it paid to keep a clear head when there were people about seeking to shoot it off—but as he got older, he'd developed an appetite for spirits,

14

especially in the company of his male friends, like some of the younger men he'd met on film sets—Bill Hart, Tom Mix, John Ford, and a tall, gangly USC footballer turned prop boy named Marion Morrison. The film people, like Wyatt, were vagabonds, dreamers who traveled West to reinvent themselves. It was a lifestyle fraught with disappointment, and alcohol helped soften the sting of near-constant rejection. The studio bosses were much the same, most men of humble means who'd struck the mother lode. And in general, these wealthy, well-connected men were distrustful of teetotalers, but instantly bonded with a man who'd share a drink with them—especially if that man was buying.

When he got Sadie home, Wyatt managed to get her to drink a glass of water and eat a sandwich—something to thin out and absorb the alcohol—and then he sat her on the bed and pulled her dress off over her head.

"I ought 'a tan your hide!" he said.

With a pounding headache and nascent nausea, Sadie responded, "Whup me and uh'll poison your cof- coffee."

"And I'll drink it," he grumbled, "if it'll give me some peace."

"Oh, Wyatt, honey, you don't mean that," she said, teetering on the bedside.

He lowered her down onto her pillow and pulled the covers over her. "That money was meant to last us through the summer!" he reprimanded. "Now what're we gonna do?"

She raised up on one elbow, squinting her eyes to clear her double vision, and asked, "Which one of you'sh talking?"

"The one in the middle." He folded her dress and laid it across the back of a chair.

"Whut about your movie conshulting?"

"I finished today."

Lying back on the pillow, she closed her eyes to keep the room from spinning—not that it helped; she still felt like she was lying on a merry-go-round. "Well, you never sheem to like that work, anyway."

"Pays the bills. Lord only knows how long it'll be before the next job comes along. How're we gonna make it till then?"

"We can borrow shum money from..."

Wyatt shouted, "Your family and mine both are sick and tired of us coming around every few months with our hands out!"

The harshness of his words, and the biting anger in his voice, stung her. Her eyes welled with tears. She looked up at him imploringly and said, "Uh thought uh could take 'em. They sheemed like rubes."

"You were hustled. They saw you for a fool and took advantage."

"Stop it!" she said sharply. She already felt like a screw-up. It didn't help to have him rubbing it in. She brushed her hand through her hair, a gesture that the booze always amplified. It was one of many minor "tells" that always signaled to Wyatt that she'd had more than a few.

He reached for a trash can and put it beside the head of the bed, where Sadie could reach it easily. "In case you need it," he said quietly, adding, "Roll over on your side." She rolled toward the center of the bed. "The other side!" he said tersely. He didn't want her to pass out and choke on her own vomit during the night, nor did he want her to throw up on his side of the bed. He stood looking at her for a long moment, and with sadness in his voice, said, "Thought you'd given up the bottle."

"I try, but... it feelsh... so good."

"Feel good now?" he asked. She didn't answer. He added, "Makes you mean and ill-tempered."

She cracked her eyes open, looked up at him. "Yeah?" she muttered. "What'sh your excuse?"

He pulled the chain on the bedside lamp, switching it off. He heard her murmur with a yawn, "Shnug as a bug in a rug." Going to the door, he paused and looked back at her with concern. He felt pity for her and, at the same time, was peeved by the precarious financial situation she'd just thrown them into.

It was the alcohol, he said to himself. Once she started, she just couldn't stop. And no amount of him yelling at her would make it any better—it was just who she was, and he had to accept it. It made life interesting and sometimes, like tonight, hard.

So why couldn't he leave this woman?

Chapter 4

MORGAN

Figuring that a dose of quiet, cool night air would settle him down, Wyatt went outside. He sat in his rocking chair on the bungalow's small porch and lit his pipe. He wasn't a heavy smoker, but as with his alcohol consumption, he'd learned that tobacco was a good ice-breaker with certain men who were worth knowing. And since he only smoked on occasion, he liked how inhaling the smoke made his skin tingle, like tiny electric shocks from head to toe. Coupled with the gentle back-and-forth rhythm of the rocking chair, it was the perfect pacifier to lift the worries of a troubling day.

As his ire at Sadie receded, he became contemplative, staring across the courtyard at the matching residences. It was almost like looking at a mirror reflection, since all the bungalows were built from identical floorplans. The exception was the larger two-story one at the end, where a mid-level studio writer lived and could sometimes be heard clacking at his typewriter deep into the wee hours.

Wyatt stared at the horizon, where the setting sun and descending night painted the sky shades of pastel orange and pink beneath an increasingly oppressive layer of deep blue-black. There was a light breeze; Wyatt could hear the tinkling of the wind chimes the writer had placed on a low limb of one of the trees in the courtyard, no doubt intended to call the Muses to him when the Jazz records he favored weren't doing the trick.

Then Wyatt's gaze drifted down to the big central lawn between the bungalows, where a few young boys had come outside to play. More

THE LAST STAGE

and more, the bungalow courtyards of Los Angeles were filling up with youngsters whose parents—usually single parents—expected to make them the next stars of the *Our Gang* shorts, or maybe the next Jackie Coogan or Mickey McGuire. But for now, the boys of the bungalow court—two of them holding cast-iron cap guns—just wanted to play Cowboy.

"I'm Tom Mix!" shouted the oldest, 8-year-old Jimmy.

"I'm Hoot Gibson!" yelled his best friend, Scott, also 8.

The youngest, 6-year-old Rudy, piped in, "I'm Buck Jones!"

"You can't be nobody!" said Jimmy. "You don't have a gun!"

"You're the Indian!" said Scott.

"Awwww!" groaned Rudy, "How come I always hafta be the Indian?"

They set about hiding behind bushes and playing around the central fountain, having a 'shoot-out' with cap guns blazing, the air soon filling with percussive pops and little puffs of smoke that smelled of sulfur.

Earpie nudged open the screen door and loped outside. He hopped up into his master's lap. Wyatt winced slightly, and moved the dog to the other side of his hip, to a spot that wasn't so tender. Rubbing Earpie's head and feeling the dog's fur soft against his fingertips, he asked, "What're we gonna do with her, Earpie?"

Wyatt wished there was some way he could stop Sadie from drinking, but he knew it was a lost cause. Anyway, when you take up with someone, you don't just get all that's good about them, you also get all that's bad, and you'd best accept it and make peace with it or move on. He'd learned that lesson with his second wife, Mattie, whom he'd met in Dodge City, Kansas in the late 1870s, when it was called "the Wickedest Little City in the West." He was an Assistant Marshal then, and she—like all too many young women who left the boring, structured lives of their home towns and traveled West seeking adventure—was a prostitute. But she was no shrinking violet, and Wyatt was attracted to her strong will. They began seeing each other, then living together, and when he moved on with his brothers to Tombstone, Arizona, she tagged along, presenting herself as his wife. By the time they arrived in the booming silver mining town, she was suffering from debilitating headaches, which she'd begun treating with laudanum.

What neither she nor Wyatt knew at the time was that the bitter-tasting medicine was ten percent powdered opium, mixed with morphine and codeine. She liked the way it made her feel, even when it eventually left her feeling practically nothing. It was only a matter of time before Wyatt lost her to the drug. Seeing no future for himself with an addict, he found companionship with a young lady newly arrived in Tombstone—Josephine Sarah Marcus, whom he teasingly called Sadie, partly because he knew she didn't care for the nickname. When Wyatt left Tombstone, after the troubles, he left Mattie behind and eventually joined up again with Sadie in California. Needless to say, Mattie was devastated.

She went along with the other Earp family members to Colton, California and lived with them for a while, expecting that Wyatt would send her a telegram telling her where to meet him, but such a message never arrived. When it became clear that she'd been abandoned, she headed to Pinal City, Arizona, heartbroken, her spirit crushed, intending to resume her former occupation. She and Wyatt had passed through the boom town on their way to Tombstone, but now, the boom had gone bust and much of Pinal City's population had abandoned it, making paying customers hard for Mattie to find. But she still had her other and most steadfast love, and on a hot July day in 1888, after drinking a copious amount of alcohol, she escaped her misery and loneliness by indulging in the warm embrace of her precious laudanum, which graciously soothed her sorrowful heart by stopping it forever.

Wyatt regretted that Mattie had given herself over so completely to the drug and been unable to break free from its grip. He still felt guilty for abandoning her, but he justified it by telling himself you can't save someone from their own self-destructive desires, especially when those desires turn into needs. Mattie was fated to have a bad end. He couldn't stop it, and he simply didn't want to be there to witness it when it came.

Wyatt never really liked to revisit his past, but the past had a habit of visiting him. As he sat there watching the boys, he soon became aware of another presence, materializing soundlessly out of the ether. It was his younger brother, Morgan, his back to Wyatt, looking out into the courtyard. He wore a coat and hat forty years out of fashion. And when he turned to face Wyatt, he had the same walrus mustache that was fashionable when he was gunned down in a Tombstone poolroom five months after the shootout at the O.K. Corral.

Wyatt's mind flashed back to that time, when a theatre company came to Tombstone for a one-night-only performance of a play called *Stolen Kisses* at Schieffelin Hall. Morgan wanted to go. Wyatt didn't

THE LAST STAGE

think it would be safe. There was a rainstorm brewing, blown in on a gusty wind. And Wyatt had heard rumblings of another storm brewing: some of the Cowboys—a gang of cattle rustlers and thieves who frequented the ranches out of town—were in Tombstone, and in defiance of city ordinance, they were armed. Wyatt asked Briggs Goodrich, a lawyer who represented the Cowboys in many of their court cases, if the Earps were in any danger. Goodrich told him, "You're liable to get it in the neck at any time." Heeding the warning, Wyatt went to his room at the Cosmopolitan Hotel. Along the way, he caught sight of two of the Cowboys, Florentino Cruz and Hank Swilling, but chose not to engage them.

A little while later, Goodrich arrived at Schieffelin Hall and saw Morgan Earp with Doc Holliday. He told them, "I saw some fellows with guns. You fellows'll catch it if you don't watch out." Morgan shrugged it off; his wife, Allie, was visiting her parents in California, and despite the wet weather, he was enjoying being temporarily out from under the matrimonial yoke and ready to relax and indulge his freedom with a night on the town.

Before the performance ended, Wyatt made his way to Schieffelin Hall to intercept Morgan on his way out. He tried to convince his younger brother to come straight back to the hotel, but Morgan was in a festive mood. "Come on, Wyatt," said Morgan. "What's it gonna hurt us to play a little pool?"

Wyatt relented, figuring as soon as Morgan finished the game they'd return to the safety of the Cosmopolitan. Dan Tipton and Sherman McMasters joined them, and off they went to Campbell and Hatch's Billiards Parlor, which had both a poolroom and a cardroom. When they arrived, Wyatt, Tipton, and McMasters sat down to watch Morgan play a game of billiards against the co-owner, Bob Hatch, who was as much a pool shark as Morgan.

At just about eleven o'clock, Morgan was giving Bob a good run for his money. But as he moved around the corner of the table and leaned in to take a shot, there was a loud bang. The window glass in the upper part of the door ten feet behind him suddenly shattered and a bullet slammed Morgan against the table. The bullet passed clean through him and ended up in the leg of George Berry, who was standing next to a stove at the entrance. A second shot came immediately afterward and struck the wall near the ceiling above Wyatt's head. Everyone in the poolroom dove for cover, including Wyatt, who watched as Morgan slid off the pool table and crumpled to the floor.

Bob Hatch and Sherman McMasters rushed into the alley looking for the gunmen. Wyatt, stunned and horrified, went to Morgan and knelt by his side. There was a look of astonishment on Morgan's face. Wyatt was alarmed by the amount of blood pouring from his brother's wound. Hatch and McMasters came back in to say there was no sign of the gunmen. Wyatt asked McMasters and Tipton to help him lift Morgan and carry him into the lounge of the cardroom. Morgan's pain was so intense, and his cries of protest so harrowing, they ended up laying him down on the floor near the cardroom door.

Word of the shooting spread back to the Cosmopolitan Hotel, and soon the Earp clan descended on Campbell and Hatch's saloon, including Virgil and James Earp and their wives, Allie and Bessie. Wailing, crying and praying, they all gathered around Morgan, as his life's blood seeped from his body. Desperate and tired of waiting for a doctor to arrive, Wyatt and his brothers decided to take Morgan to the nearest one. But as they attempted to lift him to his feet, he just grimaced and said, "Don't, boys, don't. I can't stand it." They laid him back down, and he said, "I've played my last game of pool."

Soon after, a doctor arrived, and then two more. The medical men determined that the bullet entered close to Morgan's spinal column, pierced his kidney, and came out his loin. As his blood continued to pool around him, Morgan's breathing came in shallow gasps. He motioned for Wyatt to come closer. Wyatt leaned down to him, and with his internal bleeding, it sounded like the words were gurgling up from the bottom of a pond as Morgan said, "I'm just sorry… I won't… have a chance to… to get even."

Wyatt squeezed his younger brother's hand and said, "I'll do it for you." Then, about twenty minutes before midnight, thirty-year-old Morgan breathed his last. Morgan had long been the family favorite, always ready with a witty joke to blunt the hot tempers of his older brothers, always eager to be the first to try new things. Now he was the first of the brothers to die.

A hush fell over the room.

Outside, the wind howled.

Rain fell.

And in the months ahead, Wyatt kept his word.

That was forty-six years ago, and yet now here was Morgan, looking as affable as he did that stormy night long ago. Smiling at the boys in the courtyard, he said, "Just like us, when we were little."

"'Cept our guns were just sticks," said Wyatt.

Morgan nodded at the door, from behind which came the faint sound of Sadie's snoring. "Warned you she'd be a handful."

Wyatt grinned. "I think what you said was, 'Marry an actress, expect drama.'"

"Just looking out for my big brother," said Morgan. "You'd think she'd be better with money, being a Jewess and all."

Wyatt's pipe had petered out. He struck a match to relight it. "I don't mind her gambling," he said. "I just mind she's so bad at it."

"Well, can't fault her for being unlucky. Can't everybody be as fortunate as you are. What was it? Thirty rounds fired at the O.K. Corral, and every one of us hit, 'cept you?" Morgan leaned his forearm against the post of the porch rail, again turning his back to Wyatt, who now saw the bullet hole in Morgan's coat. Morgan, watching the boys shooting their cap guns, continued, "Then they come gunning for you and get me."

"Should've been me," said Wyatt, regret in his voice.

"Aw, now, can't change what happened. Just gotta take the bad with the good and keep goin.'"

"Suppose so."

"Remember that night?" Morgan asked. "I was splayed out there on the floor, scared, in terrible pain, bleedin' like a stuck pig, worried about leaving Louisa, and you knelt down beside me, saying, 'Hold on, Morgan, hold on.' But I just couldn't. I wanted to, but..."

Of course Wyatt remembered. For years, he'd tried to clear the images of that dreadful night out of his head entirely, but no amount of whiskey, women, or wild living, and no amount of revenge, did the trick. The memories still flooded back to him at odd, often inappropriate times, like dead leaves floating to the surface of a muddy creek.

"We had a pact, remember?" Wyatt asked Morgan. "If there was an afterlife, you'd send me a sign."

"I'm here now, ain't I?"

There were more bangs from the cap guns, more of the acrid odor of sulfur in the air. Wyatt was quiet for a long moment, then asked, "Morgan, what's it like, when the end comes?"

"You just... move on," his younger brother said wistfully, casually making a sweeping motion with his arm, raising his hand at the end. "Like catchin' the last stage out."

Wyatt sat silent and still in his rocking chair. His gaze drifted to the young boys in the courtyard. Scott pointed his cap pistol at Jimmy, pulled the trigger. There was a snapping sound, and Scott shouted, "Gotcha! You're dead!" Jimmy stiffened, put his hand on his heart, and fell to the ground, the way the bad guys dramatically died in the movies. The way no one ever died in real life.

With a crack in his voice, Wyatt began, "Morgan, I... I..."

"It's alright," said Morgan. "It was my time. When it's your time, it's your time." Then he turned to look squarely into Wyatt's blue eyes as he added, "Yours is coming."

And with that, he faded into the darkness, carried away on the cool winter breeze and the tinkling of wind chimes.

The boys' mothers called them inside. Wyatt remained on the porch a while longer, staring out at the fountain, finishing his pipe, fingers stroking Earpie's fur. Would've been nice, he thought, if Morgan had stayed just a little longer.

When his pipe burned out, he gently nudged Earpie off his lap, stood, and tapped his pipe on the porch rail to empty it. The temperature had dropped with the curtain of night, and now it was just cool enough to set off the arthritis pains in the middle knuckles of his right hand. Time to go inside, he thought, away from melancholy memories and the innocent pop-pops of young boys with toy guns.

~ • ~

Wyatt, in his sleeveless, knee-length, one-piece union suit, and Sadie, in her nightgown, nestled side-by-side in the small bed, Sadie snoring peacefully, Earpie lying atop the bed cuddled against their feet. Wyatt slowly awoke when Sadie rolled up against his back, the bulk of her body pressing down on his. When they first met, he was a big strapping man and she was a wisp of a woman. Now, he was thinner and lighter, and it seemed that all the weight he'd lost over the years had migrated onto her short frame. As she snuggled closer, her bulk on his ribs made it difficult for him to breathe. But he didn't want to complain, partly for fear of hurting her feelings but also because, bothersome as it could be, he liked feeling her so close. Nonetheless, he scooched away from her just a bit, just to keep from suffocating. As he did so, she rolled over onto her side, away from him, in the process yanking all the covers off him. She had a habit of doing so—as she slept, she often wrapped the sheet and blanket around her like a cocoon, leaving him exposed to the cool night air.

Now awake, Wyatt felt a dull pain in his side and back. It was a constant with him now, one he was usually able to ignore, but right now there was an added feeling of pressure. A full bladder. He rubbed his tender abdomen. He wished he could go back to sleep and wait till morning, but no, he needed to get up now, or else risk soaking the bed. He swung his feet over the side and onto the floor, sitting on the edge—and now the pressure in his abdomen was like a searing hot knife stabbing him. With a low groan, he rose and trudged to the bathroom.

He pulled the chain to switch on the naked lightbulb overhead, unbuttoned the union suit, and let it drop to his ankles. Looking at his reflection in the three-quarter length mirror behind the bathroom door, he again rubbed his hand over his sagging abdomen. There didn't appear to be anything unusual, but there was a spot on the lower right side of his belly that felt spongy. When he pressed on it with his fingertips, there was a sudden jab of pain like an ice pick plunging into his gut.

With one hand gripping the sink to help him balance, he carefully sat down on the toilet, grunting and wincing from the pain. Once situated, he let out a long, slow breath. And there he sat, in anticipation of a release that was slow in coming. He tried a few times to exert pressure on his kidneys by tensing his abdominal muscles. All that got him were more stabbing pains and a sweaty forehead.

Though he was trying to be quiet, his grunts and groans awakened Sadie. She stopped snoring. Wyatt heard the sound of the bedsprings as she rose, and her feet half-stepping, half-sliding over the floor, and then she was on the other side of the bathroom door. "Wyatt? You okay?" she asked sleepily, her voice still somewhat slurred.

He shifted his position on the toilet. "Fine," he grunted. "Go back to sleep."

"You don't sound fine."

"It's nothing."

"Need anything?"

"Need some peace!" He was irritated, angry; he didn't want her fussing over him, especially in her hungover state. But mostly, he was embarrassed. He sat up a little straighter, held his breath, and again put pressure on his belly. And now, finally, there was the satisfying sound of an intermittent piss stream hitting the toilet water. He let out a quiet moan.

Sadie remained on the other side of the door, still concerned. "Hon?" she said.

"I'm coming. Hold your horses." Leaning forward, he wiped the sweat from his forehead. He heard Sadie step-sliding away, and the squeak of the springs as she plopped back down on the bed.

A few minutes later, after pulling his union suit back up and splashing cold water on his face, he joined her, settling gingerly down onto the mattress, exhausted. Suddenly feeling a chill, he tugged the covers away from her and pulled them up to his armpits. As he closed his eyes, Sadie rolled over, facing him.

"You need to go back to Dr. Shurtleff," she said.

"Bit late now," he yawned.

"I hate you're feeling so poorly." She snuggled close to him, and rubbing her hand over his forearm, said hopefully, "We'll get through this".

Wyatt let out a tired sigh. He tried not to wince when she put her arm over his stomach, though she might as well have punched him with a branding iron.

Chapter 5

'ROUND MIDNIGHT

Earpie climbed up onto Wyatt's stomach. Wyatt, with a barely audible groan, moved his hand slowly and weakly to push him away. Sadie immediately picked up the border collie and set him on the floor. "Go on," she said. "Leave Papa alone."

"How long has he been like this?" asked Lake.

"He was doing alright until yesterday," said Sadie. "Then he fell sick, and I called Dr. Shurtleff." She looked accusingly at Lake. "You should've come sooner."

"I know," said Lake. "I wanted to, but I had the flu, and the last thing I'd want was to be the one who finally kil—" He stopped himself, seeing a flash of anger in Sadie's eyes. Then he continued, softly, "I didn't want to pass it on to him."

Dr. Shurtleff kept his attention divided between Wyatt and Sadie. He knew there was nothing more he could do for Wyatt, so his real patient was Sadie. She was a naturally high-strung woman, and likely to become hysterical as Wyatt's condition worsened. His purpose tonight was to manage her, and her emotions, and keep her from possibly doing harm to herself.

"We should have gone on out to the mines," Sadie said quietly. "We usually do this time of year, but he just didn't feel up to it. Maybe if we had..." She let the sentence hang in the air, unfinished.

She knew her man was dying. She just couldn't accept it, even though he, too, had realized it was coming, and had sat her down a few days earlier to tell her his wishes. They made out a list of pallbearers that included several friends from their Tombstone days along with a few others. There was attorney William Hunsaker, whom Wyatt had first met in Tombstone and who afterwards became president of the California Bar Association; George Parsons, a banker who knew Wyatt in Tombstone and kept a detailed diary of his life in the Arizona Territory; John Clum, Tombstone's first mayor and publisher of the town's newspaper; playwright Wilson Mizner, whom Wyatt had befriended during their days in Nome, Alaska during the Klondike Gold Rush; and actors William S. Hart and Tom Mix. Wyatt and Mix got together on occasion to read Shakespeare plays together as part of their efforts to smooth out their rough edges and become more cultured.

But most importantly, Wyatt wanted to discuss what would happen to him after the funeral. It was a subject Sadie would rather have avoided altogether, though she was deeply moved when he said he wanted to be cremated, so he could someday be interred with her, wherever that might be.

There was a rustling on the bed. Wyatt was trying to roll onto his side—his preferred way of sleeping—but was too weak to do so. Noticing, Sadie stood and asked the men to help her reposition him.

"I think he'd be more comfortable on his back," said Dr. Shurtleff.

"You think I don't know how he sleeps?" snapped Sadie. "He likes to be on his side."

Lake pulled the covers back, and Shurtleff and Sadie gently maneuvered Wyatt onto his right side. She took the pillow from beneath his head, fluffed it, and put it back in its place. She placed another pillow between his knees, so they wouldn't get sore from the bones rubbing against each other. Out of habit, Wyatt crooked his legs slightly, and slowly moved his hand, balled up into a fist, beside his head.

Returning to her seat by the bed, Sadie rubbed her hand over Wyatt's upper body. He still had a broad, smooth back, and his hair was still soft as silk, but the muscles of his arm were looser, less rock-hard than they used to be. She clasped her hand over his fist, which he held close to his nose and mouth, and she could feel his breaths.

Her whole world was in those breaths.

They made her feel safe.

Chapter 6

LAKE

Hurdy-gurdy music filled the Santa Monica Pier's hippodrome, which had been built ten years earlier to house a colorful Looff Carousel. Young couples and children rode the brightly painted wooden horses that bobbed up and down as Wyatt and Sadie stood nearby, watching them, waiting for Stuart Lake to arrive. Wyatt held onto Earpie's leash, the little dog behind his legs, where it felt safe from the noise and bustle of the crowd. Wyatt smiled; he enjoyed seeing the children excited and laughing, and he admired the craftsmanship that went into creating the wooden horses, carved as though they were in full gallop, with mane and tail flying.

Sadie, on the other hand, was irritated by the carousel's loud and jaunty hurdy-gurdy music, feeling anything but jaunty herself. Her stomach was still queasy, and the bobbing horses almost matched the dyspeptic rhythm of her bobbing stomach. She'd rather have sat on a bench along the pier, but then she'd have the mixed odors of tar and fish to contend with, and that would have been worse.

Wyatt noticed her discomfort, and secretly reveled in it; he hoped the memory of it might deter her from going so far off the wagon again, at least for the foreseeable future. "You gonna make it?" he asked her.

"Feel like I been hit by a truck."

"Hit the bottle too hard and it hits back."

"Let's just keep this short," she said.

Both Wyatt and Sadie hoped Lake would finally be able to do his story justice. It had been a long journey to find a biographer. They'd first tried with Forrestine Hooker, daughter of Henry Hooker, a rancher whom they'd known in Tombstone, who helped Wyatt and his band elude the posse of Sheriff Johnny Behan when Wyatt took it upon himself to hunt down the murderers of his brother. Forrestine had written several children's books, and after some discussions with Wyatt and others, wrote a book called *An Arizona Vendetta* about the O.K. Corral shootout and its aftermath, but she was unable to find a publisher.

Wyatt and Sadie then decided to take matters into their own hands and asked John Flood to take a stab at it. While the rejection notices for that effort were pouring in, a Chicago newspaperman named Walter Noble Burns, who'd followed up a book about Al Capone with one about Billy the Kid, visited Wyatt in California and expressed an interest in his story. Wyatt told him Flood had already covered it, so Burns changed tack, saying he was working on a book about Wyatt's friend, Doc Holliday. Wyatt agreed to help and eventually sent Burns an eleven-page letter that covered many of the events of Tombstone. But as Burns began doing research in Arizona, he reverted back to his original plan and published *Tombstone: An Iliad of the Southwest*, a book centered not on Doc Holliday's exploits, but Wyatt's. Wyatt felt betrayed and wrote to Burns's publisher hoping to stop the book from being printed, to no avail. Now that he was in his waning years, Wyatt felt that all he had of value was his life story, and Burns was stealing it from him. He was afraid that the mere existence of the tome, from which Wyatt would earn no money, would keep publishers from being interested in his own version of events.

Then just after Christmas of 1927, after Flood's book had been resoundingly rejected by practically every publishing house, he received a belated present—a letter from another newspaperman, Stuart Lake, inquiring about writing Wyatt's biography, with his and Sadie's cooperation. Lake had known Bat Masterson, a one-time lawman and friend of Wyatt's, since they were both young buffalo hunters in the Oklahoma Territory fifty years earlier. At the turn of the century, Masterson went to New York, where he became a reporter and columnist for *The New York Morning Telegraph*. It was there that Stuart Lake, who had become a freelance magazine writer, met Masterson and first heard the newspaperman's stories of Wyatt and the Earp brothers and the gunfight at the O.K. Corral, but it was only after Lake had relocated to San Diego that he managed to finally track Wyatt down. This was about six months after Wyatt had given up on John Flood's book, so Lake found him in a receptive mood, though in their subsequent correspondences and brief meetings, Lake discovered that prying Wyatt's story out of him was rather like trying to tug a cactus out of the ground with your bare hands—impossibly prickly.

But now here he was, back for another attempt, calling Wyatt's name as he ambled into the hippodrome. Sadie heard him first, and tapped Wyatt's shoulder. Seeing the smartly-dressed author sauntering towards them, Wyatt picked Earpie up and crossed the room to greet him, Sadie at his elbow. It was difficult for them to hear each other over the loud calliope of the carousel, so Sadie immediately suggested they retreat from the hubbub of the hippodrome to the tranquility of the beach.

A strong surf roared in and ebbed out as Wyatt, Sadie, and Lake trod barefoot along the shore, across the damp area between ocean and dry sand. Sadie carried hers and Wyatt's shoes, Lake had his cradled in his arm. The men had their pants legs rolled up in case they misjudged a wave; Sadie pulled her skirt up to her knees and held it bunched up in her hand. The damp sand was cool and soothing, capturing their footprints as they strode along, past the sunbathers relaxing in their warm wool swimsuits, some under beach umbrellas, and the children who were either playing in the surf or building sandcastles.

Wyatt removed Earpie's collar, and the little dog took off like a bullet, running full bore along the shoreline, making a bee-line to a flock of gulls who, startled, immediately took to the air.

After making polite conversation about Lake's drive up from San Diego, Sadie got right to the point, asking, "When can we see some pages?"

"Soon," said Lake. "There's just one or two things I'd still like to clear up."

"Such as?" she queried, raising an eyebrow.

"I've got a list..." With his free hand, he reached into his inner coat pocket and pulled out some folded papers. He scanned down the top sheet. "Like this. Just so I can get it straight—you married Aurilla, and she died, and then when you got to Tombstone, you were with Mattie, but when you left Arizona..."

Sadie interrupted, "What's Wyatt's private life got to do with anything?! People don't care about that! They just want to know what he's done."

"I'm—I'm just trying to..." Lake sputtered.

"I don't want anything printed that makes my Wyatt look bad!" she said, sternly. Then, nudging Wyatt, she added, "Tell 'im what happened to Newton."

Wyatt stepped around some kelp, saying, "You heard about this new book that just come out, called *Helldorado*?"

Lake looked at him with consternation. "Wait—what's it called?"

Wyatt said, "Last week, Newt's granddaughter came to him with a book someone had given her called *Helldorado*, by Billy Breakenridge."

Lake knew the name. "Breakenridge? Wasn't he Sheriff Behan's deputy?"

Wyatt nodded. "He came around a while back—about the time we started working with you—and asked me all kinds of questions. Then the sonuvabitch turns around and writes a book sayin' that the Clantons and McLaury's were unarmed and threw up their hands before we shot 'em. Now, if that's so, then how come Virgil, Morgan, and Doc come up wounded?"

Lake could see that Wyatt was hurt and angry, and attempted to make light of the situation, remarking, "So you're saying his account's just a little self-serving?"

Sadie harrumphed. "Makes him look good and everybody else look bad."

"Just what we need," lamented Lake, "more competition. And all the more reason I need to sit down with you and get the information I need to finish our book."

"What information?" drawled Wyatt.

Lake again looked at his questions, while trying to keep pace with Wyatt and Sadie. "What about the vendetta ride?" he asked. "Was it you that hunted down and killed Johnny Ringo?"

Sadie snapped, "Wyatt's only ever done what he had to do. And it's made him a prisoner."

"Prisoner? Of what?"

"His reputation."

Wyatt paused, looking down at the sand, and then he stared out at the rolling surf washing up onto the beach. "Hell of a thing," he said, "to have your whole life defined by thirty seconds."

Lake smiled. "Well... it wasn't just any thirty seconds."

Thanks to the stories published in cheap pulp magazines like *Real West*, *Wild West Weekly*, *Western Story*, *.44 Western*, and *Ace High*, full of tall tales written by small men who'd never sat a horse or slept rough, and whose florid prose was the only shit they'd ever shoveled, Wyatt's exploits in Tombstone had been boiled down to either a simplistic tale of good lawmen against crooked cattle rustlers, or valiant freedom-loving ranchers against crooked lawmen, depending on the personal prejudices of the chroniclers.

The truth, as always, was much more complicated. Wyatt was nearing 80, and in all those years, he'd only spent about five years as a law enforcer. But he believed in the law. He believed that America was a nation of laws, and he believed in upholding them. But a society built on laws only worked if everyone agreed to abide by them. If there were a few renegades who didn't, who found ways to skirt the law or to hide behind it, then what was he to do? For Wyatt, the solution was to resort to a higher law, which made him the renegade.

He had no regrets about what happened at the O.K. Corral. If he had it all to do over again, he'd do everything exactly the same. The outlaws and their friends and allies—some of whom were law enforcers—imagined they could at first intimidate Wyatt and his brothers, and when that didn't work they tried to murder them. Virgil was nearly assassinated one night as he crossed a street; the attempt left him with a useless arm. Later, the outlaws were more successful, firing the shots through a pool hall window that killed Morgan. But Wyatt wasn't cowed. He avenged his brothers by forming a posse with his brother Warren and his gambler/gunfighter friend Doc Holliday. Together, they hunted down his brother's killers on what came to be called his "vendetta ride."

He began by killing Frank Stilwell at the Tucson train station, where Stillwell had come to ambush Virgil Earp, who was on his way to California to be with the rest of the Earp clan. Seeing Stilwell and a man he believed to be Ike Clanton on a train flatcar, both armed with shotguns, Wyatt confronted them. The men ran. Wyatt chased after them, and Stilwell—whom Wyatt believed had killed Morgan—fell behind. Wyatt soon caught up to him, and Stillwell faced him, too scared to fire, begging for his life. Wyatt aimed his shotgun at Stilwell's belly, and when the cowboy grabbed the weapon, Wyatt fired both barrels. Stillwell fell dead at his feet, mangled and bloody. Clanton escaped. But Morgan was avenged. And the war between the Earps and the Cowboys escalated in earnest.

The authorities in Tucson quickly labeled Wyatt's actions murder, and sent word to Tombstone for Sheriff Johnny Behan to arrest him. Behan formed a posse of twelve men that included Johnny Ringo, Phineas Clanton—the older brother of Ike whom everyone called Fin—and other members of the cattle-rustling Cowboys and took off in pursuit of the Earps.

The Earps, meanwhile, tracked Florentino Cruz to a rustler's camp in the Dragoon Mountains. Wyatt had been told that Cruz was a lookout for Morgan's murder. As Wyatt and his cohorts were riding toward Tombstone, Cruz, who was alone, spotted them and ran for the hills. Wyatt's band caught up to him and left him dead from four bullet wounds, but not before Cruz told them the names of other men involved in Virgil's ambush and Morgan's murder.

Days later, needing money, Wyatt arranged for a loan from a mine operator. He expected to collect it at a watering hole in Iron Springs, but as he approached, Earp found nine of the cowboys—including Curly Bill Brocius—waiting for him. Almost immediately, the cowboys shot and killed the horse of one of Wyatt's group, Texas Jack Vermillion. Wyatt leapt off his horse to stand and fight, expecting the rest of his posse to do the same. Doc Holliday rescued Texas Jack, whose horse had fallen atop his leg, and—like the rest of the Earp posse—the two of them rode away from the withering barrage of gunfire.

Wyatt was stuck in the midst of it. With his horse rearing, its reins over his arm, he determined that if he was going to die, he'd at least take Curly Bill with him. Curly Bill shot first; his shotgun blast peppered holes through Wyatt's long coat. But Wyatt responded with his shotgun, and the blast tore open Curly Bill's chest. He went down screaming like a demon. The other cowboys shot pistols and rifles at Wyatt, causing his scared horse to buck even more wildly. Because of the heat, Wyatt had loosened his gun belt on the ride in; it now slipped down around his thighs, hampering his attempts to climb back up into the saddle. It would have been comic if it hadn't been so dangerous. Wyatt managed to yank his pistol free, and returned the cowboys' fire, wounding two of them. After the heel of Wyatt's boot and the horn of his saddle were shot off, he was able to remount his horse and ride back to his posse. His companions were amazed not only that he had survived, but that he had once again managed to escape a hail of bullets without being hit.

After that skirmish, Earp and his party rode to Henry Hooker's ranch in Sierra Bonita, south of Tombstone, to pick up fresh horses. Afterward, they rode off to a bluff three miles away where Wyatt expected to make a final stand against Behan's posse. From there, they watched the dust clouds as Behan's group rode into Hooker's ranch and, after a brief spell, rode out again—going in the opposite direction, despite Hooker having told them where Earp was holed up. Sheriff Behan hoped catching Earp's group would help him in the upcoming elections, but he apparently wasn't willing to bet his life on reclaiming his office. As for Wyatt, he knew that he could never return to Tombstone, so he and his men continued on through the New Mexico Territory to Colorado.

After two hectic weeks, the vendetta ride was over.

One thing that Wyatt felt the scribes writing about Tombstone always overlooked was that following the deaths of Tom and Frank McLaury, Billy Clanton, Frank Stillwell, Florentino Cruz, and Curly Bill Brocius, organized, politically protected crime in Cochise County ended.

Wyatt nudged Sadie's shoulder and pointed to the surf. Not far from the shoreline, a pod of dolphins was making its way northward, their backs arcing gracefully out of the water and diving back under. They stood watching them with Lake, as the cold ocean waves lapped up onto the beach and covered their toes before receding and leaving bubbling white foam behind. Looking over at Wyatt, Sadie could tell that his energy was flagging, and she was still feeling a touch hungover herself. "Hon," she asked, "you need to go back to the house?"

This wasn't what Lake wanted to hear. He'd barely begun his interrogation. "Wyatt, please," he implored. "I drove all this way. If you can just give me a little time…"

"My man needs his rest, Mr. Lake," said Sadie. "We're taking a little trip tomorrow."

"Where to?" asked Lake.

"Going out to Vidal for a spell," said Wyatt. "Been feeling a mite off the beam. Thought a trip to the country might help me build my strength back up."

Sensing his opportunity slipping through his fingers, Lake tried a desperate move. "Okay, look," he said, "How 'bout I give you this list of questions, and maybe when you get settled out there, if you've got some time, you can just…"

Sadie took the typed list from his hands. "Thank you, Mr. Lake," she said.

"Just tell me something, will you?" said Lake, a note of irritation in his voice.

"Yes?" asked Sadie.

"Are you sure you want this? I understand you want to tell your story in your own words, but you have to know it's a double-edged sword. Once you put yourself in the spotlight, it's eventually going to shine on things you might rather keep in the dark."

"That's your responsibility, Mr. Lake," said Sadie. "You're the writer. See that it doesn't." She then gave a shrill whistle and Earpie, far down the beach, dashed towards them.

As Sadie began walking back to the pier, Wyatt knelt to reattach Earpie's leash and said, "You don't need to warn me, Mr. Lake. I know how it works. The press and public raise you up on a pedestal and then take pot shots at you until they bring you down."

"Do you want that?" asked Lake.

Having moved a ways ahead, Sadie turned back and called, "You coming?"

Wyatt gave Lake a rueful look. "Well… it's not just about what I want." He strode to Sadie and crooked his arm around hers, Earpie trotting beside them. As they walked away, Lake sighed, and trailed after them.

And a roiling wave washed up on the beach, reaching the footsteps they'd left in the damp sand, erasing them.

Chapter 7

VIDAL

Wyatt and Sadie packed clothes for their journey, Wyatt folding his shirts and pants neatly before placing them in the open suitcase atop their bed. She threw her dresses and shoes and undergarments into a separate suitcase haphazardly; she didn't have the patience for folding. As he opened bureau drawers filled not only with clothes but with mementos of his life—some old badges, a handful of calling cards from his time in San Francisco, a little box containing a lock of Aurilla's hair—his thoughts reflected back on their truncated meeting with Lake earlier that day. Given his fading memory, Wyatt feared Lake would end up being let down by him, like so many others before him.

Over the years, the various reporters, writers, and biographers who sat down with Wyatt to ask about the events of his life usually came away disappointed, feeling he was holding back, being too guarded, not telling his story the way they wanted to hear it. But for as much as some people wanted to put him into the narrow box of being a hero, Wyatt had also done much that he found hard to live with, and he didn't like to dwell on it. But sometimes, in quiet moments, those thoughts came to the fore—what if he and Aurilla had left Missouri? Would she have lived? Would his son have survived? What if he hadn't gone to Tombstone? Could he have saved Morgan? What if he hadn't allowed Ike Clanton to goad him into a bloody shootout? And how would he ever atone for all the men he'd killed, even if they had deserved it? The thoughts ran round and round in his head, like when Earpie chased his own tail, and served about as much purpose.

After packing all the clothes she thought she'd need, Sadie moved across the room to switch on the radio and went into the kitchen. She began organizing plates and cups and utensils they'd take in a wicker hamper that had leather straps to hold everything in place, which they'd picked up on a visit to her sister in Oakland some years back.

Across the crackling radio waves, they heard a florid actor with a mid-Atlantic accent reciting Shakespeare with clipped consonants, trilling his r's.

"Is that *Hamlet*?" asked Wyatt.

"Sounds like it," said Sadie.

Wyatt didn't know much Shakespeare, but he knew this one well. "Remember seeing Edwin Booth do this in San Francisco?" he asked her. "A little long in the tooth to be playing a young man, but he sure had the spirit for it."

She looked at him with a twinkle in her eye and said, "What would you know about an old man still acting like a young one?"

"Here comes the best part," said Wyatt. He stopped what he was doing to listen to Hamlet's soliloquy from Act 3, Scene 1, where the prince contemplates suicide...

"To be, or not to be, that is the question,
Whether 'tis nobler in the mind to suffer
The slings and arrows of outrageous fortune,
Or to take arms against a sea of troubles,
And by opposing end them? To die – to sleep,
No more; and by a sleep to say we end
The heart-ache and the thousand natural shocks
That flesh is heir to, 'tis a consummation
Devoutly to be wish'd. To die, to sleep;
To sleep, perchance to dream—ay, there's the rub;
For in that sleep of death what dreams may come
When we have shuffled off this mortal coil,
Must give us pause...."

As it continued, Sadie said dreamily, "Beautiful." Hearing the actor declaiming his lines reminded her of the times as a child in San Francisco when she snuck into theater rehearsals rather than attending classes at school.

"Yep," said Wyatt. "But as long-winded as Hamlet was, he wouldn't have lasted long in Arizona." Crossing the room to her, he continued, "I swear there are more killings in *Hamlet* than there were at the O.K. Corral, and with less reason. And we never killed the wrong man, like Hamlet did. Poor Polonius."

"Shhhh!" admonished Sadie. "I'm trying to listen."

He gave her an affectionate pat on the rear and went back to his packing.

~ • ~

A two-lane dirt road cut through the flat desert, with craggy mountains rising in the distance. Wyatt's Packard rolled along, pulling a small travel trailer stuffed to the gills, leaving a great cloud of dust in its wake. Wyatt sat in the driver's seat, both hands firmly gripping the steering wheel. Sadie was beside him, with Earpie standing on her thigh, his little paws crooked over the top of the passenger door and his head stuck out the window, happily enjoying the breeze blowing through his fur.

There were signs of progress along the way—poles holding aloft telephone and power lines, an occasional expanse of oil derricks—as well as reminders of the past—horses running free in corrals, cows grazing in stockyards, and the occasional tumbleweeds propelled across the roadside in the desert breeze.

Every year, thought Wyatt, more of the unknown world became known. There were no more frontiers to explore in America, and few in foreign lands; men had even been to the Poles and back. The wilds had been tamed and the Indians rounded up and forced onto reservations, where they could be so much more easily ignored. No wonder, then, that fiction writers now looked beyond the bounds of the terrestrial planet for their tales of exploration and conquest, with stories of cities under the sea and civilizations beyond the stars. Only unexplored infinities remained mysteriously infinite.

Wiping a finger over his dry lips, Wyatt said, "Throw me that thermos. Ain't got enough spit left to wet a stick of gum."

Sadie grabbed the thermos at her feet, unscrewed the top, poured some of the water inside into it, and handed it to Wyatt. He took a swig, handed it back, and readjusted his position in the seat, rubbing his aching side. Sadie looked at him with concern, saying, "You need to see a doctor when we get there."

Wyatt shot her a stern look, then replied, "He'll just say the same as the others."

"Then maybe you ought 'a start listening."

Wyatt grunted. "I thought part of the idea of coming out here was to get away from our troubles."

"Kinda hard, when the trouble's in you."

With a wry grin, he said, "My trouble's sittin' beside me."

"Oh, is that so?" she said, cocking her eyebrows. "Well…! If you weren't driving, I'd show you some trouble."

"Yeah, I reckon you would." With a smile, he added, "You know I don't mean it, Sadie-Belle."

"If I thought you did, I'd sic this ferocious dog on you."

Wyatt chuckled.

Wyatt and Sadie had set out at sunrise, taking a path across the California desert east from Los Angeles to Palm Springs, and continuing on past gnarled, twisted Joshua trees and desert cacti toward Vidal, a tiny community in the Sonoran Desert about five miles west of the Arizona border.

When the sun was low on the horizon, the Packard came down a dirt road and stopped in front of a small cottage—white with blue trim, a wide porch out front and a horse barn in back. Wyatt and Sadie had settled there just a few years earlier, purchasing the home because it was in close proximity to their mining claims, which were a few miles away at the base of the Whipple Mountains. Some years before, Wyatt had discovered several veins of ore containing gold and copper in the mountains and filed several claims under the name 'Happy Days.' The promise of great riches eluded him, but still he and Sadie returned to their desert home every fall and winter, when the weather was cooler, hoping for the strike that would set them up for the rest of their lives.

As soon as they emerged from the car, Wyatt stretched, arching his stiff back, while Earpie leapt down and immediately went about marking his territory.

Sadie tromped up onto the porch, digging a key out of her purse, and unlocked the door. She pushed it open, then came back to the car, where Wyatt was unloading luggage from the trailer. He picked up a heavy bag, with visible effort. "Let me," said Sadie, reaching for it.

Wyatt reeled away from her, not letting go of the bag's handle, and snapped, "I've got it!" After the long drive, Sadie was taken aback,

THE LAST STAGE

her feelings hurt for being reprimanded just because she wanted to assist him.

Wyatt noticed her put-upon expression, and said softly, "Man wants to feel useful, not be coddled like a basket of eggs." He made a show of not only picking up that particular bag but also grabbing another heavy one, and—walking with effort, shoulders slumped and shoes plodding from the weight of the luggage—took them inside. Sadie grabbed a couple of smaller bags and followed, kicking the door almost closed behind her.

Once they were inside, Earpie ran up onto the porch and scratched at the door, nudging it open wide enough for his little body to slip through.

~ • ~

After removing sheets from furniture and doing a bit of cleaning and arranging, they were just about settled in. Though small, the home was bigger than their Los Angeles bungalow, with a separate kitchen, a dining room, a bedroom, and a bathroom. It was, in fact, the only home they'd ever actually owned in all the years they'd been together; they usually rented or depended on the generosity of friends and relatives.

Sadie put a skillet atop the stove and began cooking some hot dogs they'd brought with them. Hot dogs were one of Wyatt's favorites, and easy to prepare, which was a boon for Sadie, since she wasn't exactly the world's best cook. Consequently, about all she ever made for Wyatt was hot dogs. She liked to split them down the middle and sear them front and back. When she had a couple ready, she removed them from the skillet and laid them into sliced buns. Having been an actress, Sadie had a "stage voice," loud and clear enough to reach the back seats of a metropolitan theater, cut through the heckling of an audience of rowdy cowpunchers, or be heard from one end of the house to the other. She used it now to call out, "What do you want on your dog?"

Wyatt, unpacking a chest in the bedroom, shouted back, "Just mustard." Unlike Sadie, he had to make an effort to get some wind in his lungs for his voice to carry. Ordinarily, he tended to be soft-voiced, unless he was riled. Now, feeling weary from the drive, he removed a wooden case from the bottom of the chest and laid it on the bed. Opening it, he looked inside to see his 1881 Colt Single Action Army pistol, gun belt, and a box of cartridges.

It had been several years since he'd had occasion to wear the gun and gear, but he always brought them along, if only for the comfort of knowing they were there if needed. The last time he used them, he reckoned, was when he crossed into Mexico to haul a couple of drug runners back over the border so Los Angeles Police Detective Arthur King could arrest them; otherwise, it would have taken up to two years to have them extradited. It was an activity that was not quite legal but wasn't entirely illegal, either; a gray area, like so many enterprises Wyatt had engaged in over the years. And it was a duty he'd performed more than a few times for King.

Wyatt closed the case and knelt down to slide it under the bed.

Sadie appeared in the doorway, wiping her hands on her apron. "Dinner's ready," she said. As Wyatt gave the case a shove, she patted the back of his head. "Getting a little thin back there."

Standing up, Wyatt grunted, "Maybe I'm just outgrowin' my hair."

"I've got something that'll hide that bald spot," she said, smiling.

"Like what?"

"A yarmulke."

"I've got a hat, thank you."

A short while later, Wyatt sat across the dining table from Sadie and was about to take the last bite of his hot dog when he looked down and saw Earpie beside his chair. Earpie gave a little whine, displaying the most pitiful look imaginable, but Wyatt was hungry after the long drive. "Sorry, boy. This is mine," he said. "Your dish is on the floor over yonder." He popped the morsel of hot dog into his mouth.

Sadie, not quite done eating her own hot dog, remarked, "Polished that off in a hurry."

"Fine eatin'" said Wyatt. Earpie stood up, his front paws against the seat of her chair, and whined. "Git," she snapped. His begging not yielding the desired results, Earpie slunk away to the rug in the middle of the room to lie down.

Upon finishing her meal, Sadie picked up their plates and took them into the kitchen. Turning on the faucet to fill the sink, she sang a song from her early days as a chorus girl.

When she was out of view, Wyatt rose and stepped to a window looking out onto the side yard. He jiggled a board underneath it, and it popped loose. Wyatt set it aside, revealing a secret compartment in the wall. Inside was a steel lockbox. He removed it, blew dust off the top, and placed it on the table. Opening it, he found a stack of bills inside. He took them out and quickly riffled through them. He guessed it was about forty dollars. Hopefully, that would be enough to buy supplies and provisions and rent some draft horses. He stashed the bills into his pants pocket, closed the lockbox, put it back into its cubby hole, and slid the board back in place.

~ • ~

After a restful night's much-needed sleep, Wyatt and Sadie woke up feeling refreshed the next morning and enjoyed a leisurely breakfast, with plenty of strong coffee. Then, while Wyatt took Earpie for a walk, Sadie dressed and put on her face powder and lipstick—"polishing up the old furniture," as she called it.

They left Earpie in the house while they drove a few miles down the road to the little town of Vidal. There wasn't much to the place—a general store, cafe, post office, jail, corral, and stables, and just on the outskirts, a railroad depot and water tower, a church, and a school, with homes of the locals scattered among and around the town. At one time, it had been a bustling place, but most of its residents had moved on; its glory days were now long gone and it was on its way to becoming a ghost town.

Wyatt and Sadie's car pulled up to Leung's General Store. They got out, both now dressed slightly more "Western" than their L.A. city duds, with Sadie in a long, loose dress and Wyatt in cowboy hat and boots; he'd once remarked to Sadie that there was something about boots that made you stand a little straighter and walk a little slower.

As they stepped up onto the boardwalk, they saw Javier, a weathered, bronze-skinned Mexican busker, sitting on a folding canvas stool wearing a battered fedora and strumming a guitar. Javier was a fixture; he could be found just about any time of the day outside the door of the store, strumming songs for handouts. He was simple-minded but very facile with the guitar, able to play practically any song someone requested—if he'd heard it once, the tune was locked in his brain forever, even if he couldn't remember much else and mostly talked nonsense. The store owners, Henry and Mary Leung, allowed Javier to sleep on a cot in a storage shed behind the store, and generally kept him from going hungry or having to face the cruelties of the world on his own. Wyatt politely tipped his hat to Javier as he and Sadie entered Leung's.

Inside the store, there were only a few long shelves stocked with food and dry goods. Near the front window, a couple of old-timers faced each other across a barrel, atop which was a checkerboard. Leaning against the wall watching them, sipping a Coca-Cola, was Jack Gunther, a slender, clean-cut, sandy-haired young man who looked to be in his late '20s.

Wyatt and Sadie stepped to the counter, where Mary Leung, a middle-aged Chinese woman with grey streaks in her dark hair, stopped restocking shelves and greeted them.

"Wyatt! Josephine! Welcome back!" Mary threw her arms around Wyatt's torso and gave him a heartfelt hug.

Wyatt responded with a warm smile, "Good to see you, Mary."

She gave Wyatt an extra little squeeze. Sadie smiled at them, but there was a glint of jealousy in her eyes.

"Grocery business been good?" asked Wyatt.

"Can't complain," said Mary, looking Wyatt up and down. "Looks like Josephine's cooking's been good." She gave Wyatt a pat on the belly. He tried to hide his wince. Moving behind the counter, Mary asked, "What can I get you today?"

"Everything," said Sadie. "Need to restock our cupboards."

Wyatt opened the cover of a book on the counter. "What's this?" he asked.

"Horoscopes," said Mary. "I found out all you Gweilo are crazy about horoscopes, so I ordered a book of the Chinese Zodiac and charge twenty-five cents for a reading. Increased my business. Want to hear yours?"

Wyatt shook his head. "I think I know my fate."

"It's on the house," cooed Mary.

"I'd like to hear it," said Sadie, genuinely curious.

Mary sidled up next to Wyatt—too close for Sadie's comfort—saying, "What year were you born?"

"1848," he answered.

Mary thumbed through her book. "Ah," she said, "you were born in the Year of the Monkey."

Sadie giggled. "The monkey..."

"No, this is good," said Mary. "It says here that for a person born in the Year of the Monkey, life is a big game. You're fast, you're smart, you have a keen mind, and play by your own rules."

Sadie's eyes went wide. "Oh, my goodness!" she exclaimed. "That's you to a T!"

THE LAST STAGE

Mary continued, "You're always extra aware of what is happening around you. Even in crowds, you're analyzing and remembering any useful information. You like to be in control of every situation, and you're not very patient."

"Are we done?" asked Wyatt.

Mary barreled ahead. "It says your life will be hard, with many ups and downs, but you always figure out the rules of the game and how to win."

"That's amazing!" said Sadie, in genuine awe.

"Hogwash," snorted Wyatt. "You could say that about anybody."

Sadie rebuked him. "Why, Wyatt Earp, that couldn't be any more on the nose! My little monkey..."

With a look to Mary, Wyatt muttered, "See what you've done?"

"Do mine!" said Sadie, excitedly.

"What's your birth year, hun?" asked Mary.

"18......" She glanced over at the men playing checkers, then leaned in to whisper the year to Mary.

Mary nodded, thumbed through the pages, and said, "You are... Year of the Rooster."

Wyatt raised an eyebrow, teasing, "Rooster, or hen?"

"Rooster," said Mary matter-of-factly. "For a person born in the Year of the Rooster, life is full of surprises. But even when things go wrong, you still believe in yourself. You like to talk..."

"And that's YOU to a T!" said Wyatt.

"Shut up!" snapped Sadie.

Mary continued, "You're very confident, and sometimes you brag and exaggerate."

"Sometimes?" said Wyatt.

Annoyed, Sadie said, "Hush! I didn't interrupt your horoscope!"

"If there's a dispute," read Mary, "you don't like to admit when you're wrong, and you like giving advice to others, even if they haven't asked for it."

"Especially if they haven't asked for it," Wyatt interjected with a chuckle, adding, "There just might be something to all this Chinese hoo-doo after all..."

Sadie glared at him and shooed him away, saying, "Will you just go on?"

Wyatt stepped away to browse the shelves, while Mary continued with Sadie's fortune. "And in your love life, you are always ready to defend your soulmate…"

Wyatt strolled down the aisle between the shelves, toward the checker players, who were too engrossed in their game and their gossip to notice him. He heard one saying quietly, "THE Wyatt Earp?"

"Used to be Marshal in Arizona," said the other, in a low voice. "Got a place over by the Whipple Mountains." He moved a checker piece, adding, "I hear tell he don't trust banks. Keeps all his money hid away in his house."

Wyatt now stepped up beside them, hovering over them. They looked up at him, embarrassed they'd been overheard. Jack, still leaning against the wall, kept a curious eye on Wyatt, wondering how the legendary gunfighter would react, secretly hoping for a flaring of tempers and an eruption of violence.

Instead, Wyatt calmly said, "If you believe that, I've got two or three mines I'll sell you." He then looked down at the checkerboard and moved one of the black pieces, jumping a few of the reds to end up at the border. "Game over," he said, before turning to go back to the counter. The men reset the checkerboard, while Jack's eyes were glued to Wyatt, sizing him up, a hint of a smile playing at the corner of his lips.

At the counter, Mary concluded Sadie's fortune. "You are reliable, sometimes annoying, but always faithful," she said.

Wyatt ambled up to them. Sadie gave him a self-satisfied look. "There," she said. "You see. Always faithful. Yours didn't say that."

Mary closed the book.

"Henry around?" asked Wyatt.

"In back," said Mary.

"How's he doing?"

Mary nodded towards the door behind her. "Why don't you go say hello?"

Wyatt said to Sadie, "Just be a minute." He stepped around the counter and opened the door, which led into a dark hallway stocked with crates. Closing the door behind him, he walked past the goods cluttering his path toward an open door at the opposite end, light spilling out around it from the room beyond.

Wyatt pushed the door open wider and stepped into Henry and Mary's living quarters, much like Wyatt's Los Angeles bungalow, with everything in one big room, except for a bathroom walled off to itself. He glanced around, seeing a table with breakfast plates still atop it, a radio that was playing a Jazz broadcast, a bed, and a couch with a wheelchair next to it. Wyatt rapped on the door, calling, "Henry?"

There was a rustle on the couch, and Henry Leung, a thin and haggard Chinese man, rose up from under a blanket, apparently awakened from a nap. "Yep. Yep. Who's that?" he asked.

Wyatt walked over to him. "It's me, you old desert rat."

Henry recognized the voice. "Wyatt? You back in town?"

"Just for a spell," said Wyatt.

Henry sat up on the couch. His face and arms were burn-scarred from a long-ago accident, and one eye was milky, blinded. He squinted his good eye to get a better focus on the big man now standing before him. "Pull up a chair," he said.

"See you got a fancy one here. Wheels and everything," said Wyatt, motioning at the wheelchair.

"Had a fall a few months ago. Legs ain't workin' so good no more."

"I hear you. I can't quite do the two-step like I used to, either." The two men smiled at each other, clasping hands. Wyatt took a seat in a worn, almost too comfortable easy chair facing Henry.

"I do a slow dance every day," said Henry, leaning back.

"That right?"

"Yep. Whenever Mary picks me up to put me in the wheelchair."

Wyatt chuckled, saying, "You got a good woman there, Henry."

"You keep away from her, you old dog!"

"Strictly business between us."

Wyatt and Henry both knew that Mary was a flirt—it was good for business, she'd always say, honey to attract the flies. And while there was once a time when Wyatt could be easily tempted by a woman's wiles, he'd never give in to Mary's flirtations. He wouldn't do that to an old friend like Henry, especially since they'd been partners once.

With all the time they'd spent together in the mines, Wyatt had come to know Henry's story well. He was first generation American, son of a man who came from Taishan, in the Guangdong Province of China, in the 1860s to work on the transcontinental railroad. The Chinese workers were paid wages half those of what the white workers earned, so the more Chinese the railroad hired, the more money was left to line the pockets of the Union Pacific's board members, allowing them to become rich. Once the railroad was finished, the Chinese were let go and set adrift. But then gold was discovered in the Sacramento Valley, and Henry's father joined tens of thousands of his countrymen who went in search of an instant wealth that never, so to speak, panned out. When the rush ended, his father headed south, settling in Los Angeles. There, he met another Chinese immigrant who became his wife, and less than a year later, Henry was born.

The family survived by running a Chinese laundry. It appeared they had found their niche in American society, so long as they tolerated being denied citizenship and accepted that all white men were created equal, but black men, Native Americans, and Asians were not included in the promise of life, liberty, and the pursuit of happiness.

Racial tension in Los Angeles came to a head when Henry was a small boy. Anti-Chinese rioters descended on his family's laundry and most other businesses in Chinatown and burned them to the ground. But that wasn't enough for the braying mob. Henry watched helplessly as his father, along with nine other men and boys, were dragged out of their homes and lynched in the street. Eight others were burned to death in their homes by white savages—and they were savages, filled with hate and bent on destruction, intent on ridding the city of the people they derided as "coolies" and "rat eaters." Henry and his mother barely escaped, heading even farther south to San Diego.

His mother wanted to return to China, but she knew her California-born son would be as much of a pariah there as he was in America, simply because he was born in a foreign land. Henry was, effectively, a child without a country, unwanted in the land of his birth and unwelcome in the land of his forefathers. For the next several years, he and his mother became nomads, bouncing around the Southwestern territories. One winter, when he was in his teens, she contracted influenza and, without adequate medical care, passed away. Henry was now on his own.

He eventually found his way to Vidal, where he met and married Mary, a woman in the same precarious situation as he, whose family ran a general store. When her father died, she inherited the business. They just barely scraped by, so Henry began hiring himself out to miners who were looking for extra hands to work their claims. This was how he met Wyatt Earp, when the former lawman and his wife came to the Whipple Mountains seeking gold and copper after having tried their luck across the border in Tonopah and Goldfield, Nevada. Wyatt needed a strong-backed man who was good with a pick-axe to help him explore his sites, and Henry came highly recommended.

"You headin' back up to Happy Days?" asked Henry.

"Yep" answered Wyatt.

Henry shook his head. "When're you gonna admit it's all played out? You ought 'a try someplace else."

With a hint of weariness and resignation in his voice, Wyatt said, "Too much work to start over. Besides, we got a deal on that hole. I find anything, you'll get your cut."

"You find anything, I'll take it."

"Least I can do, after..."

Henry interrupted him. "Wyatt—you told me if we just kept digging, we could hollow out that tunnel without blasting. Ain't your fault I didn't listen. Always in a hurry—that's my problem."

"How do you do it, Henry?" Wyatt asked.

"Do what?"

"Stay so cheerful?"

Henry shifted his weight on the couch. "Oh, I'm not cheerful all the time. I've got my infirmities and injuries and a brain that tends toward melancholy. But I manage, so long as I don't compare myself to others."

"Easier said than done."

"Not really. Just takes practice. Anyway, when people compare, they always tend to compare themselves to others who are better off, so they're always coming up short and feel sad. If they just compared themselves to the millions who are worse off, they'd be grateful, and happy."

"I suppose," said Wyatt.

"It's like a poem my mother taught me, by Li Qingzhao."

"Who?"

"He was China's greatest poet. Lived hundreds of years ago, but this verse of his still holds true..." Henry closed his eyes, concentrating, and then recited the poem slowly:

"I wake dazed when smoke
breaks my spring sleep.
The dream distant,
so very distant;

and it is quiet, so very quiet.
The moon spins and spins.
The kingfisher blinds are drawn;
and yet I rub the injured bud,
and yet I twist in my fingers this fragrance,
and yet I possess these moments of time!

And that's it," Henry said cheerfully. "That's the secret. Just be in the present, right now, and cherish each moment of time as it comes."

"If that works for you, I'm happy for you," said Wyatt.

Henry chuckled. Then, leaning forward, he said, "You really want to help me?"

"What do you need?"

"Bedpan. Think I might 'a kicked it up under the couch somewheres..."

~ • ~

Wyatt and Sadie left the store with armfuls of groceries. As they stepped outside, Javier removed his fedora and held it out for Wyatt to leave a coin, but Wyatt just shook his head "no" and kept walking. He didn't have much, and what he did have, he needed to hang onto. Neither he nor Sadie noticed Jack Gunther coming out behind them, stepping onto the boardwalk. Jack leaned against the building, watching them as they made their way to their car.

As they strolled along, Sadie said, "Shameful how that woman flirts with you."

"Don't do no harm," said Wyatt.

"Oh, I'm sure you enjoy it. Why don't you ask her out for a walk? Bet she'd welcome you with open legs."

Wyatt set his bags of groceries in the back seat, then gave Sadie, standing next to him, a reassuring smile, joking, "Ain't that how we got started?"

"Hush! If I didn't have my arms full, I'd slap the monkey out of you!"

Wyatt took the groceries out of Sadie's arms and set them in the car. And then he noticed her gaze had gone to the cafe near the store. Through its windows, she could see a poker game in progress at a table in the far corner. Giving her a little nudge, Wyatt said, "Come along, Mrs. Earp."

Chapter 8

HORSES

Wyatt's next stop was on the outskirts of Vidal, where the road was little more than a dusty trail full of potholes. He was headed to the Armendariz Corral and Stables, a location he felt one could find blindfolded once they were in the vicinity; all they had to do was follow the sweet leathery smell of horseflesh and manure.

As he drove up to the property, Wyatt could see some of Armendariz's vaqueros running a dozen horses through exercises in the corral. He pulled his car up next to the fence, where the owner, Fernando Armendariz, a rawhide-tough Mexican, was leaning on one of the top horizontal panels, watching the younger men put the horses through their paces. As Wyatt and Sadie emerged from the car, Armendariz looked back, saw them, and gave them a wave.

"Senor Wyatt!" he said, moving toward them.

"Buenos dias, Fernando," said Wyatt, careful to step around the horse dung in his path.

"Good to see you back!" said Armendariz. "But who is this mujer bonita with you?" he added, smiling at Sadie.

"Just call her Gallo," said Wyatt.

"Surely you mean Muy?"

Sadie knew some rudimentary Spanish, but this was too much for her. "What's all that?" she asked, "Gallo, Muy...?"

Armendariz beamed, "He says I should call you rooster, but surely he means hen."

"Don't pay him any mind," said Sadie. "Just go on calling me mujer bonita."

Wyatt joined Armendariz at the corral fence, watching the horses being herded from one end to the other by the wiry young vaqueros.

"What can I do for you, Senor Wyatt?" asked Armendariz.

"I need some draft horses that can pull a wagon and stand a few weeks in the hills."

"Going back to your mining claims, I see. Sure you won't be chasing any banditos?"

"Draft horses," reiterated Wyatt. "Nothing fancy and fast."

"How many caballos you want?"

"Just two—one for me, one for Sadie. And Fernando—we're on a budget."

Armendariz called out instructions to one of the stable hands. "Diego! Trae esos dos viejos sementales aquí."

Diego and another vaquero—both on horseback—went to two older, chestnut-colored Haflingers at the edge of the corral who were content to graze instead of running about like the other horses. They threw lassos over their necks and led them forward.

"Maybe these two?" asked Armendariz. "They're a few years past their prime, but they're good workhorses."

"I know just how they feel," joked Wyatt. "Have 'em delivered up to the house."

"You want any saddles? Bridles?"

"Just the drays. I've got tack in my barn."

"Sure you wouldn't rather have a mule?"

"Got one," said Wyatt, pointing his thumb at Sadie.

"Humph!" she said, "Then I guess that makes you a jackass."

As she walked back to the car, Armendariz said, "Got a lot of spirit, your woman."

"Yep," agreed Wyatt, and added in a low voice Sadie couldn't hear, "Sometimes she's so full of spirits she can't walk straight." Armendariz laughed.

~ • ~

After Wyatt settled on a price with Armendariz, he and Sadie headed home. While she put away groceries, he went to the barn behind the house to prepare for the delivery of the animals. The barn had an opening in the front big enough to drive a wagon through. In fact, there was a wagon in the middle of the enclosure, uncovered, suitable for hauling supplies from town or carting them up to the mining claims. He'd take it out later to see if the wheels needed greasing and be sure the handbrake still worked.

Along one wall were a couple of 14 x 14 stalls, each with a steel trough and a feed rack. The stalls were separated by walls almost up to the floor of the hayloft above. All he needed was to kick a couple of bales of hay down and spread it around the stalls for bedding.

Hanging on the wall at the front of the barn, beside the wide door, were tools for working around the property—a shovel, an axe, a scoop, a broom, etc. And along the adjoining wall were saddles, bridles, and other tack, as well as an old leather quirt—a short riding whip with a braided leather lash—that Wyatt had received from a Mexican woman who was incarcerated in the Yuma penitentiary. Since she'd murdered her husband, Wyatt was fond of saying that it was a good quirt made by a bad woman.

Wyatt had spent the better part of his youth around horses and barns. He was born in Monmouth, Illinois, the fourth of what would eventually be nine children, if you counted his half-brother Newton, from his father's first marriage. When he was two-years-old, his father, Nicholas, set out to take the family to San Bernardino, California. They were on their way there with about a hundred other homesteaders when Wyatt's older sister, five-year-old Martha, fell sick as they crossed into Iowa. The rest of the caravan continued Westward, but Nicholas stopped and bought a 160-acre farm northeast of Pella. Martha died there six years later.

In April of 1861, the Civil War erupted, and in November, Wyatt's older brothers Newton, James, and Virgil enlisted in the Union Army. Wyatt's father Nicholas had served in the Mexican War in the late 1840s in a company commanded by Captain Wyatt Berry Stapp, whom he held in such esteem that he named Wyatt after him, and now that the nation was at war again, Nicholas spent much of his time away recruiting and drilling soldiers for the Union cause.

This left 13-year-old Wyatt as the man of the house, charged with tending to 80 acres of corn along with younger brothers Morgan and Warren. Wyatt never particularly liked farming, and often tried to run away and join the Army. Each time, his father found him and brought him home. When he was 16 and the war was winding down, his father again decided it was time to go Westward, so the family once again pulled up stakes and lit out for San Bernardino, joining a train of forty wagons. They arrived in December of 1864.

By the spring of the following year, Wyatt was assisting older brother Virgil, who'd taken a job as a driver for a stagecoach line in the Imperial Valley. Sometimes they carried supplies for the Union Pacific railroad, which was then edging its way westward. The job took Wyatt into Wyoming Territory and, while there, he found he had a facility for gambling. He also tried his hand—or rather, both hands—at boxing, but pretty quickly found it was less bruising to officiate than participate in pugilistic matches.

For a young man just turning twenty, the postwar years were a heady time, full of promise and adventure. But when his father decided it was time to take the family back east, he insisted that Wyatt come along, so Wyatt's adventures in the west came to an end.

For a while.

Chapter 9

SADIE'S CONCERN

Wyatt's breathing became more labored. Sadie rubbed a damp washcloth over his lips, which were dry and chapped from a day of inhaling and exhaling mostly through his mouth.

Outside, rain continued to pour, with an occasional rumble of thunder adding to the ominous feeling in the small, stuffy room. It had been warmer than usual that year. Even though it was wintertime, temperatures were hovering in the 80s during the day, and only dropping into the 60s at night. But the rain made it feel cooler, and now—past midnight—Sadie felt particularly chilled. The candle in the Menorah was almost gone, the flame flickering, threatening to go out and plunge the bungalow into darkness. She went to a dresser and took out a wool shawl to cover her shoulders.

Ambling into the kitchen, she opened a drawer full of odds-and-ends and found a box of long, tapered candles. She took a couple out and went to the table, where Stuart Lake had come to offer help. "Allow me," he said. She handed him the candles. He lit the new ones from the flames of the ones that were almost burned out and pushed them into the empty cups on the Menorah branches. The room now brightened with a steadier, golden glow.

Sadie went back to Wyatt's side, but Lake's attention was drawn to a manila envelope among a stack of papers and unopened mail at the corner of the table. Scrawled on the front of the envelope was his name, LAKE. He reached inside and pulled out several sheets of paper with typewritten questions. His anticipation rose as he realized these were the pages he had given Wyatt and Sadie on the beach in Santa

Monica. But as he flipped through them, he saw that the questions were still unanswered. His heart sank.

He went back to his seat by Wyatt's bedside, where Sadie kept her eyes trained intently on her husband's unmoving form, as though she were trying to will some of her own life force into him.

It had been fifty years since she first arrived in Tombstone and crossed paths with the man with whom she'd spend over two-thirds of her life. Looking at him now, she couldn't help but reflect on the journey that had brought her to this time, this place, this situation.

If her father hadn't left Posen—now a part of Poland since the Kingdom of Prussia was dissolved at the end of the world war in 1918—she might have lived her life in Europe as the daughter of a Jewish baker. But in the 1850s, Hyman Marcus set sail for America hoping to find better opportunities and less prejudice. Arriving in New York, he was disappointed to find the burgeoning population of expatriate German Jews in the city looked down on what they considered to be the less sophisticated Eastern European Jews, or 'Polacks,' as they were derisively called.

Not long after settling in the disease-infested, crime-ridden slums of Five Points in lower Manhattan, Hyman married a widow named Sofia Lewis, another recent refugee who had a daughter named Rebecca. The couple had three additional children: Nathan, Josephine, and Henrietta. Josephine, or Josie, being the middle child, struggled to find her place in the family. While her parents and siblings were humble, modest and hardworking, Josie was brash and loud and ambitious, a radiant butterfly among a family of worker bees.

She was only eight years old when her father decided that their prospects might be better in the newer city of San Francisco—recently a rough-and-ready gold-rush town—than in the socially stratified slums of Five Points. After a three-week voyage that involved steerage passage on a steamship south to Panama, then a train across the Isthmus, and steerage in another steamship north to California, they arrived in the bustling Bay area. But even in a city that was considered to be more progressive, they found that German Jews still discriminated against Polish Jews, and her father still struggled to provide for the family. Over the next ten years, they moved six times from one low-rent neighborhood to another. Somehow, through it all, Hyman and Sofia always managed to keep their children well-fed and in school.

THE LAST STAGE

Josephine's younger sister Henrietta, or Hattie, was the star student in the family. Older brother Nathan, lazy by nature, was less so, while step-sister Rebecca secured her future by marrying a clothing salesman shortly after their arrival in California. Josephine, being less practical and more rebellious than her siblings, preferred theater performances to school lectures. After much begging and pleading, her mother enrolled her in dance classes.

Shortly after she turned eighteen, Josephine escaped San Francisco and, along with her friend Dora Hirsch, daughter of her dance teacher, joined a touring company of Gilbert and Sullivan's hugely popular comic opera H.M.S. Pinafore. Soon, they were on their way to the wilds of the Arizona Territory. When she arrived in the west, she was determined that she would no longer be seen as a lower tier citizen and told anyone who asked that she was the daughter of a wealthy German-Jewish merchant.

The touring company eventually brought her to Tombstone, a silver-mining boomtown which, at that time, had only about a hundred residents living mostly in tents and shacks. While there, Josephine caught the eye of the town's handsome Deputy Sheriff, Johnny Behan, 16 years her senior. His engaging smile, dark hair, and coal-black eyes captivated her, and it wasn't long before he began finding excuses to come around her boarding house. Conveniently ignoring that he was married and had a child, he began an affair with her. He justified their courtship by telling Josephine that his marriage was effectively over and that he would soon be divorced from his wife, whom he was no longer living with. For her part, Josephine was flattered by his attention, and found the affair a welcome diversion from her feelings of homesickness. But she was not enamored enough of him to claim that she loved him, nor enough to stay in Tombstone when the theatrical troupe moved on to Prescott.

Shortly after arriving there, the troupe dissolved. Josephine was now stranded in the Arizona Territory, receiving letters from Behan pledging his love but never mentioning marriage. At a seeming dead end, she decided it might be best to return home to her family in San Francisco. Before she left Prescott, she wrote Behan a letter saying, "when you get your divorce, come see me."

After her adventures in the Territory, life in her parents' home seemed exceedingly dull. It wasn't long before she began to feel the wanderlust again, and she was elated when Johnny Behan showed up one day on her parents' doorstep and presented her with a diamond ring. Behan asked the Marcus's for their daughter's hand in marriage. After his departure, Josephine was still uncertain if she wanted to hitch her future to Behan's prospects, so Behan dispatched a friend who was the wife of a prominent Tombstone lawyer to plead his case. The friend proved to be a successful advocate; Josephine was soon on her way back to Arizona.

She arrived to find that in the short time she'd been away, the city had grown to ten times its former size, now with over a thousand residents and the tents replaced by actual homes and shops. Behan had lost his bid to be re-elected Deputy Sheriff and was now angling to become County Sheriff. His divorce from his wife had been particularly acrimonious, leaving him living in a house with his young son, Albert. Though he began introducing Josephine around town as "Mrs. Behan," he continually evaded setting a formal wedding date. After the initial glow wore off, it seemed to Josephine that instead of finding wedded bliss and respectability, she had traveled nearly a thousand miles only to become, in effect, Behan's mistress and unpaid governess.

And so she remained for the next year, as the miners found silver harder to come by and the town became overrun by a rougher element—an organized crime group called the Cowboys, comprised of the Clantons, the McLaurys, Curly Bill Brocius, Johnny Ringo and others who were carrying out stagecoach robberies and engaging in cross-border cattle rustling while newly-elected Cochise County Sheriff Johnny Behan turned a blind eye. There was also a greater influx of prostitutes into Tombstone, and ladies' man Behan enjoyed their companionship, a vice that landed him in hot water with Josephine after he contracted syphilis. Too embarrassed to return to her parents for a second time, and too humiliated to stay with Behan, she lived at the homes of various friends over the next six months.

Meanwhile, she'd seen the Earp brothers—Virgil, Morgan, Wyatt, James, and Warren—around town; they'd arrived beginning at the end of 1879 with their mostly common-law wives intending to establish a stage line. Since there were already two well-established lines there, the Earps changed course and bought interests in mines and water rights, bartended, and gambled. Virgil was now the deputy U.S. Marshal for the Tombstone mining district, responsible for covering the entire

THE LAST STAGE

southeastern area of the Arizona Territory, and Wyatt found work as a shotgun messenger on Wells Fargo stagecoaches, a job he passed on to Morgan after Virgil appointed Wyatt as his deputy.

Josephine was often in town, buying groceries or mailing letters, and on one of those occasions a mutual friend introduced her to Wyatt Earp. She never could remember exactly what words they first spoke to each other; it was probably a dull pleasantry along the lines of "pleased to make your acquaintance." But it wasn't the words that mattered—it was the electric shock she felt up and down her spine when she first looked into his piercing blue eyes.

What was it that drew her to Wyatt? It wasn't social climbing; there were plenty of available men, and sons of available men, who were better connected and better off financially. Nor was it a youthful rebellion against the mores and attitudes of her parents; she'd never really adopted their mores, so there was nothing to rebel against. And it wasn't some misguided notion that this towering 6'3" giant was a great romantic who would worship and adore her and spend his life trying his damnedest to make her more comfortable. No, it was more basic than that. It was pure animal lust.

She was a ravishing, raven-haired, smooth-skinned, rosy-cheeked, dark-eyed 21-year-old with small hips and a big bosom, just over five feet tall, always immaculately dressed in finery that accentuated her bountiful curves. Wyatt was a tall, blonde, broodingly handsome 33-year-old who moved with the grace of a jungle cat and had twice the ferocity bubbling beneath a quiet surface. He was brave, courageous, and bold, effortlessly exuding charisma, and quick-tempered. Josephine sensed there was something inside him that was broken, that fueled his gruffness and fits of anger. And she thought maybe, just maybe, she could fix him. Perhaps she was spirited enough to match him, maybe even break this wild Mustang and tame him for polite society.

It wasn't long before they'd begun an affair, and she was delighted to discover that he was a passionately aggressive and adventurous lover. She'd once heard Bat Masterson describe Wyatt as "manhood extreme."

Bat had no idea.

Sadie's reverie ended as she noticed Dr. Shurtleff wrapping a steel hot water bottle in a towel. "You think he's getting better?" she asked him.

Giving her a concerned look, Dr. Shurtleff said, "Infection's spreading."

Sadie trembled, trying to hold back her tears.

Dr. Shurtleff placed the hot water bottle just below Wyatt's belly, and pulled the cover up over it. "This might give him some relief." Looking at Sadie with concern, he asked, "Why don't you let me give you a sedative?"

"I don't want a sedative," she responded. Brushing her fingers through Wyatt's fine white hair, she said quietly, "I want my husband."

Chapter 10

HAPPY DAYS

"Gettin' a mite warm," Wyatt grumbled. Armendariz's drays pulled Wyatt and Sadie's rickety wagon, stocked with all the mining supplies they needed as well as water and food to last a few days, up the long, blistering-hot rise toward the foot of the Whipple Mountains. The mountain range was named for an Army lieutenant who surveyed the area for the transcontinental railroad in 1854 and declared it unfit. With the sun bearing down on him and dust filling his nostrils, Wyatt was inclined to agree.

As they traveled north to their campsite, sitting on the wagon's spring seat, their feet resting on the toe board, with the reins in Wyatt's hands and Earpie on Sadie's lap, the desert became a craggy mess of sand and rocks. There was a considerable amount of Sonora creosote bush scrub at the beginning of their journey, thinning out as they began the incline up to the mine, replaced by various species of cacti—mostly cholla and prickly pear, but also the ever-majestic saguaro. Wyatt took a handkerchief from his pocket and wiped sweat beads from his brow, as Sadie unscrewed the lid of a canteen and handed it to him. He took a long draw of the refreshingly cool water.

Earpie alerted and Sadie had to hold him back whenever the occasional jackrabbit or chipmunk dashed across their path. And as they continued up the slope, Wyatt had to pause to move a slow-moving desert tortoise out of the way. Thankfully, their trek kept them on the broad wash to the foothills, avoiding the uneven terrain of steep-walled canyons, cliff bands, and eroded formations that began farther up. The mountain itself rose to over 4,000 feet at its highest peak, a geographic monolith visible from just about any point in a ten-mile radius.

Both Wyatt and Sadie were dressed for the desert, with Sadie in a skirt shorter than the ankle-length ones she usually wore, and made from durable corduroy rather than cotton, along with stout high-laced, low-heeled boots and a wide-brimmed sun bonnet. She'd always had an aversion to wearing any kind of clothes she considered "mannish" —like trousers—no matter how practical they might have been; she felt they were unbecoming on any woman past the first blush of youth. Wyatt, meanwhile, was in his working gear: blue jeans, long-sleeved shirt, well-worn boots, cowboy hat, and a neckerchief.

As they reached their destination, they passed a claim marker sticking out of the ground bearing the crudely painted name:

EARP—HAPPY DAYS

He was home.

~ • ~

Wyatt and Sadie spent the morning setting up camp in a flat spot under a scraggly Juniper tree. A line was pulled taut between two creosote bushes to tie off the horses, which Sadie then tended to. She poured water for them from a bucket, which she'd filled from a 50-gallon drum of fresh water on the back of the wagon.

There was a tent, of sorts, still there from their previous sojourns at the mine. Wyatt had thrown it together with poles, scraps of lumber, ropes, and big canvas tarpaulins. It was more like a canvas room than a tent or teepee. He inspected it for damage, replacing tarps that were weather-damaged and rotting and tightening rope bindings that desert animals had used for sharpening their teeth. Earpie, meanwhile, made a few circuits around the desert, exploring and marking territory, before claiming a napping spot in the scant shade from the Juniper tree.

When Sadie was done with the horses and Wyatt had prepared the tent for another stay, he and Sadie went to work on the inside, setting up folding cots and canvas chairs. They then gathered rocks to place in an oblong square outside, a short distance from the door flap, where they could pile brush to burn for cooking. Over the square, Wyatt set up a couple of iron tripods connected by a rod at the top—rather like a thin sawhorse—from which hung hooks for a Dutch oven and a hanging iron grill. The Dutch oven—a covered pot—would be handy for warming beans or soup, while the grill would be used for cooking in the cast iron skillet or heating up the coffee pot.

When it was all done, the camp looked almost good as new. Wyatt glanced across their "front yard," such as it was, and gave Sadie a big grin. He was happy, a man in his element. And seeing Wyatt so comfortably at ease made her happy, too. But he could see her enthusiasm didn't quite equal his, even though she'd shared this experience with him many times before. It seemed that with each passing year, she got a little more skittish about being in the wilderness.

"You gonna be okay?" he asked her.

"You know I don't feel all that comfortable out here," she said.

"Then why'd you come?"

"'Cause you're here. And I imagine you've got courage enough for the both of us."

She went to the wagon and returned with a few provisions for lunch. There was a deeper fear she left unspoken, that if anything happened to her man in that unforgiving place, though she wouldn't want to leave him alone, she'd have to go an awful long way to find help.

~ • ~

After a quick lunch of bread, apple slices, and beef jerky, Wyatt and Sadie set out to explore the mine. She helped him take a wooden extension ladder off the wagon. Unexpanded, the ladder was ten feet, but when the smaller top section was pulled out and locked into place, it extended to eighteen. They hoisted it over the rim of a pit and slowly lowered it until its feet were secure on the rocky ground below. About three feet of ladder extended above ground, and Wyatt tied one of the rungs off to a deeply-rooted bush nearby for added stability.

He and Sadie unloaded empty buckets, a couple of rock hammers, and a kerosene lantern from the wagon. They threw all but one of the empty buckets into the pit. The final one Wyatt loaded up with their tools and the lantern, tied the bail to a length of rope, and slowly lowered it down to the bottom of the pit. Then he climbed down the ladder, with Sadie following after him.

Left alone up above, Earpie barked up a storm. He didn't appreciate being abandoned, even if there were rabbits and chipmunks to chase.

"Don't think Earpie wants us to come down here," said Sadie.

"I wouldn't worry about it," said Wyatt. "He'll tire himself out pretty soon and go sleep in the tent."

Having reached the bottom of the pit, Wyatt lit the kerosene lantern and, holding it aloft in front of him, entered the mine tunnel. Sadie followed close behind. The tunnel was narrow—if they'd put their arms out, they'd have touched the sides—and not very high; every so often Wyatt had to duck to keep from bumping his head. The farther they walked ahead, the narrower it became. There were a few timbers here and there shoring it up, and some others left lying on the sides for possible future use. The lantern light glinted off violet veins of amethyst in the rock wall, sparkling in the lantern's glow, and the air became cooler and mustier, faintly scented with the ammonia-like odor of bat urine and guano.

After walking for about thirty feet, passing by the occasional dried husk of a rattlesnake's molted skin, they came to a place where the tunnel let out into an area that was pretty well excavated. This is where Wyatt had struck copper on one of his first excursions here, when Henry was helping him and decided the quickest way to accomplish the job was to blast his way through the earth, a plan that began well and ended badly. The vein Wyatt and Henry uncovered played out pretty quickly, but Wyatt felt there might be more in the rock walls, so that's where he and Sadie had concentrated their digging ever since. Over time, they'd excavated enough to create a space about the size of a large igloo's interior—confined, but one in which there was room to stand up straight and move about a little.

There were a couple of fresher, narrower exploratory tunnels dug into opposite sides, but their clearance was so low they'd have had to crawl on their bellies to get into them.

"Here goes nothing," said Wyatt. He set the lantern down, then he and Sadie got to work. They pounded the stone walls with the rock hammers, chipping away bits of worthless igneous rocks and amethyst that collected in the buckets they held underneath.

After half an hour had passed, though Wyatt kept chipping away with the rock hammer, his rhythm was slowing. He sat down on a rock and put down his bucket and hammer, then wiped the sweat from his brow and rubbed his aching belly. Sadie noticed. She stopped hammering. "You need to go outside," she told him.

He replied testily, "You need to leave me be."

"Leave you be? You think I don't see you're in pain?"

"Dammit, woman, hush! If I want your help, I'll ask for it!"

Sadie wasn't in the mood to be snapped at. She dropped her bucket, slung her hammer beside it, stomped over to him, and put out her hand. Wyatt looked at her, fire in his eyes. But her gaze was just as defiant. Two immovable objects colliding... until Wyatt gave in. Letting out a sigh, he extended his hand. She grabbed it, yanking him to his feet. She followed him as he trudged slowly through the tunnel to the ladder. He ascended slowly, tuckered out. She followed close behind him, hoping his feet wouldn't slip or his hands lose their grip, because there'd be little she could do to stop him from falling if they did.

Once he was back above-ground, Wyatt felt like he should set up the dry sifter, but he just wasn't up to it. Instead, he relaxed on a canvas chair outside the tent, feeling the slight breeze that kicked up as the moon appeared low on the horizon. Though blazing hot in the day, the desert could become a mite chilly at night, which was a welcome relief. Sadie started a fire and warmed a Mason jar full of soup for their dinner, pouring it into the Dutch oven to heat while she brewed a pot of coffee on the grille. When they finished eating, she put the dishes aside and brought a fresh mug of coffee to Wyatt.

"Feel like I got a bellyful of bricks," he grumbled.

She sat in the folding chair beside him and rubbed his lower back. He moaned his appreciation. She said, "Even pack mules need a little rest now and then."

"You calling me a pack mule?"

"Stubborn as one. Should've rested a day or two after that long drive."

Earpie sauntered over and laid down in the sand in front of them. Wyatt took a sip of coffee and stared at the ground. "Just the indignity of it, is all," he sighed.

"I know, Shug."

"I've stood toe-to-toe with some of the meanest, toughest sons of bitches around, bullets flying, never even got nicked. And now I'm being done in by a piss infection." He took another sip of coffee, set it down. "Help me up."

She stood and pulled him to his feet. Looking down at his little round belly drooping over his belt, she said, "Mary's right."

"'Bout what?"

"You are getting fat."

"Well," drawled Wyatt, "you know how it is—when a man gets done with his tools he puts a shed over 'em."

She guffawed, and gave a light slap to his bicep. "Hush your mouth!" she said. Looking into his blue eyes, she added, "Anyway, we might find a use for those tools yet."

He gave her a peck on her forehead, and moseyed off into the shadows. Of course she was right. His belly was bigger, visibly so, bloated from his infection and water retention, tight and round like a melon, hard in some areas, spongy and painful to the touch in others. And it was all the more noticeable on his otherwise lanky frame, like a pencil stuck through a plum. But he didn't want to have another discussion about his ailment with Sadie, so he'd brushed off her comment with a joke.

As he walked along, Earpie caught up to him, sniffing around at his heels. "Careful where you put your nose, Earpie," said Wyatt. "Might get snake bit." Rattlers were common in the mountains. But Earpie didn't go too far astray—he stuck close to his master. Wyatt went to some tall rocks that were nearby, but not too close to the camp. He unbuttoned his fly, reached inside, felt around for his tallywag, found it, and pulled it out. And then he just stood there. Waiting. Trying to urinate. His distended stomach rumbled.

His malady had made Wyatt become preoccupied with his abdominal region. His gut made such strange noises now. Sometimes it sounded like a frog croaking, sometimes like a spring vibrating, sometimes like water gurgling through a funnel. And sometimes, it was all three at once. He sensed his body was beginning to break down, like an old wagon misused and abandoned to dry out in the sun. But he hoped he'd get a little farther down the line before he was totally beyond repair.

He looked down and saw Earpie close by, sitting on his haunches, panting, his eyes fixated on Wyatt. "Earpie, git!" commanded Wyatt, but Earpie didn't budge. Wyatt sighed, "You know I can't do this with you staring at me." Earpie kept happily panting. So, Wyatt called out, "Sadie! Come get this dog!" He heard Sadie call Earpie's name and whistle. Earpie ignored her. But then she banged a spoon against the side of his food dish. That did it—Earpie's ears perked up and he took off like a shot.

THE LAST STAGE

Now, finally, Wyatt had some peace. He gazed out at the horizon, where the distant mountains appeared like pale blue phantoms in the fading light. There, in the encroaching darkness, he saw a faint cloud of dust moving across the desert. Hard to tell from this distance, but as he narrowed his eyes to focus, it looked like a white stagecoach pulled by white stallions, racing across the valley floor at a good clip and kicking up a dust cloud, until it finally disappeared behind a hill.

Wyatt feared he might end up standing out there beside the rocks for half the night. Concentrating on his breathing, he tensed his stomach muscles. At last, he felt relief as his kidneys emptied themselves in the dust and rocks in an unsteady stop-and-start stream.

~ • ~

Afterwards, Wyatt sat side-by-side with Sadie, staring into the campfire, which cast a muted red-orange tint on the desert sand, while glowing red embers rose into the sky, blending with the stars before fading out.

He was quiet, and so was she, looking at his profile in the faint light of the campfire. The soft glow it cast was magical, smoothing out his wrinkles, putting a bit of glow back into his cheeks. Seeing him this way, it was easy for her to recall how handsome he'd been when she first met him, with his dark blonde hair, mustache, and blue eyes under a brooding brow. Back then, he was a force to be reckoned with. Now, he'd become fragile. He was ill. He was old. But nonetheless, her most fervent wish was that she could keep him by her side forever.

Wyatt saw how intently she was staring at him. He gave her a little smile, and took her hand in his. "Sadie-Belle," he said, "all my life I've been hustling and scrambling. Make money, lose money. Never had much of nothin' I could hang onto and call my own. 'Cept you." He kissed the back of her hand.

"What'd you go saying all that for?" she asked.

Wyatt shrugged. "Just want to let you know I care about you."

Wyatt seemed to always stop short of referring to his affection for Sadie as love. She'd learned to accept it; the fact that he had trouble expressing his feelings didn't mean he didn't have them. He was just naturally reserved.

"Well…" she said, "I love you, too."

She leaned in to give him a peck on the lips.

"Good thing," he said. "Ornery as we are, I reckon nobody else'd have us."

~ • ~

The next morning, Wyatt and Sadie had some eggs, hardtack and coffee and then Wyatt helped her feed and water the horses. Sadie gathered some desert grasses and scrub for them, while Wyatt toted a bucket of water, drained from the water barrel on the wagon, to fill their troughs.

As Wyatt poured water for one horse and Sadie put down a pile of grass for the other, they suddenly heard a rattle. Sadie caught a glimpse of the snake, a three-footer, undulating out around the trough where she was standing. The horse tethered there saw it too, and panicked. It reared up, it's shoulder bumping Sadie and knocking her off-balance. She fell, twisting around, putting her hands out to break her fall, but her left foot caught on a rock.

Meanwhile, Wyatt picked up a stick, which he jabbed under the snake and quickly flicked upward, sending it sailing out into the desert. With the threat gone, the horse settled down. Wyatt rushed to Sadie, still on the ground, and knelt beside her, grabbing her shoulders to raise her up to a sitting position. She reached for her ankle, her eyes squinting in pain.

"You okay?" he asked.

"Don't know," she said, blinking away tears. "Banged my foot. Feels like I might'a broke it."

Wyatt looked at her foot. Her ankle was cut and scraped, some blood trickling. Wyatt clasped his hand around it. She whimpered.

"Don't think it's broken," he said. "Probably a bad sprain. But I don't expect you're gonna be climbing ladders anytime soon. C'mon, let's see if we can get you on your feet."

She clasped her hands behind his neck and he raised up, lifting her. Once she was upright, she faltered, but he held her up. "What do you think we should do?" she asked.

"Not much we can do except take you home. Maybe have the doc come around and look you over."

"Perhaps if I just rest for a day or so…"

"You're no use here," he said bluntly. "Need to be at home, resting, and healing."

THE LAST STAGE

She knew he was right, but she also knew this meant separation from Wyatt—he'd surely want to come back out to work the claim, and she'd be in the house by herself.

She was never very good by herself.

"Come on," he said. "Let's get you in the tent for a spell."

She moved with a sort of hop, trying to keep her weight off the injured foot, keeping an arm around Wyatt's solid shoulders. He helped her into the tent and lowered her down onto a cot, then he went back out to take a saddle from the wagon to throw on one of the horses.

When the horse was ready, Wyatt gingerly helped Sadie up into the saddle, then he climbed up to share it with her, sitting behind her. They started down the long sloping incline at a walk, then gently galloped over the flats, to make the ride as comfortable as possible for her. Earpie kept pace alongside.

Nearly an hour later, they arrived home. Wyatt took Sadie inside, laid her down on their bed, and cleaned and dressed her wounds as best he could. Earpie, nearly dehydrated, drank a bowlful of water and nestled in beside her. Wyatt left them resting while he got into his car and drove into Vidal to fetch Dr. Cork, who followed Wyatt back to the house.

Dr. Cork was a short, balding man with bifocal eyeglasses and a pleasing smile whose cheery bedside manner was helped considerably by a lilting Irish accent. He confirmed Wyatt's diagnosis of a sprained ankle, adding that Sadie also had a torn ligament. Before he left, he prescribed plenty of rest, cold compresses, and aspirin. And to help with her immediate pain, he reached into his black bag, pulled out a quart bottle of Irish whiskey, and poured her a double. As he handed it to her, she stared at it with both trepidation and anticipation.

"Oh, I don't know if I ought 'a…" she began.

"Young lady," Dr. Cork said with a commanding voice, "who's the doctor here?"

Well, she thought, if he insists…

After Dr. Cork collected his payment and left, Wyatt came into the bedroom with a couple of plates, having made fried baloney sandwiches for both of them. He sat next to her on the bed, facing her. "Feeling any better?" he asked.

"A little bit," she said, taking a bite of her dinner. "You're not going back tonight, are you?"

"Tomorrow," he said. "I'll stay with you tonight. The mine ain't goin' nowhere."

"I don't like the idea of you up there all alone," she said. "What if you were to have an accident? How would anybody know? You need somebody up there to look after you."

"Maybe Mary'll come with me," he said, teasing her.

"UNH!" she exclaimed. "You would, wouldn't you? And I know just what you'd be mining!"

Wyatt chuckled. "Might have to drill a little deeper…"

"Hush!" she said. Then smiled. "You're awful." They ate in silence for a moment, and then she said, with seriousness, "What you need is some strong-backed, weak minded young buck to do all the heavy lifting. A man your age ought to be supervising, not working."

"I don't need any help," he grumbled.

"'Course you do!"

"Why don't you let me handle the mine?"

"You're not twenty years old anymore, Wyatt!" she shouted, losing patience with his obstinance. "Just go into town and hire somebody. Maybe get one of those horse wranglers from the stables."

"With what?" Wyatt said sharply. "What am I gonna pay 'em with?"

She'd hit a nerve. As calmly and sweetly as possible, she said, "Well… don't we have money?"

"Did," said Wyatt. "Till I paid the doc just now."

Sadie put her hand on his forearm and looked into his blue eyes. "Oh, honey," she said, "you know how to get money."

Chapter 11

THE GAMBLER

The next morning, Wyatt left Sadie at the house and drove his Packard down the dusty road to Vidal. He went to the cafe, where he found a table in the back and pulled out a deck of cards. It didn't take long for the vultures to come circling, and by noon he was engaged in a tense poker game with three rough-looking men—Gib Hayden, Clete Jenkins, and Wes Hightower.

Hayden was a hot-tempered ranch hand, or railroad worker, or whatever odd job he could rustle up that week, his face drawn and tight from thirty-plus years of hard living. He was condescending to everyone, all the time, not because he believed they were lesser than him, but because he knew damn well they were better, and the only way he could rise above them was to cut them down to size, with a combination of mean-spirited wisecracks and a general demeanor of unbridled menace.

Jenkins was a decade younger and had the disposition of a chicken on a hotplate—gangly, obnoxiously loud, and sporting a wide-brimmed sombrero that looked considerably more well-seasoned than the fidgety, anxious, impetuous, overgrown man-child wearing it.

Hightower, by contrast, was a stout, tall, dark-haired native, probably a Chemehuevi, one of the bands of Paiute that wandered around the Mojave Desert. Hightower didn't speak much in the presence of strangers, particularly white men. In Wyatt's estimation, he was as imposing as a giant Sequoia tree, and had about as much personality.

Each man had a stack of bills in front of him. As they kept playing, Wyatt gauged his progress by how their piles of money grew as he drew them in, and then dwindled as he cleaned them out. After a couple of hours, almost all of the legal tender on the table was in front of Wyatt.

They began a new round. It was Wyatt's deal, and he couldn't resist showing off with a well-practiced riffle.

"Where'd you learn all them fancy shuffles?" groused Hayden.

"My grandma," said Wyatt.

"Hunh!" Hayden scoffed, adding, "You a card-creaser?"

Wyatt looked into Hayden's eyes, saying, "Just a man who enjoys a good hand."

Wyatt dealt the cards, then glanced at what he held. He took the cigar he was smoking from between his lips and tapped its ash into the heavy glass ashtray in front of him. A quick look around the table and he instantly measured the expressions of concern in his opponent's eyes. Bad hands, all of them. Wyatt took a sip of water from his glass, and casually, but purposefully, sat it down close to the ashtray.

Jenkins shifted in his seat, and Wyatt looked over at him. Jenkins noticed. "Like my hat?" he asked. "Got it from a captain at the battle of Tia Juana."

"What'd you give him for it?" asked Wyatt.

"A bellyful of lead."

"Mind taking it off at the table?"

Jenkins smirked, a dangerous gleam in his eyes. "What if I do?"

"Shit, Jenkins," said Hightower, defusing the tension, "you bought that lid at a flea market."

Jenkins' face flushed, as he yelled, "I GOT IT AT THE BATTLE!"

"That battle was fifteen years ago," Wyatt said coolly. "You must 'a been the fiercest ten-year-old at the front."

"You skin that back!" Jenkins spat.

He began to leap up, but Hayden put a hand on his forearm, commanding him, "Sit down."

Jenkins obeyed, reluctantly. Hayden jerked the sombrero off Jenkins' head and flung it to the floor. Jenkins shot a fiery look at Wyatt, who played it cool, meeting Jenkins' gaze.

THE LAST STAGE

"You in or out?" asked Wyatt.

"You sure are powerful lucky, Mister," said Jenkins. "Powerful lucky."

Wyatt said nothing. But Hadley piped in, "Don't seem natural." He looked at Jenkins, adding, "Does it?"

"Sometimes luck ain't required," said Wyatt.

Jenkins asked, "What's that s'posed to mean?"

"Stupid people play stupidly."

Bristling, Jenkins began, "Are you callin'—"

Wyatt snapped, "If you ain't got at least a pair of Jacks, fold and be done with it!"

The air was thick with tension. Hayden's eyes took the measure between Jenkins and Wyatt. Jenkins threw his cards down.

Right at that moment, Tom Wendler—a rancher from the community who was well-known to Wyatt—walked towards their table, giving Wyatt a curt little wave. "Wyatt Earp, as I live and breathe!" he said, slapping Wyatt's shoulder. Hayden reacted, surprised, as Tom continued, "When did you get back in town?"

"I think you're mistaken, Mister," said Wyatt, with a terseness that alerted Tom that he'd made a faux pas.

"Oh, sorry," Tom apologized, nervously. "My mistake. You sure do bear a powerful resemblance to him, though."

"'Preciate the compliment," said Wyatt dismissively.

Tom tipped his hat to the men and stepped on out of the cafe. When he was gone, Hayden took a long, measured look at Wyatt. "Wyatt Earp?" he said. "I thought you said your name was Barry Stapp."

"It is," said Wyatt coolly.

Jenkins muttered, "Man don't want to tell his true name, usually means he's got something to hide."

"Wait a minute..." said Hayden, thoughtfully. "I remember now... I read about a Wyatt Earp! He was in the shootout at the O.K. Corral..."

Jenkins asked, "The what?"

"O.K. Corral," said Hayden. "Famous gunfight." He fixed Wyatt with a knowing gaze. "This old coot's a famous lawdog, boys."

Wyatt's jaw flinched. He tried to ignore them, asking, "How many cards you want?"

"Two," said Hayden, discarding two from his hand. Wyatt dealt him two new ones. Hayden studied his new hand, saying, "I seem to recall readin' in some book or other that that shootout was more like a massacre."

"Don't believe everything you read," said Wyatt.

"Why, it's gotta be true," teased Hayden. "If they put it in a book, it just has to be true."

"Then I guess the truth ain't what happened," said Wyatt, "it's what somebody says happened. Even if they weren't there." He eyed the men. "What'll it be?"

Hightower reluctantly folded. Then Jenkins threw his cards down, looking peeved. But Hayden threw in a five-dollar bill, saying, "Raise you five."

Wyatt added fifteen dollars to the pot. "I'll see your five, raise you ten."

Hayden studied his hand. Looked at Wyatt, stone-faced, then turned his attention back to his cards. And with a look of disgust, he threw them down. Wyatt scooped the money on the table towards himself.

Jenkins spat, "Show me your cards!"

Wyatt kept his cool. "Beg pardon?"

"Show me your cards!"

"Don't have to," said Wyatt. "You folded."

Jenkins slammed his fist on the table so hard the ashtray and drinking glasses bounced. "I want to see your hand, Mister!"

Hightower leaned back in his seat. "I'd like a look, too."

Wyatt said calmly, "Well, fellas, that ain't a right, it's a privilege. You only earn it if you call my bluff. Now are we gonna play poker, or —"

Jenkins seethed, "I said I want to see your cards!".

"Yeah, Mr. High-and-Mighty Earp," said Hayden. "We'd all like to know what you got."

With a sigh, Wyatt picked up his cards, along with the rest of the deck, and shuffled his cards in among them. He slapped the deck on the table. "They're all in there," he said. "Look at 'em all you want." As he said it, Wyatt accidentally knocked his glass over, spilling water on the table. Embarrassed by his clumsiness, he whipped a handkerchief out of his coat pocket to sop up the mess.

"Thirty years ago…" said Hayden, his voice dripping menace.

"Come again?" asked Wyatt.

"San Francisco. The Fitzsimmons fight against Tom Sharkey. You refereed it—or should I say, fixed it? Everybody went home empty-handed that night, except you and your cronies."

THE LAST STAGE

"I made an honest call. Fitzsimmons punched Sharkey below the belt."

"He punched him in the stomach! I saw it! I was standing next to my daddy's knee at ringside! That was as legal a punch as I ever saw, above the trunks! And you disqualified him!"

"Well, I saw different."

The Sharkey-Fitzsimmons fight was a stain on Wyatt's character that he'd never been able to erase. The prizefight was set for December 3, 1896, at San Francisco's Mechanics' Pavilion, where Bob Fitzsimmons and Tom Sharkey were scheduled to box using the new Marquis of Queensberry rules to determine which one would become boxing's world champion. The new rules dictated that the men would fight wearing gloves rather than bare-handed, and could only land blows above the waist.

At this time, Wyatt was living in San Francisco with Sadie, where he owned race horses and considered himself a capitalist and horseman. He and Sadie both bet on races and cultivated friendships with the city's most prominent citizens, including publisher William Randolph Hearst and gambler Lucky Baldwin. As the night of the boxing match approached and the fighters could not agree on a referee, two representatives of the fight's sponsor, the National Athletics Club, approached Wyatt. They played to his ego, telling him it would be an honor if he would referee the bout. Wyatt finally relented.

The next night, after five preliminary rounds, the big event was about to begin. The boxers' managers entered the ring and held a discussion about Earp; earlier that day, Fitzsimmons's manager had heard rumors that the fight had been fixed. He objected to Wyatt calling the contest and argued with Sharkey's manager, who steadfastly refused to switch referees at the last minute. Eventually, Fitzsimmons's manager gave in. Sensing things might be going sideways, Wyatt himself asked to be excused, but was urged by one of the National Athletics Club's reps to continue. So he did.

As Wyatt stepped into the ring, the police commissioner noticed a bulge in Wyatt's coat rdedpocket and asked if he was carrying a gun. "Yep," said Wyatt. The commissioner asked him to hand it over. Wyatt did so. It was a careless error; Wyatt, as was his custom, had spent all day at the races, and by the time the last race was run and Wyatt had tended to his duties at the stables, he had to cross over from the stables to the car parking lot after everyone else had left. He often carried his winnings and was never sure whom he might encounter, so he made a habit of keeping a pistol for protection. He'd become so used to it that he'd simply forgotten the gun was hidden in his jacket pocket until he went to enter the ring.

After Wyatt handed over the pistol, the fight got underway. Though Fitzsimmons was the favorite, the two combatants seemed pretty evenly matched until the eighth round, when Fitzsimmons unleashed a barrage of blows. Sharkey went into the ropes and fell, one hand going to his groin, his face contorting in agony. Fitzsimmons laughed at Sharkey's antics, considering it a badly acted put-on, but Wyatt believed that Sharkey had been hit below the belt—a foul—and immediately declared Sharkey the winner by default, a decision that earned Sharkey the $10,000 purse. While Sharkey was carried away on a stretcher still writhing, angry spectators leapt from their seats and rushed the ring. Fitzsimmons and his manager loudly proclaimed the fight had been fixed.

Wyatt returned home to Sadie, who immediately saw that he was not only tired but also distressed. He told her he was sorry he had ever been drawn into refereeing the fight, but that he was not sorry about his decision. "It's all I could do," he said. Wyatt considered himself a man of honor, and he'd called it as he'd seen it.

Wyatt was fined $50 for having carried a concealed weapon into the ring, and Sharkey's $10,000 pay-out was frozen while a court determined whether the fight had, in fact, been thrown. After a week-long trial that gained national attention, the judge effectively tossed the case out on the grounds that it should never have been brought in the first place since prizefighting was, after all, illegal in San Francisco. Sharkey was allowed to cash the check for his winnings, but Wyatt's character had been dragged through the mud in the national press, with scurrilous falsehoods and spurious accusations leaving him depressed and dispirited. After that brief time under the lens of the national microscope, all he desired was to return to relative obscurity.

And now, here he was, in Vidal, about as remote an outpost as one could imagine, and yet still, after all this time, the stain of the San Francisco fiasco followed him.

"My daddy lost all his money that night," said Hayden. "Ten whole dollars."

"Is that all?" asked Wyatt, giving Hayden a sharp look. "I lost my reputation."

Hayden leaned forward, saying, in almost a whisper, "I think that reputation's spot on. What kind of fancy card sharp tricks you pullin' here? Bendin' the corners? Dealin' off the bottom?"

With his hands beneath the table, Wyatt grabbed opposite corners of the water-soaked handkerchief, twirled it, and tied a tight, tiny knot in one end. His eyes narrowing, he looked at Hayden and said, "I won, fair and square. Nothing you say'll change that."

"What if we just break your fingers?" Hayden said ominously.

Wyatt's jaw flinched. "Son, there's two things you need to know..."

"What's that?"

"I've got a short temper and a long memory." Wyatt palmed the wet, tightly wound handkerchief. Keeping a wary eye on the men, he stood and began pocketing the money.

"You can't just leave!" hissed Jenkins. "You gotta give us a chance to win it back!"

"I'm giving you a chance to keep what little you still got."

"Sit down, Mister," barked Hayden. "We're not done with you yet!"

Wyatt glanced at all three of them, seeing the danger in their eyes, and said, "Well, I'm done with you. Try me again when you learn how to play this game."

Jenkins leapt up, pulling a switchblade out of his coat and flicking the knife open. Hayden and Hightower also jumped to their feet, Hayden knocking his chair over, ready for a fight.

"I tell you, he's a card-creasin' cheat!" shouted Jenkins.

Wyatt's steely blue eyes fixed on Jenkins. "Them's strong words for a weak man."

Jenkins sneered, "You won't talk so big after I slice that turkey neck of your'n!"

With sobering calmness, Wyatt said, "You wanna put that thing away, or do you wanna be carried out of here in a box?"

Jenkins lunged at Wyatt with the switchblade.

Quick as lightning, Wyatt snatched the ashtray off the table, and used it to knock the knife from Jenkins' hand, then backhanded it across the young punk's jaw. Jenkins staggered back, stunned.

Hayden, meanwhile, threw his coat back and reached for a World War I issue 1910 Browning pistol. As he raised it, Wyatt flicked his hand out and snapped the sopping handkerchief, the knot slapping Hayden's eye. Hayden reflexively put his hands to his stinging eye, dropping the pistol—which Wyatt snatched up by its barrel.

Then, as Hightower lunged at him, Wyatt buffaloed him, smacking the side of his head with the pistol's handle. Hightower plopped back into his chair, semi-conscious. Wyatt released the magazine clip from the pistol's grip, pulled back the slide to pop the bullet out of the chamber, and slung the gun across the room. Putting his cigar back between his lips, he pocketed the rest of the money.

As he strode out, he passed a table where a young man was sitting. Wyatt turned back for one last look at the humiliated men—Jenkins on the floor, rubbing his jaw, Hightower massaging the knot on his noggin, and Hayden rubbing his sore eye.

"Just so you know," he called to Hayden, "all I had was a pair of deuces."

He dropped the pistol's magazine into a trash can beside the door, and calmly walked out.

The young man looked back over his shoulder as Wyatt exited. It was Jack Gunther, who had noticed Wyatt a few days earlier in Leung's store. In his hand, Jack held a crumpled slip of paper. In handwritten block letters, it said: 'HELP WANTED,' with directions to Wyatt's home beneath. Jack felt there was no time like the present.

He followed Wyatt out the door.

Chapter 12

JACK

After leaving the cafe, Wyatt strode down the boardwalk to an ice cream parlor. He'd acquired a taste for ice cream ever since enjoying his first bowl of it in Tombstone, where practically every day, he'd stop in to a parlor called the Ice Cream Saloon, situated on Fourth Street between Allen and Fremont, and leave with a sticky mustache and ice cream drip-stains on his coat.

In those days, ice cream was served in a saucer, but roughly twenty years later, around the turn of the century, an Italian immigrant in New York City invented the ice cream cone, a clever way to sell ice cream in an edible container that the customer could take away with them. Wyatt felt it was about the best damn thing ever invented—excepting maybe his Colt shooting iron.

As Wyatt sat licking the cold treat, Sheriff Hank Ledbetter entered the shop and sauntered to the counter. Ledbetter was a tall, lean man with dark brown skin who was nearing 50 but was more fit than many men half his age. His deep voice reeked of authority even when he was barely talking above a whisper; when he was riled, it thundered like a cannon. Often, that was all it took to make a miscreant toe the line.

Like a lot of people in the west, Ledbetter had come from back east, having grown up in Alabama after the Civil War, when conditions for blacks were mighty precarious, to say the least. When he was in his late teens, he lied about his age and joined the Army. They had special regiments for men of his racial heritage; Ledbetter became a Buffalo Soldier, serving with the 24th Infantry Regiment in the Spanish American War. Charging up San Juan Hill to seize Spanish blockhouses, he was shot in the thigh, which angered him so much he put a bullet through the ear of the Spanish soldier who shot him. His injury earned him a Purple Heart.

A year later, he was fighting guerillas in the Philippines, and seventeen years after that, ended a twenty-year career of Army service after participating in the Punitive Expedition that crossed the border into Mexico and fought against Pancho Villa's men in retaliation for Villa having launched a raid on Columbus, in the New Mexico Territory.

After leaving the Army, Ledbetter remained in the West, eventually settling in Vidal. When it turned out that no one among the declining and aging population was terribly interested in the job of Sheriff, he ran for the job and was elected, mostly on the strength of his reputation as a soldier and marksman, but also because the town's predominantly white businessmen were happy to have someone as fearsome as him guarding their homes, even if they'd never deign to invite him inside them.

Over the years, he'd earned the town's respect as a fair and honest lawman. As he saw it, his primary job was just to keep the town boring. If people were generally behaving themselves and getting along with one another, he was fine. And if anyone got out of line, a night or two in the pokey usually straightened them out.

Wyatt understood Ledbetter's philosophy. It was similar to when he was a lawman, first in Lamar, Missouri, then Wichita and Dodge City in Kansas and finally Tombstone, Arizona. In those bygone days, the job didn't involve solving crimes and tracking down murderers so much as it did just keeping the peace. When the cowboys came storming into town at the end of a long cattle drive, they were ready to drink and carouse and raise the roof. Sometimes a few of them would get wild and unruly and cause a ruckus or threaten violence. When that happened, the main job of the lawman was just to keep 'em from killing the people they were supposed to be doing business with the following day.

Ledbetter settled onto the stool next to Wyatt. "Hello, Hank," Wyatt said with a welcoming smile.

Ledbetter got right to the point. "Hear you ruffled some feathers over at the cafe."

"Just some damn fool boys playing a man's game."

"If you don't mind my asking," said Ledbetter, "how much longer you plan on gracing us this time with your sunny disposition?"

THE LAST STAGE

Wyatt looked at the Sheriff, seeing where this was leading. "Just got here, and you're already trying to run me out of town?"

"Well, Wyatt, Vidal's generally a quiet little place, until you come 'round. You tend to attract all kinds of pests." Ledbetter pointed to a gummy yellow fly-ribbon strip hanging from the ceiling. "You're like that fly trap up there. Trouble just sorta sticks to you."

Taking the Sheriff into his confidence, Wyatt said quietly, "Hank, I ain't exactly making public knowledge of this, but between you and me, my days are numbered. And if my time's running out, I'd just as soon have it run out here."

"Alright," said Ledbetter. "But let me just say this—if you're entertaining any dreams of going out in a blaze of glory, go burn up somebody else's town, why don't you?"

Wyatt took the last bite of his ice cream cone, licked his sticky fingertips, wiped his mustache with a napkin, and slid off the stool, saying, "I ain't looking for any trouble."

Ledbetter nodded. "Good."

Picking up his hat from the adjacent stool, Wyatt added, "But if trouble comes a' calling, I'll damn sure answer it."

With that, he put on his hat and ambled out, leaving Ledbetter shaking his head and sighing.

Wyatt wound his way back to his car, and just as he was about to open its door, Jack Gunther trotted up to him, holding the slip of paper, calling, "Mr. Earp! Mr. Earp!"

Wyatt turned to him.

"You are Wyatt Earp?" asked Jack.

Wyatt looked the fresh-faced young man up and down. "Who's asking?"

"Jack Gunther."

Jack put his hand out to shake. Wyatt just gave him an icy look. Unnerved, Jack held up the slip of paper. "I saw this notice you put up at the stables. Looking for help in your mine?"

"Got any references?"

"Well," Jack said nervously, "I was helping Bill Tatum out over at his ranch, but now that he's shipped his cattle out…"

"Done any mining before?"

"No, sir."

Wyatt was quiet for a moment. Jack certainly seemed eager, and had the kind of slight, wiry build that was deceptive—there wasn't much meat on his bones, but what was there was pure muscle and gristle. "Two dollars a day suit you?"

Jack smiled. "Yessum, that'll do fine."

Now Wyatt put his hand out to shake Jack's. "Guess you'll do."

~ • ~

The next day, Wyatt led Jack to the Happy Days mining site, both of them traveling on horseback. Wyatt had left the wagon at the mine after Sadie's accident, with a tarp tied over it as tightly as he could get it, but as he approached it now, it looked like a couple of critters had tried to chew through one spot to get to the jerky and other goodies underneath.

The tools and buckets used by Wyatt and Sadie were still down in the mine tunnel, but not the lantern. Wyatt refilled it with kerosene, handed it to Jack, and led him to the pit. He went down the ladder first, then Jack followed, climbing a bit clumsily since the fingers of his right hand were wrapped around the lantern's bail and he was unable to fully grip the ladder rungs. When both men were at the bottom, Wyatt struck a match, lit the lantern, and moved into the tunnel, Jack close behind.

They soon arrived at the chamber where Wyatt had been working with Sadie. Wyatt demonstrated the technique—hold a bucket up high with one hand, chip off bits of the rock wall with the other. They both set to work, Jack banging at the rocks at a faster pace than Wyatt, with a young man's energy. There was a ferocity to his hammering, like he was releasing some bit of inner anger with every blow. "Don't swing the hammer too hard," Wyatt cautioned, "unless you enjoy getting an eyefull of rock splinters."

Jack tempered his swings, but nonetheless, after half an hour, his bucket was half full of rock chips, while Wyatt's was only about a quarter full. "Go ahead and take it up," said Wyatt, knowing if Jack filled the bucket any more it would be too heavy for him to carry up the ladder. Jack did as he was told, and reaching the top of the ladder, left the bucket on the rim, and came down to start filling up a fresh one.

After his second trip up the ladder, the blush was fading off the rose for Jack. "Is this it?" he asked Wyatt. "Is this all we're doing?"

"This is it," affirmed Wyatt, striking a blow against the rock wall.

Jack scoffed. "This ain't mining. This is just moving dirt."

"Well, what do you think mining is?"

Jack sighed, and got back to work. Wyatt knew this wasn't what the kid had expected, but hell, at least he would get paid. So far, about all Wyatt had gotten out of years of mining were callouses and blisters.

In the late afternoon, Wyatt called a halt to the proceedings. He and Jack were both soaked with sweat, and both had made several trips up and down the ladder. Wyatt had half-filled four buckets, Jack almost topped off six. After they carried up their final hauls for the day, they took a coffee break—or at least Wyatt did, drinking the last of the cold coffee still in the pot. Jack, who finished off the water in his canteen, smiled at Wyatt and said, "As much coffee as you drink, I'm surprised your heart doesn't beat right out of your chest."

"Well, if I didn't drink it, it probably wouldn't beat at all," Wyatt replied.

After the brief break, Wyatt enlisted Jack's aid in taking a portable dry sifter off the wagon and setting it up near the mining pit. The sifter was like a compact box that unfolded into a rickety contraption with a hopper up top that funneled rocks into a down-slanted basin comprised of a series of catches and screens in a long frame. There was a hand crank on the side that turned a flywheel causing a bellows underneath to blow puffs of air into the basin. Between the puffs of air and the shaking of the basin, the dust would get blown away and the rocks and pebbles would separate. If there was any gold or gold dust in the mix, it would end up on the bottom, since gold was denser than the other minerals and gravity would drag it down.

Once the sifter was set up, they lined their buckets of pebbles and rocks beside it. Wyatt pulled his neckerchief up over his nose. Jack followed his example. Then Wyatt lifted one of the buckets and began pouring its contents into the hopper, a little bit at a time. "Turn that crank," he ordered Jack.

As Jack turned the crank, the bellows began pumping and soon there was a great cloud of dust around the machine. The rocks and pebbles went through the hopper and rattled down the basin. When the bucket was empty, Jack stopped cranking and watched as Wyatt picked through what remained in the basin.

"See anything?" asked Jack anxiously.

"Lot of silt and a little bit of amethyst," growled Wyatt.

"That worth anything?"

"Not enough to matter."

Jack noticed that one of the stones had a bright spot that glinted in the fading sunlight. "Hey!" he said, "what about this?" He picked up the stone and held it in front of Wyatt. "Think that's gold?" he asked, excited.

"That's leverite," said Wyatt.

"Oh, good!" Jack said, relieved. "I was afraid it might be pyrite."

"You know what leverite means, don't you?"

"Nuh-uh."

"Means leave 'er right there. It's worthless."

After going through a couple more buckets with the same result, Wyatt could see that Jack was becoming frustrated. Finally, the young man shook his head, saying, "Seems like an awful lot of work for nothing."

Wyatt, sorting through the basin, cast a wary eye at him. "Nothing?"

"Well, ain't it?" said Jack. "How long you been at this?"

"'Bout twenty years."

Jack guffawed, "Twenty years?! What in the world would keep you going at it that long?"

Wyatt sighed, "Just the hope that every hammer blow brings me that much closer to striking the mother lode."

"Sounds like a fool's errand to me."

Wyatt understood Jack's impatience. He'd been that way himself, when he was Jack's age. Now that he was older, he'd learned that things didn't always come when he wanted them to, but rather when they were meant to. That was the definition of patience, which was something that seemed to multiply with each passing year. Indeed, he thought, patience was a paradox of aging—the less time you had, the more time you were willing to take.

Wyatt rubbed his sore lower back. "I've heard it said prospectors are optimists," he explained to Jack. "At any moment, you can either be two feet from a million dollars or a million feet from two dollars. Don't know till you get there."

"And what if you don't find nothin'?"

"Well, Jack..." he said, "it's not about whether you ever get the gold or not. It's just that you keep searching."

~ • ~

As the sun began descending on the horizon, the desert air turned cool. Jack gathered some scrub brush and built a fire to make dinner, and now he and Wyatt sat in canvas chairs by the fire's warmth, eating soup that Wyatt and Sadie had brought up with them a couple of days earlier, having emptied the jar into the Dutch oven and heated it over the campfire.

Wyatt took his time eating, but Jack gulped down his dinner ravenously. When he was done, he cleaned out the bowl with a piece of hardtack. As he chewed on it, he made an attempt at small talk, saying to Wyatt, "You and Mrs. Earp been married long?"

Wyatt chuckled. "Oh, we ain't married."

Jack was taken aback. "You're not?"

"We're just two cantankerous sorts who enjoy each other's company," said Wyatt.

"How'd you end up out here?"

"Prospecting. We spend our summers in Los Angeles, or go out to see family in 'Frisco or San Diego. Then when it cools off, we come back here."

There was a lot more Wyatt could tell, like how when they visited Sadie's family, he sometimes sat for Seder with a yarmulke atop his head, but he tended to be wary of strangers and wasn't prone to revealing too many details of his private life. However, he made a slight allowance for Jack, seeing as they were now working together and needed to build trust in one another.

"How long you been together?" asked Jack.

"Forty years," answered Wyatt.

"Forty years? How've you managed that?"

"Mighty precariously."

Jack chuckled, and said, "That's a long time to be with somebody you're not actually married to."

"I reckon the reason we've lasted so long is because we're not actually married." Wishing to shift the focus off himself, Wyatt asked Jack, "You got a girl?"

Jack smiled. "I don't stick to just one. I got girls all over."

"That right?"

"Yep," boasted Jack. "A redhead, coupla brunettes, some blondes. Even got a little Mexican girl I roll around with sometimes."

Wyatt couldn't help but smile. "Busy man."

"I see something I like, I just go after it," said Jack. "'Specially women." Amused, Wyatt shook his head, grinning. Jack noticed. "You think I'm lying?" he asked.

"Either that or awfully ambitious."

"What's wrong with being ambitious? One of these days, I'm gonna be a millionaire."

"Might happen," said Wyatt. "Ain't that hard to be a millionaire."

"What do you know about it?"

"I done been a millionaire two or three times over." Wyatt wiped his forefinger around the inside of the bowl and licked the soup off his finger. "Makin' money's easy," he said. "Hanging onto it's hard."

Jack looked at him for a long moment. Putting his bowl aside, he leaned forward. "Folks in town, they say you've got all kinds of money squirreled away somewheres."

Wyatt looked up and saw the reflection of the waning fire dancing in Jack's eyes. "If that was true," he said, "you think I'd be busting my ass out here with you?"

Wyatt stood up, stretching his long arms out to the starry sky, working a kink out of his back. "But seriously, Jack," he said, "the rich man is the one who finds the right woman to settle down with and spends the rest of his life with her. That's all you ever really need."

"I've thought about it," said Jack. "But if I do that, it'll have to be with a girl who's got a good personality, fun to be with, wholesome, loves the outdoors, and maybe has a bunch of freckles from bein' out in the sun, and a callous or two on her hands from paddling a canoe or swinging an axe. I just ain't found one like that, yet."

"Oh, there's girls like that," said Wyatt. "Trouble is, they usually ain't looking for a good man. They're looking for a good woman."

Chapter 13

AURILLA

In the inky blackness of night, Wyatt laid on his cot, under a wool blanket, wide awake. How could he not be? Jack, having exerted all his youthful energy during the day, was sleeping the sleep of the dead, out cold, snoring so loudly Wyatt swore it was rattling the tent flap. After tossing, turning, and tossing again, Wyatt finally gave up, sat up on the side of the cot, and reached for his pants and boots.

Once dressed, he trudged out into the night, under the faint light of stars that sparkled in a way it was becoming increasingly difficult to notice in Los Angeles, where there were now so many electric streetlights they washed out the starlight and covered the city in a dim, dull, hazy glow. A few moon-white clouds crawled slowly across the dark sky, and there was the occasional sound of small animals—lizards, probably—skittering over the rocks.

Wyatt had picked up his pipe on the way out of the tent. He took a small box of matches out of his pocket and lit it. A few deep inhales pulled the flame to the bottom of the pipe bowl, lighting the tobacco so it would burn from the bottom up, and warming his tongue. The nicotine tingled the base of his brain, and the sensation slowly washed over his entire body.

He wandered over to the sifter. There were a few stones on the rim of the basin. He picked one up, held it between his thumb and forefinger, brought it close to his eye to study in the dim light. Amethyst. Practically worthless. He tossed it away.

From the far distance came the sound of a wolf howling. Wyatt went back to where they'd had the campfire burning earlier and plopped himself down in his folding canvas chair. He puffed on his pipe. Leaning forward, he scooped up a handful of sand, and when he opened his fist, a gentle breeze blew the white grains from his palm.

Suddenly, the gales blew a little dust devil over the dune. It moved in an arc around and behind him, out of his line of sight. And then, after a moment, he felt the hair on the nape of his neck rise. There was the unmistakable sensation that someone was there—an eerie presence behind him. After a moment, he felt a delicate hand caress his cheek. It was a familiar gesture from his ancient past. Even before she moved in front of him, he knew that it was Aurilla. Barely 20, with her golden hair and green eyes, she looked just as she did when they were first married and happy. In her soothing, soft voice, she asked, "Why aren't you sleeping?"

Wyatt nodded back toward the tent. "Kid snores worse than you did. Might have to move my cot out here." He closed his eyes, luxuriating in her touch, in the trace of her fingertips on his face. "I miss you, Aurilla," he said. "Never wanted anyone more'n you."

"Not even Mattie?" she asked.

He reopened his eyes, looked into hers. "Mattie had her problems..."

"More than Sadie?"

Wyatt said quietly, "It's... different with Sadie." He let the words hang in the cool night air, then said, "After you passed, I swear I just went plumb mad. Didn't know if I'd ever find my way back. Turned hard. Mean." He paused again, and added, "Sadie's a mite like that."

Aurilla took his hand in hers. "But you love her?"

Another long pause from Wyatt, then he muttered, "Why'd you leave me? Everything would've been so different if you..."

"Wasn't my choice."

"It hurts, these thoughts of you."

"It was lovely, wasn't it? A home of our own, a garden to grow, our baby on the way."

"Best part of my life."

And it was.

Wyatt met lovely, chestnut-haired Aurilla Sutherland after his family moved back east to settle in Lamar, Missouri in the spring of 1868. Her father, who owned the Exchange Hotel, was doubtful of Wyatt's prospects as a husband until November 1869, when, at age 21, Wyatt was elected town constable. Six weeks later, he married 19-year-old

Aurilla, confident he'd found his lifelong soulmate. Wyatt's father, Nicholas, Lamar's Justice of the Peace, married them in Mr. Sutherland's hotel. Afterwards, Wyatt spent $50 on a lot outside of town where he built a farmhouse for himself and his new bride. They moved into it eight months later, expecting the rest of their lives together would be peaceful and happy. By the time they settled in, Aurilla was expecting a child, which Wyatt hoped would be a boy.

"But that's not the Wyatt Earp people want to hear about," Aurilla said. "They want the gunslinger. The violent man. The Lion of Tombstone."

"I never figured on being that."

An air of melancholy suddenly settled over Aurilla. "And I didn't figure on getting typhoid fever," she said. "We start on one path, end up on another..."

The epidemic swept through Lamar in the winter of 1870 and when it was finished, it had swept Aurilla away, too, along with her stillborn child, Wyatt's son, the only child he would ever have. When she died, Wyatt's dream of an uneventful, settled life died with her. He fell into a pit of despair, desperation, and destruction. But no matter how much whiskey he drank, he couldn't turn off his thoughts or erase his memories of her. The house was overflowing with reminders of Aurilla, her belongings, her scent, her essence. So he sold it, and incinerated all her belongings in a blazing bonfire.

His deep, abiding grief and the deadening effects of the bottle changed him. He became reckless, impetuous, consumed by anguished heartbreak. His passion for Aurilla morphed into a compulsion for self-destruction. He was a wild wolf among a community of sheep, a community that turned on him when he began abusing the powers of his office as constable and dipped into community funds to cover his gambling debts. And then came the last straw—he was caught stealing a horse. In that place, at that time, stealing a man's horse could mean stealing his livelihood; it was a mortal sin as contemptible as murder.

Facing certain conviction, Wyatt escaped Lamar and headed West, where he continued to gamble, get in fights, and steal. It was only after he spent time on the open prairie as a buffalo hunter that he began to reevaluate his life. In the solitude of the wide-open spaces, he screamed his suffering out to the endless sky, which was almost big enough to absorb it. But he wasn't yet fully reformed—he moved on to running brothels, until after several shakedowns he discerned there was more money to be made as a peace officer than as a pimp. This dark side of Wyatt's past was what Sadie hoped to keep forever hidden from the world. And it was a path he might never have taken, if only Aurilla had lived.

"You always feel like you have to protect everybody," said Aurilla. "And the burden of all that responsibility weighs on you and makes you mean. And when people get hurt, or get killed, you blame yourself, and that just makes you meaner. But you can't control everything, Wyatt. And you can't change what's happened. What's done is done. Accept it. Stop blaming yourself. Stop torturing yourself. Then you'll be free to move on."

With pleading eyes, he looked at the lovely young woman in front of him and said, "Come back to me, Aurilla."

"I can't. But you can come with me."

"I… I want to," he said. "But…"

"This isn't your place now, Wyatt. You don't belong here. Not anymore."

He looked down at the ground. "I'm… just not ready to go."

She leaned down and tenderly kissed his forehead, her cool fingers delicately tracing the contours of his cheeks. God, how he'd missed that touch! He closed his eyes, wanting to hold on to the sensation of her skin touching his for all time.

"Aurilla," he whispered, "stay."

And then her soft touch faded away.

And when he reopened his eyes, so had she.

Chapter 14

A WHISPER IN THE NIGHT

Earpie alerted.

He had been up on the bed, nestled against Wyatt's hip, until his ears suddenly went straight up and his body stiffened, as he stared at Wyatt's face. This caught Sadie's attention, and then she realized Earpie wasn't staring at Wyatt, but rather at a spot just above his head, like he'd seen a spider on the headboard. But so far as she could tell, there was nothing there.

"Earpie, what are you looking at?" she asked.

Across the room, Dr. Shurtleff and Lake had been speaking in hushed tones. But they also sensed something was different; the bungalow had suddenly become cooler. Lake wondered if one of the upper windows had slid down, allowing a chill draft into the room.

Dr. Shurtleff turned his attention to Sadie and Wyatt.

She scooted forward in her chair, closer to her husband. His lips trembled almost imperceptibly. No, thought Sadie, they're not trembling—he's trying to speak. She leaned in closer, her ear almost touching his mouth, to hear what he was saying. In the faintest of whispers, barely audible, he said, "Au… ril…….. la…."

Curious, Dr. Shurtleff and Lake moved closer to Sadie. Lake asked, "What'd he say?"

With a hurt look on her face, Sadie leaned back in her chair, and said quietly, "Nothing. Gibberish."

Sadie knew she was being petty, but she couldn't help herself. She'd always felt jealous of any woman who won Wyatt's affections, whether it be women from his past or women in the present. She wanted Wyatt, all of Wyatt, all to herself. And yet, conversely, she was still hoping that Lake would help her share him with the world.

If it weren't for his indignity at being maligned in so many of the books about the events of Tombstone, Wyatt would have been content to let sleeping dogs lie, but he'd often said that there was nothing so sacred as honor. That had been enough to motivate him to work with Flood and, later, with Lake, but as disappointments mounted and his health declined, he seemed to care less and less about what people might say about him after he was gone, if they said anything at all. She, on the other hand, would still have to live with the aspersions to his reputation. She would never be introduced socially as Josephine Marcus Earp, one-time singer and dancer on the Territorial stage, but always and forever as Mrs. Wyatt Earp.

And since Wyatt had no assets to speak of, once he was gone, how would she survive? The most valuable thing Wyatt possessed was his story, and that was something she could continue to profit from for the rest of her life, if they could just get a workable manuscript. Just a few weeks earlier, she had raised the issue with Wyatt, when she discovered that he still hadn't made any attempt to answer the questions Stuart Lake handed to him on the Santa Monica beach. Growing impatient with her prodding, he eventually barked, "Why don't you just tell him your story?"

"Because I'm a woman," Sadie shouted in reply. "I've never done anything—except take care of you. A book of my life would just be a few sentences. Wouldn't even make a page. Your life'll fill up a whole bookshelf." And then with a shrug, she added, almost as an afterthought, "Unless we clean it up."

That made Wyatt chuckle. But he still procrastinated, putting off answering the questions until… well, until now, when it was certainly too late.

If he didn't survive, then her future security might not, either.

Nor would her sanity—without him to tend to, what would she do with her days? And how empty would they be if she was all alone, abandoned by the one person she knew loved her totally and unconditionally and would do so for all their days?

He had to recover. Had to.

For her sake.

Chapter 15

HE LOVED HER WELL

Jack kicked the leg of Wyatt's chair, waking him with a hearty, "Rise and shine." Wyatt's eyes blinked open, adjusting to the yellow sun rising on the pale pink horizon. He began to stand, but abruptly stopped and plopped back into his seat. While he slept, the chill in the night air had crept into his bones, stiffening his joints and aggravating his arthritis. He rubbed the back of his aching neck and grumbled, "Help me up, will you?"

Jack clasped Wyatt's hands in his and pulled him to his feet, asking, "What're you doing out here?"

"Came out for a smoke. You were snoring like a chocked bull." Wyatt yawned. Aching from sleeping in the chair, he stood with knees slightly bent and shoulders crooked. He needed to move around a bit to limber up. After another, louder yawn, he asked Jack, "You know how to make coffee?"

"Make a whole damn breakfast, if you want," smiled Jack.

"Good man," said Wyatt, as he shuffled off to the privacy of some tall rocks. Once out of sight of the camp, he unzipped his pants. Dug around for his bush-whacker, found it, pulled it out. And then, bracing himself with one hand against a rock, he stood there. Let out a pained grunt. And stood a while longer. And then emitted another grunt.

Meanwhile, Jack put some fresh wood on the fire and lit it with a cigarette lighter. He went into the tent and came out with a cast iron skillet and the coffee pot. He put the skillet on the grate over the fire. Then, stepping over to the larder on the wagon, filled the coffee pot with water from the water barrel and dug out some eggs and a hunk of bacon.

Looking off toward the rising sun, he could see Wyatt standing among the rocks, like a statue, waiting to piss.

Wyatt had been feeling the effects of cystitis for some time. It began weeks ago, with a little pain that came and went, usually when he'd drank a lot of water or coffee and his bladder was full. It was just a minor irritation to begin with, a nuisance. But as time went on, the pain persisted. He'd begun to feel it in his testicles and penis. Relieving himself became irregular. Sometimes, try as he might to force the urine out by tensing his stomach muscles, nothing happened; the discomfort in his nether regions only increased.

Over the past couple of weeks, the pain had spread to his abdomen and, sometimes, his lower back. Most times the pains were sudden and sharp, like being stabbed. Other times they were dull and lingering, lasting all day and making it uncomfortable for him to move about, no matter how willfully he tried to push through it. In the past few days, in addition to all those discomforts, he'd felt aches in his pelvic area, and behind his scrotum, and had felt a more frequent need to piss, not only during the day but also at night. The latest manifestation of his illness was a constant sense of urgency, a feeling that he needed to pee even when he didn't. And worse, on occasion there was no feeling at all, and no warning except for the warm dampness spreading over his legs as he wet himself. Thankfully, that had only happened twice, and both times he was at home and alone, sparing him public humiliation.

Now, Wyatt waited, eyes closed, concentrating on pushing on his bladder with his stomach muscles. After another minute, he finally felt some satisfaction, as a slight trickle of urine pooled in front of his boots. When he was satisfied that he was finished, he buttoned his jeans. And as he looked down, he saw the urine was stained with streaks of red.

~ • ~

Following breakfast—which Wyatt had to admit was one of the best he'd had in a while, since Sadie's culinary talents didn't stretch too far beyond hot dogs—he and Jack returned to the mine.

Jack was well-rested, chipper, and bursting with youthful enthusiasm. Wyatt, on the other hand, was already stiff and sore, and the day's work hadn't yet begun. In addition to his usual morning aches, pains and annoyances, his shoulders and neck were cramped from sleeping in a sitting position, and his old hip injury had decided this would be a good day to pay him a visit. Wyatt masked it all as best he could; the last thing he wanted was to appear weak in front of the kid, who was tossing their empty buckets down into the pit, raring to go.

Once they made their way into the bowels of the mine and set to work, Jack got a good rhythm going, chipping away at the tunnel wall, collecting the rock fragments in his bucket. But for Wyatt, the more the morning wore on, the more he struggled. He pounded the wall as though his hammer weighed a hundred pounds. He was sweating profusely, short of breath, and began to let out a little grunt with each blow. Jack couldn't help but notice. He put down his hammer and bucket and stepped over to Wyatt. "Why don't you go home, get a good solid rest in your own bed?" he said. "I'll take care of things here."

Defiance flashed in Wyatt's eyes. Ignoring Jack, he struck the rock with the hammer again... and again... but each blow had less force behind it than the one before. It was clear he'd run out of steam. He was breathing hard, short of breath, heart beating rapidly. He let his arm hang at his side, weighted down by the heavy hammer in his hand, and panted.

"Go on," said Jack. "I promise when you come back, there'll be a whole pile of rocks up there to run through the sifter."

Wyatt didn't want to admit it, but he knew Jack was right. No matter how much he'd like to stick with it, his body was screaming for a proper rest. Sure, if he really pushed himself, he could put on a good show of keeping at it, but what if he dropped dead down here? Is that the kind of ending he wanted? No, he decided, that wasn't going to be his fate. Better to swallow his pride and return another day, when he was feeling more of his usual self.

He set his bucket and hammer down, and with a little nod of acknowledgement to Jack, trudged out of the tunnel without speaking.

~ • ~

Wyatt sat hunched over his saddle as his horse trotted up to the house, stopping in front. He slowly climbed down, tethered the horse's reins to a hitching post at the side of the house, and walked inside with heavy steps.

Earpie dashed up to him, barking excitedly, bouncing and jumping up at him, his tail spinning like a pinwheel. Wyatt scratched the dog's ears and said, "Whoa, Earpie. Settle down. Where's your ma?"

Moving farther into the cottage, Wyatt looked about. There were dishes piled in the sink. A newspaper tossed carelessly atop the table, a couple of pages of it on the floor below. Even at the best of times, Sadie wasn't much of a housekeeper; it was Wyatt who made the beds, and if he didn't stay on Sadie's case, she'd never sweep the floor and she'd let the sink overrun with dishes—as she appeared to be doing now that she'd injured her ankle.

The radio was turned on, with Paul Whiteman's orchestra playing a lively waltz to accompany Jack Fulton's high tenor voice singing "In a Little Spanish Town ('Twas on a Night Like This)", coming in through occasional bursts of static.

As Wyatt wandered into the kitchen, he heard more singing in the air, but unaccompanied by music. He went to the back door, looked out its little window, and saw Sadie, a house slipper on one foot and the other wrapped in a bandage, hanging damp clothes from a wicker basket onto a clothesline. She'd set the basket up on a chair to be higher and easier to reach, and continued singing as she pulled out a damp sheet and attached it to the line with clothes pins. With a grin, Wyatt pushed open the door and strode out.

Sadie didn't notice him at first, too preoccupied with singing a tune from her distant past, when she was a young woman touring with George N. Pring's Hayne Operatic Company. When that outfit folded due to Pring's financial mismanagement, Pauline Markham re-organized it and renamed it the English Opera Company. Sadie was in the troupe as a member of the chorus; their bread-and-butter was performing Gilbert and Sullivan's *H.M.S. Pinafore* for audiences of cowboys, miners, and occasionally Eastern businessmen who'd gone West seeking riches. In a lively mezzo-soprano, she belted out a song from the operetta's Act I Finale:

"Of life, alas! his leave he's taking,
For ah! his faithful heart is breaking;
When he is gone we'll surely tell
The maid that, as he died, he loved her well…"

Hearing the crunch of footsteps behind her, she stopped abruptly and turned around, slowly, favoring her still sore and tender ankle. She was surprised to see Wyatt coming toward her. With a welcoming look of elation, she dropped the skirt she was about to hang back into the basket and threw her arms open wide, exclaiming, "Wyatt!"

He stepped into her embrace and hugged her tightly. He was dirty and dusty from the desert and wet with reeking sweat, but she didn't care. To her, he was the answer to a prayer. And since he was a foot taller than her, when they caressed, the top of her head only came up to his shoulder. She turned her head aside and pressed it against his chest, the better to hear his heartbeat.

"Thought you were going to stay off your feet," he said.

"Been waiting for you to come sweep me off them," she smiled. He kissed her, happy to be home, comfortably content in her arms.

Sadie could see that Wyatt was plumb exhausted and, after he'd washed the sweat and trail dust off, she soon had him safely ensconced in bed. As he settled in, she pulled the sheet up to his chest, tossed a blanket over his legs, and fluffed his pillow, anxious to make him as cozy and comfortable as possible. "I been worried about you down in that mine," she said. "What if there's a cave in?"

"You worry too much."

"How's the new helper?"

"Pretty good worker. Awful cocky. Reminds me of me at that age."

"Is that a good thing?"

Wyatt chortled. Then Sadie gave him a look of cautious concern. "You trust him up there by himself?"

"I'll get back to check on him tomorrow."

She picked up a glass of crimson liquid from the bedside table and handed it to him. "Here. Drink this."

He looked askance at it. "What is it?"

"Cranberry juice. Mary told me it'd be good for, uh, your problem."

Wyatt felt a tinge of embarrassment. "How does she know about my problem?"

Sadie shrugged, "Word spreads."

"Uh-hmm," said Wyatt, with a pretty good idea of who'd been spreading it. "And what were you doing going into town with that bum foot of yours?"

"I didn't," said Sadie. "Dr. Cork told her I was laid up, so she came by to see if I needed anything."

"Mighty thoughtful of her."

"Mighty smart of her. Sold me three dollars' worth of groceries 'fore she was through. Including that," she said, with a nod to the cranberry juice.

Wyatt took a tentative sip, raised his eyebrows appreciatively, then took a more hearty gulp. "Pretty good," he said, as he handed the glass back to Sadie. She set it back down on the bedside table, next to the half-empty bottle.

"Rest of it's right here, if you get thirsty," she said. "Now get some rest."

She bent down to hug him, and he patted her back. As she straightened back up, he caught her hand in his and said, "Sure you don't want to get off your feet?"

Sadie gave him a warm smile. She kicked off her slipper, shucked off her dress, and lifted up the bed cover. Wyatt slid over to make room for her, and she scooted in and cuddled up against him. Earpie waddled to the side of the bed and barked. "Come on, Earpie," said Wyatt. "We ain't forgot you." He patted his thigh. Earpie scrunched like a spring coiling and sprang up onto the bed. Finding a good tight spot to squeeze into between Wyatt and Sadie, he settled in.

"Snug as a bug in a rug," said Wyatt.

It was only late afternoon.

It didn't matter.

Chapter 16

SMOKE BREAK

Earpie snuggled against Wyatt's legs, his sad round eyes locked onto Wyatt's, hoping they would open. Sadie dozed in her chair beside the bed, while Lake sat in another chair across from her, fixated on Wyatt's near-comatose form, finding it difficult to accept that the vibrant and violent hero of Tombstone could now be this frail, helpless, ordinary old man. Dr. Shurtleff stood up, wandered several steps away, and yawned audibly. Returning to the bed, he caught Lake's eye. The doctor took a cigarette case and lighter out of his coat pocket and gave Lake a silent invitation, nodding towards the door. Lake nodded his acceptance, got up, and followed Dr. Shurtleff outside.

As they stepped off the porch, it was eerily dark. The power was still out, but the rain had abated for the time being, leaving a sheen on the road and the sidewalks that glistened as the moon peeked out from behind the storm clouds. There was a light breeze, just enough to tinkle the wind chimes.

Dr. Shurtleff and Lake strolled out into the courtyard, standing near the fountain. The doctor lit up a cigarette, then gave the case and lighter to Lake, who took a smoke for himself, lit it, and handed the case and lighter back to their owner. They spoke in low tones, so as not to disturb the other occupants of the bungalow court.

"What do you think?" asked Lake.

Dr. Shurtleff bowed his head and sighed, "Frankly, I'm surprised he's still hanging on. But he is a stubborn old cuss." Then, raising his head, he took in a deep, calming breath. "I love the way the air smells after a rainstorm," he said. "Fresh and clean."

Lake also took a deep breath. "Oh, that's good. I needed that." He nodded at the bungalow. "That ammonia smell was getting a little thick in there."

Dr. Shurtleff nodded. "Yeah. It's his kidneys shutting down. His urine's backing up and getting into his bloodstream. Comes out in his breath."

Lake just shook his head. What a terrible way to go, he thought. "Known him long?" he asked the doctor.

"A few years, just casually. Can't really say I know him well."

"I'm not sure anyone does," said Lake. "Wyatt's so reserved he's like a monolith, a blank. You see what you want to see in him."

"What do you see?"

Lake thought for a long moment before answering, "A man who's searching. Searching for something that… well, I'm not sure even he knows what it is anymore."

There was the sound of rainwater swishing as a car rolled past. And now they noticed a glow in the apartment at the end of the courtyard, a faint lantern light illuminating the silhouette of a man sitting at a desk near the upstairs window. After a moment came the sharp tap-tap of typewriter keys.

"Poor guy," said Dr. Shurtleff. "Must have a deadline. Speaking of which, how's your book coming?"

"Still gathering material," said Lake, flicking ash into the wet grass. "Getting Wyatt to open up is like pulling teeth. Should 'a got a lot more out of him when I had the chance." There was a moment's silence, then Lake continued, "Last time I saw him, I gave him a long list of questions to answer when he was able. Guess he never did."

"You could always see what he told Flood," said Dr. Shurtleff with a grin.

"You read it?" asked Lake.

Dr. Shurtleff shook his head "no."

"It's awful," Lake continued. "No wonder they couldn't find a publisher. But then again, I guess Flood had the same handicap I do." He gave the doctor a knowing look.

"Josephine?"

Lake nodded. "She keeps rushing it. Scared I might dig up something she doesn't want me to tell."

"Have you?"

"Well... I just remember years ago, sitting in a bar and having a drink with Bat Masterson, talking about Wyatt, and he just casually mentioned that Josephine was the belle of the honkytonks in Tombstone. 'The prettiest dame in three hundred of her kind,' he said."

"Her kind?" asked Dr. Shurtleff. Then he saw Lake's raised eyebrow. "Oh."

"She thinks all I know is just what she and Wyatt have told me. And in their version of things, the Clantons are the villains and the Earps are the heroes who ran 'em out of town, and of that there is to be no doubt or disagreement whatsoever. But that's not the whole story." Lake took another drag, exhaled a plume of smoke. "Before she took up with Wyatt, she was Sheriff Behan's woman. There's some who think that that was the real powder-keg that set the whole thing off."

Dr. Shurtleff felt the thrill of getting insider information. "Sherriff Behan? So Wyatt started seeing the Sheriff's woman, and then..."

"And when the Earps left Tombstone, Wyatt left his common-law wife behind."

"The one that was an opium addict?"

"Laudanum," Lake corrected. "She died not long after. And I think Josephine feels responsible for it."

"You ask her about it?"

"No use bothering. She's covered up her past with a tissue of lies so transparent a child could see through it. But it's her version of things and there's no getting her to budge."

There was another silent pause, as the men enjoyed their smokes. Then the doctor said, "Well, I guess that explains all her meddling with your book."

"I just feel sorry for her," said Lake. "She can't control what's happening to Wyatt, so she tries to control everything else."

"Including biographers."

Lake nodded. "And she's done a pretty good job of muddying the waters. At this point, it's hard to say what's true and what isn't." He took another drag from the cigarette. "There's only two people that really know, and one of 'em won't give me straight answers and the other one's dying."

"So what do you do?"

"Only thing I can do," Lake said with a shrug. "Make it up."

Behind them, the door to the cottage opened. Sadie stepped out onto the porch and saw the men smoking by the fountain. "What're you fellers doing out here in the cold?" she asked. "Come on in. Just brewed up a fresh pot of coffee."

Dr. Shurtleff dropped his cigarette, stubbed it out. Lake flicked his into the wet lawn. As they headed back inside, Lake crossed the threshold before Dr. Shurtleff, and touched the mezuzah. Turning his head to Dr. Shurtleff behind him, he whispered, "Touch that box." Dr. Shurtleff was puzzled, but did as he was told. Sadie, holding the door open for both of them, smiled as the men entered.

She hadn't always been devout in her faith, but somehow, tonight, it mattered.

Chapter 17

JOSEPHINE

Once inside, Lake and Dr. Shurtleff watched as Sadie pulled back the curtain to the kitchen area. She took a pot of coffee off the stove and walked it to the dining table, where she'd already placed a few cups. A fresh candle burned in the Menorah atop the table, near the unfinished puzzle. She motioned for Lake and the doctor to sit, and as they did so, Sadie filled their cups.

She'd liked to have poured the scalding coffee over their heads.

What they didn't know is that she'd awakened sooner than they realized, and was just about to open the door when she heard them talking. She paused and eavesdropped as they spoke about the possibility that, during her time in Tombstone, she might have been a soiled dove. Of course, she never had been. It was true that she began sharing a bed with Wyatt Earp while he was still living with Mattie, but Mattie and Wyatt weren't married, and though they still presented themselves as man and wife, Mattie had clearly given herself over to her laudanum addiction, and by doing so had effectively abandoned him. As for Sadie, she'd moved on from Johnny Behan, tired of his philandering and empty promises. It was Wyatt's loneliness, and her own, that brought them together, and so they remained.

That was life on the frontier—it was full of outcasts and free spirits creating new societies, often risking their lives to flee the restrictive bonds of Eastern conservatism. But as time went on and the new transcontinental railroad took much of the risk out of venturing westward, Eastern conservatism came a-calling, imposing a veneer of respectability over the cow towns and mining camps that came with a considerable amount of judgement and shaming. All "wanton women" were considered by the more staid types who came later as whores, whether they actually charged for the pleasure of their company or not. And all actors and entertainers—including former dancers from a traveling H.M.S. Pinafore troupe—were considered to be low-class vagabonds, drunks, libertines and sexual deviants. So what could she do? Sue for libel? In court, she'd be asked all sorts of humiliating questions; there'd be as much burden of proof on her as on her accusers. And what proof would she have? Dens of iniquity were known for their discretion, which was anathema to record-keeping. If a list of all the ladies employed by a particular brothel even existed, and your name was not on it, so what? Who among those ladies ever used their real name? How could you prove you weren't working there under an alias?

In Sadie's instance, the situation was made even murkier by a woman named Sada Mansfield, who had been Johnny Behan's favorite prostitute in Prescott and who, after his divorce, made her way to Tombstone and back into his bed. She was known as "Forty-Dollar Sadie," and since Wyatt teased Josephine by calling her Sadie—derived from her middle name of Sarah—gossips conflated the two women, and surmised that they were one and the same. That aside, Josephine couldn't have cleared her name without shining a light on how she'd 'stolen' Wyatt from Mattie, and again, she'd come off as being immoral. So, she just went on enduring the rumors, ignoring them as best she could, hoping they'd eventually fade away with the passage of time.

"Thanks, Josephine," said Dr. Shurtleff, as she filled his cup.

"Josephine..." she smiled. "I don't hear that name much. He always calls me Sadie" she said with a nod towards Wyatt's bed. "I never cared much for it."

"Then why does he do it?"

"He likes to tease."

After pouring her own cup of coffee, she put the pot on the table. Then she went to a cabinet, opened it, and took out a half-full bottle of whiskey. She looked at the men with a mischievous twinkle in her eyes. "How 'bout some sweetener?" she asked. She returned with the bottle, pouring a shot into her coffee before passing the liquor to Lake and Dr. Shurtleff. Then she sat down in a chair facing Wyatt's erratically-breathing body.

With a worried tone, she asked, "Think he'll last another day?"

THE LAST STAGE

Dr. Shurtleff decided it was better to be blunt than to give her unrealistic expectations. "I wouldn't bet on it," he said.

Sadie gave him a sharp look, saying, "I'll take that bet." Lake grinned, and Sadie, noticing, continued, "I know. I'll bet on anything. Biggest gamble I ever took—hitching myself to that man. Took up with him and never looked back. He's always said I don't know when to leave the table. And I haven't. After all these years, I'm still here."

She thought of all the detours her life had taken with Wyatt. From Tombstone, Arizona to Silverton, Colorado, Idaho's Coeur d'Alene, Nome, Alaska, then Seattle, Washington, San Francisco, San Diego, Tonopah, Nevada and finally back to California, bouncing between Los Angeles and Vidal—one boom town to the next, always on the move, often with the two of them together running saloons and gambling dens.

Cheeks inflamed with emotion, Sadie said, "What am I gonna do? Forty-seven years I've been by his side... how can that just end?"

"It won't end," said Lake. "He'll live on in your heart, and in the hearts of everybody that knew him. And he'll live on in the stories that are told about him."

"Like in your book," said Sadie.

"Our book," said Lake. This made Sadie smile.

Dr. Shurtleff said, "Indians say a person doesn't truly die until the last one who remembers them speaks their name. So by that measure, think of all those pharaohs of Egypt and Roman emperors and great generals and presidents who are still with us. Cleopatra and Caesar, Michelangelo and Mozart. Even Abe Lincoln's just as alive in our hearts today as when he was flesh and blood. Maybe more so."

"Or the idea of him is," said Lake.

"That's what important," said Dr. Shurtleff. "The idea of him. The spirit of him. The body's just a vessel. It's finite. But the spirit it contains... that goes on and on."

Lake raised his mug. "To Wyatt. Long may his story be told."

Sadie's eyes welled with tears. She and Dr. Shurtleff also raised their mugs, and the three of them clinked their coffees together and took a drink. As a tear rolled down her face, Sadie said, "If he pulls through, I promise I'll be a better wife. I won't nag, I won't drink, I won't gamble—I'll just take care of him."

A heavy solemnity hung over the room. In the silence, Lake could hear a clock ticking. He looked around and, atop a shelf, spotted a tintype photo of a much younger Sadie, seductive, in a gauzy dress that left little to the imagination, with long, cascading hair accentuating the curve of her breasts. "Is that you?" he asked.

Sadie was mildly embarrassed. Nodding, she said, "I used to be a looker. Used to be."

"You're still a fine figure of a woman," Dr. Shurtleff assured her.

"And you're a liar, God bless you." Staring into her coffee, she said wistfully, "Maybe if I'd kept my looks..." She sighed. "It's not easy being married to a man of notoriety... but when you're loyal to someone, you're loyal to everything about 'em... even… even the bad parts."

"Bad parts?" queried Lake.

Sadie's head lowered, eyes downcast. "The women," she said. "The women."

In the beginning, Wyatt had a strong sex drive, and believed that he should be able to exercise it whenever the opportunity allowed. She didn't agree, of course, and considered retaliating by taking a lover of her own, but she never followed through. For one thing, she'd never met another man who could measure up to Wyatt. For another, she feared that Wyatt would not be as quick to forgive in that department as she was, and she never, ever wanted to do anything that might cause her to irrevocably lose her man.

Besides, Sadie knew he enjoyed the excitement of the hunt and the thrill of the conquest. She was willing to turn a blind eye to his dalliances, so long as they didn't become long-term affairs, and so long as he always returned home to her. As he aged into his 40s and 50s and was still consorting with women in their 20s—women much younger than herself—she figured he continued doing it because he wanted to indulge in as much pleasure as he could while he was still able, and while such women still found him attractive, before he began to get a paunch around the middle and his hair began to recede and fade from dark blonde to white.

"Sometimes, my feelings run away from me," Sadie said, brushing a palm over her moist cheeks. "There are times I feel so excited and happy I think I'm just gonna bust. And there are other times when I get so melancholic I wish I could just fade away and disappear. So I drink. I drink to take the edge off the excitement, and I drink to keep me from feeling the misery of my darker moods. And Wyatt… he never knows what to do with me when those deep emotions come over me. He just isn't one to show his feelings so strongly. Likes to hold his cards close to his vest. Too close, more often than not." She sighed. "I swear, he's the only man I know that you can be with and still sometimes end up feeling… so alone."

Lake felt he was finally getting a peek behind her veil of secrecy. Both he and Dr. Shurtleff looked at Sadie with sympathy. She suddenly became acutely aware of the two men giving her pitiful looks, and as much as she loved being the center of attention, she hated being pitied. So now, her veil of secrecy closed back up, tight as a drum.

She fixed her gaze on Lake, and said firmly, "You need to hurry and finish that book."

"It'll get done," Lake assured her.

"Has to. One way or another, we have to keep my man alive."

Chapter 18

COLLAPSE

The glow of sunlight filtering through the curtains awakened Sadie, who was cozy beneath the covers. She rolled over, expecting to see Wyatt in the bed beside her, but there were only rumpled sheets and Earpie, who was snoring lightly. Sadie let out a long, loud yawn.

Wyatt emerged from the bathroom tucking his shirt into his denim jeans. He smiled at her, saying, "Mornin.'"

Rubbing the slumber from her eyes with her fingertips, she asked, "Heading out already?"

"Figure I better go check on the kid," he said. He sat down on his side of the bed, his back to her, to pull on his boots.

She rubbed her hand over his lower back. "Don't go," she cooed. "I like you here with me."

"Didn't come here just to laze around." Having wiggled both feet into the tight boots, he stood up.

"Please, Wyatt. Stay." She put her hand out towards him.

He clasped his hand around hers. "What's got into you?"

"I don't know," she said, gazing up at him. "I just don't like being here all by my lonesome. Especially with this bum foot. Don't you want to stay and take care of me?"

He leaned down and kissed her. "I reckon you'll survive without me."

Wyatt went out to the barn to saddle his horse and then took off on the dusty path into the Whipple Mountains. Although he liked automobiles and the feeling of speed one got in an open-topped car, for him, nothing could ever compare to the experience of riding a good horse.

THE LAST STAGE

A car was all steel and rubber and noxious fumes and wasn't much good on uneven terrain. But a horse... a horse was a living, breathing beast, an engineering feat in its own right, with a broad body sized just right for carrying a man, legs long enough to gallop at fast speed and hooves that allowed it to navigate precarious ground, even steep rocky inclines—places an auto couldn't go. And sure, you could carry more, or haul more, with a car or truck, but a horse's saddle could be kitted out with bedrolls, saddle bags, rifle scabbard—all a man really needed to survive a journey from one place to another.

And even though some fools took to naming their vehicles, a car had no actual personality. Horses, on the other hand, were as individual as people. Some were firebrands, ready and willing to carry you into dangerous situations. Others were timid, built for slow treks in peaceful surroundings. Over time, a horse could become as close a friend as a human being, a companion to share experiences with and tell your secrets to. And unlike a human, a horse never betrayed your secrets. No wonder, thought Wyatt, that there were some men he'd known who would rather go on a long trail ride with their horse than a long car trip with their spouse.

If fortune ever smiled on him again, thought Wyatt, he'd buy a ranch and invest in some fine horses, because a man who invested in horses was investing in himself.

Besides which, a man looked pretty silly sharing secrets with his car.

When Wyatt arrived at the camp, he was pleasantly surprised to find everything in order and Jack already in the mine—he could hear the slight pings of Jack's hammer striking the rock wall echoing up from down below. And Jack had, as promised, left several buckets of rocks and a good-sized pile in addition near the sifter, so he'd obviously worked for quite some time after Wyatt headed home the previous day. Wyatt felt fortunate to have found such a diligent young man to work the mine with him, someone who would give him a hard day's work for a hard-won dollar.

Gathering his gear, Wyatt climbed down into the pit and entered the tunnel, feeling refreshed and eager to show Jack how it was done. The night's rest had done him well. After only a short while, his bucket was already nearly half full. Then he struck a blow that knocked loose a piece of rock that immediately grabbed his attention. About the size of a biscuit, it had a white striation running through one side. Wyatt held it closer, and as he inspected it, his face broke into a satisfied smile.

"Jack," he said calmly, "c'mere and look at this." Jack stepped over, wiping his forearm over his sweating brow, and took the rock from Wyatt. "See that white streak?" Wyatt asked. "That's quartz. Now, take a closer look and tell me if you see anything else there."

Jack held the piece of rock closer, tilting it toward the light from the lantern. Among the streak of white was a little dot of yellow. "Some little speck of something," he said. Jack's eyes grew wider. "Is that…?"

"Gold," said Wyatt. "And if there's a speck, there might be a peck."

Jack looked at him, confused. "Are you joshin' me?"

"Where you find quartz, you're pretty likely to find gold," Wyatt said. Grinning at Jack, he added, "So… you still think all this moving dirt around is stupid?"

"Well…" said Jack, taking a moment to think about it, "I reckon so is chasing girls, until you catch one."

Jack soon joined Wyatt at his section of the wall, both chipping away, hoping to find more of the quartz and yellow specks. After a while, Jack was hot, sweaty, and had a bucket filled to the point that it was almost too heavy to hold up. He set it down. Picking up his canteen, he tilted it up for a sip. It was empty. "I'm gonna take this load up and get some more water," he announced to Wyatt. "You need any?"

Wyatt picked up his canteen, shook it, heard the satisfying sound of the water sloshing inside. "I'm fine," he said.

Jack left, carrying his bucket load of rock and mineral chips. After he was gone, Wyatt resumed work, but at a less vigorous pace now that he was all by himself. After a few more hammer blows, he heard a sound from farther back in the tunnel like a pebble had loosened and bounced down the wall to the floor. Wyatt hoped it was just rats making nests in one of the smaller, narrower tunnels. But then he felt a sensation like being on a boat riding an ocean wave, the ground seeming to undulate beneath his feet. And at the same time, there was a low rumbling sound, growing in intensity to a cacophony. Pebbles, and then rocks, shook loose from the tunnel walls as the sound became a roar.

Wyatt quickly tied his neckerchief over his nose and mouth and flattened himself on the ground. The trembling and shaking lasted for several seconds that seemed like eons. There was a thunderous crashing sound, and all went dark. Wyatt felt a cloud of dust wash over him,

THE LAST STAGE

and heard some larger rocks thumping nearby. One smaller rock struck his thigh; Wyatt hoped it would do no more damage than leave a nasty purple bruise.

The shaking didn't stop so much as dissipated, dying off to an ominous stillness. Satisfied that the quake was over, Wyatt got up on all fours, then slowly stood up, afraid the quake might have either raised the floor or lowered the ceiling. But he was able to stand upright, so it seemed the pit had mostly survived. He was in total, absolute darkness, and it disoriented him. He felt panicked, his heart beating wildly, the swirling dust finding its way past the barrier of his neckerchief and getting into his nose and mouth, making him cough so hard it rattled his ribs.

Hands shaking, he got back down on his knees and felt around for his canteen. Finding it, he picked it up. Whipping off his neckerchief, he took a big swallow to wash the dust down, then poured water over the neckerchief and tied it again over his nose and mouth. He then reached into his pocket for the box of matches. Sliding it open, he could feel that there were only two left. He struck one, and a wisp of dusty air put it out instantly. One match left. He struck it on the side of the box and cupped his hand beside it to keep the flame alive. It provided scant light, but enough to see that he was well and truly entombed.

The tunnel had collapsed near the middle of the excavation area, blocking access to the spot Jack had spent the past couple of days working and—more ominously—blocking Wyatt's egress to the tunnel leading outside. To make matters worse, the lantern was on the other side of the barrier.

He stepped slowly toward the mound of earth and rocks that now blocked his exit, dust still swirling in the air. The match was about to burn his fingertips, so he shook it out and dropped it. But as the dust from the collapse settled on the other side of the barrier, tiny slivers of light began to poke through the rocks trapping him. He began tugging away at some of the stones at the top of the pile, letting them roll behind him, hoping to clear a path.

And then he heard Jack's voice, calling to him from the other side—"Wyatt! WYATT!"

"I'm here!" Wyatt said with a cough.

From the other side, he could hear Jack digging rocks loose with his hammer and pulling them away. With a little more light ebbing in, Wyatt got down on all fours and felt around on the cave floor until he located his own rock hammer, finding it under a layer of dust. He picked it up and went to work, digging into the dirt surrounding the stones until he could loosen them and yank them free.

With Wyatt working from one side and Jack from the other, they soon created an opening about the size of a cannonball. Wyatt put his face up to the hole and gulped in fresh air. Jack held the lantern aloft, shocked by Wyatt's appearance—covered in dust, he appeared ash gray, like a statue. "You okay?" he asked.

"Think so," croaked Wyatt. "Banged up a little, but don't feel anything broken."

A beam of lantern light shone through the opening, creating a luminous shaft in the dust-filled air. Wyatt took a step back from the hole, and with his head no longer blocking the lantern light, the beam cut through the smoke-like dust as though it were a spotlight. And behind him, Wyatt saw an exhilarating sight.

"Jack!" he called, "Look here!"

Jack put his eyes up to the opening, moving the lantern out of the way, which made its shaft of light disappear.

"Raise the lantern up!" Wyatt said, excitedly.

Jack held the lantern back up to the hole, beside his face, and now the beam once again cut through the dust... and landed on a bright, glittering yellow ribbon embedded in the rock wall opposite, running in a thin line through a lengthy swath of quartz, expanding into occasional pockets ranging from golf ball to baseball-sized.

It was gold. Precious, sparkling gold.

"Lord have mercy!" said Wyatt, in awe. "We've hit the mother lode!"

Overwhelmed with joy, they both whooped and laughed and, with renewed vigor, went back to the hard work of clearing the tunnel.

Chapter 19

A LAUGH

Sadie, Dr. Shurtleff, and Lake—half-dozing in their chairs—were startled to attention when they heard what sounded like a weak laugh escaping Wyatt's lips.

"Did you hear that?" gasped Sadie. She rubbed her hand over Wyatt's forehead, hoping for another sound, another indication that he hadn't left her yet. But there was nothing. His eyes remained closed, his hands still.

"Wyatt," she said, "if you can hear me… if you can hear me… you…" She batted her eyes, fighting back tears. "You need to come back to me. You can't just leave me. Not after all we've seen, and done—all we've been through. Come back to your girl. If you don't… if you don't… then…" Her voice cracked. "What am I gonna do?"

She bent forward, resting her head on his chest, sobbing. And then, raising back up, she grabbed his shoulders and shook him violently, her grief replaced by rage.

"Wake up!" she screamed. "Wake up! Come back to me! Come back!"

Dr. Shurtleff shot a look at Lake, who rushed forward to help him pull Sadie away from Wyatt. Each man grabbed one of her arms, dragging her back into her chair. All the while, Sadie shouted furiously, "Get your hands off of me! Let go!"

"Please, Josephine!" said Lake. "Calm down!"

"Shut up!" spat Sadie. "You don't understand! You'll never understand!"

Dr. Shurtleff opened his bag, found a sedative, and filled a hypodermic needle. Meanwhile, Lake tried his best to restrain Sadie, who squirmed in her seat. Dr. Shurtleff knelt beside her, holding the needle aloft. "This is for your own good," he said.

"Get that away from me!"

"It'll relax you."

"I don't want to relax!" she shouted. "I want to scream! I want to scream until this nightmare ends and Wyatt rises off that bed and holds me!"

Dr. Shurtleff pleaded, "Josephine! Please!" He leaned in with the hypodermic needle. She jerked her arm loose from Lake's grip and slapped the needle out of Dr. Shurtleff's hand.

So he slapped her.

Sadie was shocked. Stunned. Both she and Lake looked at Dr. Shurtleff, dismayed. Though trembling, Sadie quickly recovered. Her eyes narrowed. Through gritted teeth, she said, "I've never let any man hit me without hitting back."

Lake let go of Sadie and stepped between her and Dr. Shurtleff, hoping to defuse the tension. He said quietly, "Josephine... understand, we're not just here because of Wyatt. We're here for you." He looked to Dr. Shurtleff. "Right, Doctor?"

Dr. Shurtleff was contrite. "I'm sorry," he said. "I just... you need to be calm."

She stared daggers at him. "Why?" Taking a deep breath, keeping her feelings shakily in check, she stood and stepped beside Wyatt's bed. Sitting on the edge, she put a hand on his shoulder, rubbing it gently. "How can I be calm when my whole reason for living..." She wiped a tear from the corner of her eye. And when she looked down again at Wyatt, there was just the hint of a smile curling his lips. Seeing it gave Sadie a jolt of hope. "Doctor?"

Dr. Shurtleff took his stethoscope from his pocket, put the earpieces in his ears and pressed its diaphragm against Wyatt's chest, listening intently. At the same time he flicked his stopwatch open and watched the second hand make a full revolution, silently counting the faint thumps. "Heartbeat's increasing," he said.

"Is that good?" asked Sadie, with a mixture of desperation and hope. Dr. Shurtleff just gave her a sympathetic look. "Is that good?" she repeated.

"Maybe," said the doctor, doubtfully.

It had to be good, thought Sadie.

It just had to be.

Chapter 20

THE ALMIGHTY

Bursting with excitement, Wyatt galloped his horse to the house. As soon as the animal stopped, he could hear Earpie barking from inside and the banging of the door as the little dog repeatedly leapt against it. Wyatt dismounted. As his feet touched the ground, the front door opened and Earpie came dashing outside, tail twirling, followed by Sadie, who limped onto the porch, her ankle still bandaged.

"What's all the commotion?" she said.

Wyatt scooped the dog up in his arms and strode up to Sadie. She was taken aback by his appearance—covered in chalky grime, looking almost like a ghost, yet smiling happily as a lark. Putting Earpie down, he reached into his pocket and pulled out a few tiny, glistening gold pebbles. Her eyes went wide. Then she leapt at Wyatt. He caught her in a tight hug and spun her around, laughing. In his dirty, calloused hand, he held the fulfilment of a dream they'd both sought for decades. Finally, after years of boom and bust, they had real security. They'd found their safety net, the promise of an easier future, their entrée into the uppermost echelons of respectable society, all literally within Wyatt's grasp.

Now Sadie would never again have to worry about Wyatt getting on to her about sweeping the floor or washing the dishes; they'd have a fine mansion with servants, and she'd have all the time in the world to get involved with a local theater or arts council or to go off to the Santa Anita racetrack with Wyatt and play the horses to their heart's content.

~ • ~

The next day, Wyatt and Sadie arrived at the Assayer's office with Earpie in tow, traipsing along on his leash, to find Jack waiting for them, sitting in a chair on the boardwalk. Wyatt had invited him to be there. After Jack's initial disappointment with prospecting, Wyatt wanted him to experience what happened when one beat the odds and got lucky. They all strode into the Assayer's office together, and Jack and Sadie stood back while Wyatt went to the counter, Earpie trotting at his side, and rang the little bell. Baur, the assayer, was in the midst of eating a sandwich in the back room, but he put it down and came out to greet his customer.

While Jack glanced around at all the bottles of chemicals and beakers and test tubes and retorts and Bunsen burners on the tables and shelves behind the counter, Sadie found a seat off to the side, where she could take a load off her injured ankle.

Wyatt explained to Baur that he'd had some luck digging around up in the mountains, then pulled a few pebbles out of his pocket and handed them over to the assayer. Baur smiled and nodded encouragingly and said, "Let me just check these out."

He went to one of the work areas behind the counter to apply various chemicals and run tests on one of the pebbles, while Wyatt and his cohorts waited patiently. Earpie found a cool spot on the floor and plopped his belly down. When Baur finished, he came back to the counter and carefully laid the pebbles out in a row between himself and Wyatt.

"So what do you think?" asked Wyatt. "Is it worth mining, or do we leave it in the ground?"

"How much more is there?" asked Baur.

"Don't rightly know yet, but… more than a little."

Baur nodded, and said, "Mr. Earp, this is about as pure a gold sample as I've ever seen. I'll give you fifteen dollars an ounce for these three right here."

"How about twenty?" asked Wyatt.

"That's market value," said Baur. "I have to be able to make a little money, too." Wyatt just smiled and began to reach for the nuggets. Baur waved his hand away and quickly added, "Will you take seventeen?"

Wyatt countered, "Eighteen."

"Seventeen-fifty?"

Wyatt thought about it for a moment, then looked back at Sadie. She gave him a little nod. He turned back to Baur and said, "That'll work."

THE LAST STAGE

Baur reached below the counter and brought up a lockbox. Using a tiny key dangling from his watch chain, he opened the lockbox, reached inside, pulled out a handful of cash, and counted out five ten-dollar bills, two ones, and two quarters. Wyatt folded all the bills save one and put them in his pants pocket.

Stepping away from the Assayer's window, he handed the other ten-dollar bill and the two quarters to Jack. "Here's your cut," he said.

Jack's face broke into a wide smile. "Dang!" he exclaimed. "That ain't bad for a few days' work!"

"You earned it," said Wyatt.

Sadie put out her hand for her cut. Wyatt simply gave her a smile, and went to hand her Earpie's leash. She huffed and began limping for the door. Wyatt thanked the assayer and tugged on the leash, the signal for Earpie to get up. "C'mon, boy. Let's go."

As they left the Assayer's office, Wyatt, still holding the dog's leash, stepped down into the dusty area between the road and the stores, while Sadie and Jack strolled along the boardwalk. Wyatt couldn't help but give Jack a little fatherly advice, saying, "Don't let that money burn a hole in your pocket."

"What's it matter?" scoffed Jack. "There's gonna be a lot more where that came from."

"Well, you be careful who you mention it to," Wyatt cautioned. "We don't want to welcome any trouble, if you know what I mean."

"I understand."

Sadie was warming up to Jack, but then she always appreciated a young man with manners. She asked him, "You want to join us for an ice cream cone?"

"Now, Sadie," said Wyatt with a teasing wink, "Jack wants to go celebrate with his lady friends."

"Well, we won't keep him long, if he wants to join us."

Jack gave her a lopsided grin. "Be honored to, Mrs. Earp."

As they kept strolling along, Earpie, his leash trailing behind Wyatt, paused, jerking Wyatt back a little. He stopped for Earpie to do his business. Sadie and Jack paused, also, politely waiting for them. Wyatt looked at the dog and shook his head. "Not fair," he muttered. Jack gave him a quizzical look. Indicating Earpie with a nod, Wyatt said, "He makes it look so easy."

Jack chuckled, but Sadie said grimly, "What ain't fair is God lettin' a man suffer so."

"Now, Sadie, don't go jinxing us," said Wyatt. "Not after my prayers were just answered."

"You mean the gold strike?" asked Jack. "How do you know that wasn't just dumb luck?"

"I consider an earthquake an act of God," Wyatt said, regarding the young man warily. "Don't you believe in the Almighty?"

Jack hesitated, fumbling for an answer—and that told Wyatt everything.

Earpie finished and scratched the sand and continued on down the path. Wyatt and the others fell in after him.

"Well... if there is a God," explained Jack, "I think he's a pretty cruel one, the way he lets some worthless bastards live a long time, and lets good people die before they ought 'a."

"Maybe some things are just out of His hands," said Sadie.

Wyatt paused again for Earpie, and so did Sadie and Jack.

"How, though?" asked Jack. "Ain't he supposed to be all-powerful?"

"Well..." began Sadie, not sure what to say.

Wyatt came to her rescue, saying, "He is, but He gives us power, too, to make our own choices. And if you choose badly, you pay the consequences."

Once again on the move, they entered the ice cream parlor.

~ • ~

Wyatt moved away from the counter holding three ice cream cones. He stepped to a table where Sadie and Jack sat, Earpie on Sadie's lap. As he approached, Wyatt heard Sadie ask, "Do you play cards, Jack?"

"Sometimes," Jack answered. "Not much good at it."

"Neither is Sadie," said Wyatt. "But I reckon she's a tad more experienced than you, so... I wouldn't advise playing against her." Sadie gave her husband a frown, taking her ice cream cone from his hand. Wyatt handed one of the other cones to Jack, and kept the last one for himself. He sat down with them and, as they began enjoying their desserts, Sadie continued quizzing Jack.

"Your parents... were they churchgoers?" she asked.

"Every week," said Jack. "Until one Sunday, after the service, we were on our way home when a big truck come over a hill and ran into us head on. Killed Daddy right off. And Mama... she bled to death."

There was silence for a moment, then Sadie quietly asked, "And where were you?"

"In the back seat. Got a little scar up here." He pointed his finger at the top of his head. "You can't really see it 'cause of my hair, but… when that other car slammed into us, it threw me forward into the back of the front seat and split my scalp open. I just… I just laid there screaming for momma and daddy, and…she reached back for me. I was crumpled up there in the floorboard, looking up at her fingers, reaching to comfort me, with her blood dripping off 'em onto my cheek."

"Oh, dear," Sadie said quietly.

Jack was silent for a moment, a faraway look in his eyes. Then he said, "It seemed like a long time before the police showed up." He shifted in his seat, inhaled a deep breath. "Sumbitch driving the truck was drunk. Walked away without a scratch. So, you tell me, was that one of them acts of God? And if it was, why'd He have to go and do that? Leave me fending for myself, and me just twelve years old?"

Sadie looked at Jack with pity. "Guess there's nothing really anybody could say that would make any sense of it," she said. "But sometimes… well, sometimes you just have to make a leap of faith."

Jack shook his head. "I don't know. I just can't believe in some magical man in the sky. But… y'all do?"

Wyatt shrugged. "I'm coming 'round to it."

"How?"

As Wyatt considered how to answer, Earpie jumped up into Jack's lap, looked at him with his puppy dog eyes, and whimpered, his little tail whipping side to side .

"Earpie! Get down from there!" snapped Sadie.

Jack waved her off. "He's alright," he said. "Ain't hurtin' nobody. Are you, boy?" He rubbed Earpie's head. Earpie, pleading eyes on Jack's ice cream cone, whimpered again. He was a well-practiced beggar, and Jack was an easy mark. After a few moments of having a stare-off, Jack finally relented and let Earpie have a few licks of his ice cream.

With a smile, Wyatt exclaimed, "Ice cream and puppy dogs."

"Hunh?" said Jack, puzzled.

"Ice cream and puppy dogs," Wyatt repeated. "You get a dog cozied up in your lap and share your ice cream with him, and you can't help but think there must be a God, 'cause you're already in Heaven."

Watching Earpie lick the ice cream cone, Jack grinned.

Made sense.

Chapter 21

HENRY'S CUT

After parting ways with Jack, Wyatt and Sadie walked Earpie on down to the entrance of Leung's General Store. Javier, at his usual spot outside the entrance, sat on his canvas stool, strumming his guitar. Wyatt paused, fished a dollar out of his pocket, folded it and stuffed it into Javier's shirt pocket. Javier gave him a broad smile. Wyatt tipped his hat to him, then he, Sadie, and Earpie went inside.

They found Mary sweeping between the aisles. Seeing them, she stopped and put the broom away. "Oooh, Mr. Earp," she cooed, "you're looking very handsome today."

"Had my weekly bath," joked Wyatt.

"Really?" said Mary. "Look what we just got in…" She went to a shelf and came back with a small box. "Bath salts."

"What'll these do?"

"Makes your skin so soft. Feel." She held her arm out. Wyatt stroked her forearm, while Sadie's eyes shot daggers at him.

"These make you soft all over," purred Mary.

"Wouldn't want to be soft all over…" said Wyatt. Then he caught Sadie glaring at him. Cleared his throat. "Maybe you ought to show this to Sadie."

Sadie said icily, "I've seen all I need to."

"Henry up and about?" asked Wyatt.

Mary gestured to the door behind her. "You know where to find him."

Wyatt handed Earpie's leash off to Sadie, walked around the counter and opened the door into the dim hallway. He strode toward the door

THE LAST STAGE

at the opposite end, opened it, and, as he stepped across the threshold into the living quarters, rapped on the wall, calling, "Henry?"

Henry responded, "Yep. Yep. That you, Wyatt?"

Wyatt discovered Henry in his wheelchair, beside the console radio, turning the dial. "Just got this in," said Henry. "A little boxful of sorcery. All I have to do is turn it on and twist the dial, and I can hear music without having to go anywhere—it comes to me, whole orchestras! And I hear stories from all over the world. And news—I don't have to wait for Mary to read the newspaper to me anymore. I can hear news anytime. And I know what's going on before she does—by the time it's in the papers, it's already a day old, or more."

"Yep," said Wyatt laconically, "That's what a radio does."

"Ah!" said Henry, "You're much too practical. No vision. No romance. You'd take the fun out of an orgy."

Wyatt chuckled, "Been known to happen."

Henry hoped to find a good station, but as he twisted the dial, all he got was a sound like eggs frying in a skillet. "Static," he said. "Nothing but static. Must be a storm coming."

"Maybe you just need an antenna. Here—this might help." Wyatt stepped across the room to Henry and placed a ten-dollar bill in his hand.

"What's that?" asked Henry.

"Your cut."

Henry gasped, excited. "You didn't!"

"I sure as hell did!"

Henry let out an excited yelp. "Well, I'll be a suck-egg mule!" He immediately began feeling around for a key under the radio, and soon retrieved it. "How good a strike is it?"

"Not sure yet," said Wyatt. "Might be just a pocket, might be a vein. Gonna have to explore a little more."

Henry wheeled over to what appeared to be an end table and pulled up the tablecloth. Beneath was a Wells Fargo Overland Stage strongbox. There was a hasp on the lid, held closed by a padlock. "Sure wish I could be down there with you," said Henry.

"You're there in spirit."

"Spirit! To hell with that! I want to smell the dirt! Feel the cold rock! Blister my hands with a pick axe!" He stuck the key into the padlock, opened it, and raised the strongbox lid. There was cash and jewelry inside. He asked Wyatt, "What are you gonna do with your money?"

"If it's a big strike, probably sell it to some outfit or other."

Henry deposited the cash into the strongbox, locked it, and pulled the tablecloth back over it. "Sell it? What for?" Henry wheeled back to the radio to return the key to its hiding place.

"Security," said Wyatt. "I'll make me and you and Sadie and Mary stockholders, and we'll be collecting dividends the rest of our lives. Maybe enough to keep Sadie in gambling money after I'm gone."

Henry gave Wyatt a wide grin, and said, "If you're aiming for that, you better hope that whole damn mountain's full of gold!"

As Wyatt stepped back through the hallway to the front of the store, he saw Sadie at the counter with a sack of groceries. Mary, at the cash register, shared a conspiratorial whisper with Sadie as she counted out her change. Moving farther into the store, Wyatt caught sight of Hayden, Jenkins, and Hightower huddling near the door. The men talked in low tones, all three with their eyes now trained on Wyatt.

"Wyatt, sure you don't want a sample?" asked Mary, holding up the small box of bath salts.

Sadie took the box from Mary's hand, saying, "Much obliged."

She put the box into the sack, and was about to lift the grocery bag off the counter, but Wyatt said, "Let me." He hefted up the groceries. As he turned to go, he saw Hayden, Hightower, and Jenkins moving to block their path.

"There he is!" bellowed Hayden. "The man himself! Mr. Stapp! Or is it Mr. Earp today? Oh—and his little lady! What do you call him, Miss……"

Sadie's eyes narrowed. "I call him my husband." Earpie growled at the strangers. Hightower gave the little dog a wild-eyed look and barked at him, loudly. Frightened, Earpie went behind Sadie. She picked him up, cradling him in her arms, and glowered at the men. "Shhhh," she said to the dog, "it's okay, Earpie. Mama won't let 'em hurt you."

"Earpie?" said Hayden. "Well. I guess that settles it. Reckon you're going by Mr. Earp today."

Jenkins and Hightower stepped to either side of Wyatt. "Buyin' anything good?" asked Jenkins, as he peeked into the grocery sack. He pulled out an apple and bit into it. "Little sour," he said, putting it back.

THE LAST STAGE

Sadie put Earpie back down on the floor and squeezed Wyatt's arm. She could feel his bicep tensing, knew this could get ugly in a heartbeat. But Wyatt controlled himself, keeping his volcanic temper in check, even as Hayden stepped close—uncomfortably close—and looked into the sack. "Got something for the little one?" he asked. "Oh—no. That's right. Y'all don't have no little 'uns, 'cept that mutt.. Wonder why that is?"

"Maybe he can't," said Hightower.

Taunting Wyatt, Hayden said, "You mean to say the biggest, bravest gunman who ever lived shoots blanks?" He cast a glance at Sadie. "Does he?"

"That's enough," said Wyatt.

"Or maybe we're wrong..." continued Hayden, leering at Sadie. "Maybe ol' Wyatt's just been planting his seeds in barren ground." Sadie looked stung by the remark; it obviously hit close to home. And Wyatt's patience had reached its limit.

He calmly set the grocery sack down on the counter. "Wyatt..." Sadie said softly, fearful of what was about to come. The men moved forward, purposefully crowding him against the store's counter, but he remained cool and unruffled. Mary, still at the register, slowly lifted a baseball bat from beneath the counter and let the business end of it come down onto the countertop with a loud, persuasive thud. Wyatt glanced at her, gave her a little smile. But he didn't want there to be any trouble. Not now. Not here.

Looking back at the men, he said, "I know you're tryin' to rile me up, but to tell the truth, I'm pretty flattered you think me and the missus are still active in that department." He reached slowly into his pants pocket and pulled out two of the ten-dollar bills. This got the men's—and Sadie's—attention.

Wyatt continued, "The other day, I knew pretty quick you boys weren't up to snuff on your card playing, and I reckon I took advantage, and that wasn't very Christian of me, so... here." He handed the money to Hayden, who took it with uncertainty, not sure where this was heading. "That ought to cover what I won off you," said Wyatt. "I'll let you figure how to divvy it up."

And with that, he picked the sack of groceries back up from the counter. With a nod to Mary, he and Sadie walked calmly out of the store, Earpie at their heels, as the dumbstruck men looked on.

When they were gone, Hayden, Hightower, and Jenkins were left confused and speechless—until Mary again slammed the baseball bat loudly on the countertop and said, "Hey—you gonna buy something?"

"C'mon, boys," said Hayden. They ambled to the door.

"What the hell was that?" asked Jenkins.

"A down payment," said Hayden.

"Hunh?"

He held up the ten-dollar bills. "Bet there's more where this came from." He nodded his head toward the counter, and behind it, the door to Henry's room.

Chapter 22

THE GUNFIGHTERS

On the drive home, Sadie was unusually quiet, staring out the car window at the desolate, dusty desert, Earpie curled in her lap. Wyatt could tell something was gnawing at her, so he asked, "You all right?"

After a long moment of silence, she sighed and said quietly, "I'm sorry I never gave you a child. God just didn't make me right for having babies."

"Prob'ly for the best, anyhow."

She pondered that for a moment, then looked around at Wyatt, his tanned, weathered hands gripping the steering wheel. Reaching out, she put her soft, pale hand atop his.

"Is it?" she asked. "Our brothers and sisters have children and grandchildren. Why don't we?"

"Just wasn't meant to be."

"But why couldn't it have been? Couldn't God hear my prayers?"

"We got Earpie."

She guffawed. "You know that's not the same." She looked back out the passenger window and continued, "And never mind all that. What I want to know now is… why can't he answer my prayers for you? Every day I ask God to take away this damned infection that's afflicting you, and every day it gets worse. Why is that? Can't he see how much I need you?" She was quiet for a moment, reflective. Then she said quietly, "What if Jack is right? What if there is no God?"

Wyatt glanced at her, and saw the sadness in her eyes. "Now, Sadie-Belle…" he began.

She looked at him and said, voice cracking, "I don't want to lose you. I don't know how I'll live without you." She wiped a tear from her eye.

Wyatt let out a long, deep sigh. He eased down on the brake and wheeled the car into the gravel at the shoulder of the road, rolling to a stop near a large saguaro cactus. Turning to Sadie, he said, "Listen, hun, nobody lives forever. And anyway, most fellers only get three or four decades, some even less than that. I've had eight."

He slid his arm over her shoulder, pulled her closer. "Only one thing lasts forever, and that's the love we give each other. And you'll still be feeling mine long after I'm gone." He kissed her forehead, and added, "And to tell you the truth, the nearer I get to the end, the more certain I am that there is a God. And far as I'm concerned, He made you just right."

Embracing Sadie in his arms, he gave her a long, lingering kiss. When their lips parted, she whispered, "You're still my man, Wyatt Earp."

He whispered back, "Always will be. And you'll always be my girl, Sadie-Belle." They just sat there in the peaceful silence of the desert for a while, holding each other, and then Sadie eased back onto her side of the seat. Wyatt put the car into gear, wheeled back onto the deserted roadway, and drove on.

~ • ~

When they arrived at the house, Wyatt grabbed the grocery sack and let Sadie support herself on his arm as she limped up the front steps. Once inside, he set the groceries on the kitchen counter and began to unpack them, but she came limping after him and said, "I'll do that. You take Earpie out and water the horses."

"Yes, Ma'am," he said. He went to the front door and held it open for Earpie to come bounding out.

While Earpie made his rounds around the perimeter of the house, re-marking all his favorite spots, Wyatt pumped fresh water for the horses and made sure there was plenty of hay in their troughs and fresh hay to lie down on in their stalls. As he worked, he heard the faint sound of music coming from the radio inside the house. He waited to hear Sadie singing along; singing always lifted her spirits.

But this afternoon, there was only the radio.

After dinner, Wyatt and Sadie went out onto the front porch and sat in the bench swing, gently swaying. Sadie cuddled against Wyatt, her arm intertwined with his, while Earpie was on the other side of him, nestled against his leg. He looked out at the darkening sky, with the ruby red sun sinking on the horizon, and the sky changing shade from sapphire blue to black onyx.

Resting her head on his shoulder, staring out at the dark outline of the mountains, she said, "Let's go back to Los Angeles."

"Already? What for?"

"I don't know. I just got this feeling like it's time."

"Soon," said Wyatt. "Got a few odds and ends to tie up here first, before we go hightailing it back to our bungalow."

"Oh, no," she said. "No more staying in that cheap little bungalow. Let's get something bigger."

"How big?"

"Maybe a nice big house on a hillside with a garden and a swimming pool and a verandah…"

"Sounds mighty fancy."

"Nothing's too good for my Wyatt. And then we can invite all our Hollywood friends over on the weekends and you can sit out there with Mr. Lake and finish your book."

"Forget the book," he grumbled.

She looked at him, surprised. "What do you mean, forget the book?"

"You'll have plenty of money now to keep you comfortable after I'm gone. No need to bother any more with that nonsense."

"Don't you want to set the record straight?"

"Not gonna matter much to me when I'm dead. Shouldn't matter that much to you, either."

"But it does matter," she said. "I heard a prayer once that said we're like leaves on a tree, and when a leaf dies, it falls to the ground, and that dead leaf nourishes the soil, so new trees and flowers and plants can grow."

"Am I supposed to be the dead leaf?"

"I'm just saying, your story could have a fine influence on people that come after—if we tell it right."

Wyatt let out a deep sigh. "Is that leaf thing from one of your Jewish prayers?"

"Maybe. But wouldn't that be a splendid legacy?"

Wyatt considered it for a moment, and answered, "Well… what if, maybe, having a legacy has nothing to do with what you leave behind, or leave for the future?"

"What is it, then?"

"What if it's just how you live right now? Who you help, whose spirits you lift with a funny story, or who you cheer up with a visit, or a meal, or just a kind word? What if it's just those everyday things, all the little kindnesses that make other people's lives more bearable? What if that's your legacy?" He looked in her eyes. "Ain't that enough?"

Sadie gave him a smile. That was about the most words she'd ever heard him say in a single utterance before. "Maybe," she said, circling her arms around his chest, and snuggling her head against his shoulder. "For you."

They stared off into the sunset. The last red rays were fading, the desert shifting from a golden orange to gray-blue. The pinpoint white glow of stars emerged through the dark night sky, shining over a patchwork of moonlit clouds.

Sadie's gaze drifted to Wyatt's hand as he gently rubbed it over Earpie's back. The little dog rolled over on his back, exposing his belly. Wyatt obligingly gave him a belly rub. Sadie smiled, but then her thoughts drifted to the events of the day. Looking up into Wyatt's eyes, she asked, "You sure about giving Jack a share of the mine?"

Wyatt could tell she had some misgivings about their new partner. "You heard him," he said. "He ain't got none of his own people to help him, so maybe we ought' a look after him."

"We're not really obliged to."

"Well… I reckon we can afford a little generosity now."

She once again looked out at the desert, the stars, the clouds. And in her silence he could read that she still had her doubts.

When the night air turned cool, they went back inside. Sadie sat down, with Earpie at her feet, to listen to her favorite radio program, a Classical music show highlighting popular symphonic pieces and operettas. The music didn't quite appeal to Wyatt, so he excused himself.

All day long, he'd been concerned about protecting their newfound gold strike. Entering their bedroom, he switched on the light and, kneeling down, reached under the bed and pulled out the wooden case. Standing up, he laid it atop the bed and opened it. He took out his holster, his Colt Single Action pistol, the box of shells, and a cleaning kit.

He sat on the edge of the bed and picked up the six-gun. He had hoped he would never have to use it again, but he'd held onto it just in

THE LAST STAGE

case. After all, this was the pistol he'd worn in Tombstone. The one that started the infamous gunfight.

Over the years, Wyatt had found he could always make a few bucks by buying a cheap Colt pistol, cleaning it up, and taking it with him into a bar or casino. Invariably—especially in the first couple of decades after the incident—someone he was gambling with would ask if he had a gun on him, and then ask if it was THE gun, and then wonder if they could hold it, and then eventually, without fail, they'd get that star-struck look in their eyes and ask what he'd take for it. He always said he could never part with the pistol, given its history, but in the end, he always did, and walked away a little richer; the more he resisted selling, the higher the eventual price would be. He sometimes wondered what would happen if any of those gullible marks who thought they had the actual pistol Wyatt used at the O.K. Corral happened to cross paths with some other fool who'd bought one. Would they draw down on each other in the street, like those phony gunfights in the movies, or would they band together and come looking for the fox that fleeced them? Wyatt wasn't terribly concerned about the latter prospect; few of those guns he sold could shoot worth a damn.

Wyatt took time to carefully clean his pistol, using a bore brush to make sure the barrel was unobstructed and the cylinder chambers were clear. With an old toothbrush and some strong-smelling cleaning solvent, he scrubbed the muzzle, the rear cylinder opening and the cylinder's extractor rods, then he cocked back the hammer and cleaned it. Once he was done, he made sure the mechanisms were still working smoothly. He cocked the trigger with the joint of his thumb—not the ball of his thumb as amateurs did; if your hands were sweaty or moist, the thumb ball could slip off the trigger and cost you precious seconds that could mean the difference between continuing to breathe and taking a permanent dirt nap. Then he pulled on the trigger, to make sure it had the right amount of resistance.

The older he got, the heavier the pistol felt in his grip. How many men had he buffaloed with this gun, slamming their heads with the steel butt to knock them unconscious? How many more had he wounded?

How many had he killed?

After all this time, he wasn't sure.

Sometimes, being forgetful was a blessing.

~ • ~

Wyatt rode up to the mining camp the next day, with his gun belt strapped around his waist. He arrived to find that Jack had already put out fresh water and hay for the horses, and was now moving his and Wyatt's buckets to the pit. Wyatt dismounted and tied off his mount. Approaching Jack, he saw that the younger man was also wearing a holster and pistol. "What are you doing heeled?" he asked.

"Better safe than sorry," said Jack. "Looks like you had the same idea."

Wyatt nodded at Jack's pistol. "That a Colt?"

Jack pulled the gun out of its holster with a flourish, saying, "Gun that won the West."

"Guns didn't win the West, plows did," Wyatt scoffed. "Know how to use that thing?" Jack twirled the pistol like Tom Mix, plopped it back into its holster, and smiled, proud. "That's real pretty," said Wyatt. "But try it in a gunfight, and before it spins around once, you'll have a ventilated skull."

"I'm too fast for that."

"Uh-huh. Well, I've known lots of fellers who were faster'n rabbits. And fast is alright, but accuracy's better. You get in a gunfight, you gotta take your time in a hurry."

Feeling his oats, Jack took a long look at Wyatt, and challenged, "Bet I can outdraw you." He whipped his gun from his holster, twirled it, slapped it back in place. Looking expectantly at Wyatt, itching for action, he asked, "You game? Come on—pull that plow handle."

Wyatt chose not to take the bait, saying, "I never draw a gun unless I mean to use it. And anyway—that was a mite slow. I could 'a put two slugs in you 'fore you got that gun up and ready." Jack stared at Wyatt dumbfounded. Was this old man just pulling his leg?

Although he'd done a fair amount of shooting with rifles and pistols as a buffalo hunter, Wyatt didn't learn any real gunfighting skills until he arrived in Kansas in the early 1870s, when he was still a young man in his twenties. Tom Speers, Kansas City's town Marshal, and his deputies educated him to shun flashy gun tricks and focus instead on being consistently accurate. On the prairie, Wyatt had come across men who liked to impress and intimidate with their skills at gun spinning and gun throwing, but all those pistol acrobatics were useless in an actual gunfight, where the real trick was to keep your nerve and use that split second before the other fellow pulled his trigger to be sure you'd got him clearly in your sights. If you hurried, you might miss. And if you'd been showing off your twirling tricks, the extra concentration required to keep your hand muscles from doing the extra maneuvers you'd trained them to do might slow you down. Any man who fanned his gun, using the hammer instead of the trigger to fire quickly, or who shot from the hip, stood little chance against one who focused, concentrated, and made his trigger pull count.

Wyatt began his climb down the ladder, Jack following after him. "Truth be told," said Wyatt, "I prefer using a rifle."

"Why's that?"

They reached the bottom of the pit, where Wyatt lit the lantern and picked up his bucket and hammer. As Jack grabbed his, Wyatt said, "If I've got to shoot somebody, I'd rather shoot 'em from a distance, before they figure out I'm there." Lantern held out in front of him, Wyatt began his trek into the tunnel, Jack close behind.

"That don't sound fair," said Jack. "What about the Code of the West?"

"What Code of the West?" scowled Wyatt. "That's all dime store novel crap."

"You mean, you'd shoot a man in the back?"

"The back, the front, the side... if you're settin' out to kill a man, kill him."

"Just like that?"

Wyatt turned looked into Jack's eyes. "Ain't that hard when they're trying to kill you."

They continued on in silence, until they came to the chamber where they'd been working. Before they began hammering at the rock, Jack said, "Hey... is it true you knew Doc Holliday?"

"'Bout as well as anyone could," said Wyatt.

"What's that mean?"

How could Wyatt describe Doc Holliday? He was scrawny and well-educated, spoke with a Southern drawl as smooth as a well-mixed julep, and had an acerbic wit offset by a mercurial, volatile temperament. He'd trained as a dentist, and when he left that profession behind in Georgia and headed West, he used his nimble fingers and steady hands for gambling and, on some rare occasions, gunslinging. Wyatt first met him in Dodge City, where Doc saved his life by tossing him a pistol at an opportune moment in a shootout. They were close as brothers after that, even though Wyatt's own brothers didn't care much for either Doc or his frequent companion, a prostitute named Big Nose Kate, with whom Doc fought constantly. Wyatt felt that Doc's bitterness came from being condemned for an act of kindness; he cared for his mother when she was dying of tuberculosis, and was rewarded for his charity by contracting it, as well.

"Doc could be prickly," Wyatt told Jack. "He didn't really let people get too close to him. And he had a powerful ornery temper, like a powder keg just waiting for the right spark to set it off."

"I hear when it come to gunfights, he was a wild man."

"Well, I'll tell you this," said Wyatt, "I never knew him to be a coward. Never showed any fear at all. I reckon he figured he was practically dead already, what with his tuberculosis and all, so he just never thought twice about leaping into harm's way."

"So he had a death wish?"

"Maybe," said Wyatt. "I certainly thought so at the time. But now I figure that, the closer you get to the end, the less you care how it comes. You just want it to be quick when it does."

"Here I grew up thinking all them old-time lawmen were heroes," said Jack. "But after listening to all your stories, I've 'bout decided that y'all weren't much better than the outlaws. You were all a bunch of drinkers, gamblers, womanizers, cold-blooded killers…"

"Son," Wyatt said, his words echoing off the cavern walls, "you gotta remember it was a frontier. A lot of those places we settled didn't have any civilization at all until we came in and imposed one."

"At the barrel of a gun," quipped Jack.

Wyatt gave him a stern glare. "It was a different time. Different attitudes. Different values. Don't go judging what we did back then by today's standards. That just ain't fair." Wyatt picked up his hammer, but before striking the first blow, he said, "Anyway, you know what the vaqueros say…"

"The who?"

"Mexican cowboys. They say you come into this world scared, cold, crying and covered in blood. And if you play your cards right… you'll live that way all the time."

~ • ~

After bringing up several buckets each of quartz and gold, Wyatt and Jack were ready for a lunch break. Having an exact location in the pit to concentrate on, and knowing it was filled with gold, took the guess-

THE LAST STAGE

work and uncertainty out of the operation. And now, as they brought up their buckets, they didn't even bother running them through the sifter, since they were mostly filled with gold, anyway. Instead, they emptied them into short burlap bags with ties at the top, which they cinched shut when full. They then hoisted the bags onto the wagon, underneath a tarp, to be taken into town at the end of the day.

At mid-day, as they downed their lunch of hardtack and beef jerky, Jack asked Wyatt, "You reckon maybe we ought to get some help?"

Wyatt scoffed, "You know anyone you'd trust not to stab you in the back?" Jack was unable to come up with a name immediately, and remained silent. "That's the problem," said Wyatt. "Money warps people. I've known men who were bosom buddies since birth, some of 'em even kin to each other, who fell out and tried to kill each other over money. It's just human nature. No matter how much they swear to each other they'll be partners and split everything fifty-fifty, when the prospect of riches becomes a reality, one of 'em always thinks he deserves a bigger slice of it than the other. Never fails."

"Never?"

"I'm telling you—all it takes to turn two lifelong friends against each other is the promise of easy money. That, or the promises of an easy woman." Wyatt shook his head. "Greed's a powerful emotion. I've seen it infect a lot of fellers and turn good men into bad ones."

Jack considered what Wyatt was saying, and said, "You trust me?"

Wyatt gave him a measured look. "Don't have much choice out here, do I? But I tell you what, Jack, just to keep it on the up and up, when we take that wagonload into town, we're gonna stop by a lawyer's office and have papers drawn up, and we'll both sign 'em. Then if one of us gets greedy, it won't matter—we'll be bound to abide by what's on that paper." He looked into Jack's eyes. "That sound alright to you?"

"I reckon," said Jack. "But what's the cut?"

"You'll get thirty-three-and-a-third."

"You're gonna take sixty percent?" Jack asked, sounding affronted.

"I'm splitting the rest with Henry Leung. We'll all get a third."

"Why do you want to give any of it away to some Chinaman?"

"That Chinaman damn near killed himself blasting those holes we're digging. We wouldn't be anywhere without him." After a moment's silence, Wyatt asked, "That's the deal. So… can you live with it?"

"Have I got a choice?"

"No."

Wyatt could tell Jack wasn't happy with this turn of events. He'd probably been figuring on half and now he felt gypped. But hell, thought Wyatt, since he'd been paying the kid wages, he didn't have to offer him any cut at all. He could just pay him off and be done with it. Was Sadie right to worry about Jack? Or would Jack come to realize that he'd stumbled into the lucky break of a lifetime? Or would he just keep simmering until—

What was that sound? There was a strange buzzing overhead. Wyatt and Jack craned their necks and saw an aeroplane come over the ridge of the mountain and pass over their camp, heading in the direction of Tucson.

Jack shielded his eyes from the sun with his hand, watching the plane soar over the cacti, and said, "Can you imagine being up there in one of them things?"

Good Lord, thought Wyatt. When he was born, everybody needed a horse to get around, and pretty much everything west of the Mississippi was wilderness. Now there were cars, transcontinental trains, and aeroplanes, and cities popping up all over the once-wild West. He tried not to be too nostalgic for the old times, but he couldn't help himself. In many ways, the longer he lived, the faster the world around him moved. And the older he got, the more he appreciated a pause, which is why he returned to Vidal every year—it was a little town that seemed frozen in time.

The plane disappeared into the distant clouds.

"I'd rather keep my boots on the ground," said Wyatt. "I fell off a street car in San Francisco thirty years ago and broke my hip. Had to put off going to Alaska for a while until I recuperated. That was bad enough. Fall out of one of them things and you break everything."

He noticed that Jack suddenly had a paranoid look in his eyes. "You don't reckon they're claim jumpers, do you, trying to see where our gold's at?"

Wyatt chortled and shook his head. "Lot cheaper ways to do that than hire an aeroplane. Damn near the whole town knows where my claims are."

As they headed back to the pit, Jack asked, "What were you doing in Alaska? Mining?"

"In a manner of speaking."

"What's that mean?"

"I ran a saloon."

Jack grinned. "You went all the way up north just to be a saloonkeeper?"

"Well," said Wyatt, "Miners like to drink, like to gamble, and they like women. I figured as long as I could give 'em all that, I could mine the miners."

He picked up his bucket and rock hammer and trudged back into the dark tunnel.

Chapter 23

DOC

The confines of the mine faded away and Wyatt felt that he was floating in limbo in a space that was blacker than black, devoid of all light. Had he passed out? Was it heat stroke? He became aware of voices that were nearby and yet far away. He recognized Dr. Shurtleff's somber tones, and Stuart Lake's, and then heard Sadie speaking quietly. He couldn't make out what they were saying, but it sounded like they were in another room, or at the bottom of a well. Yet he knew they were present, within reach, if he could only call out to them. He tried, felt his lips quiver ever so slightly, but couldn't force enough breath through his voice box to push the words out.

He felt Sadie's hand clasp his, her fingers intertwining with his own. He wanted to reassure her, give her a signal that he was there, that he could hear her, that he could feel her touch. But his fingers were limp, unresponsive, unyielding to his commands, unable to simply squeeze her hand.

His legs ached. His joints ached. His shoulders and neck ached. His stomach was tied in knots. And his abdomen felt like it had been split open and filled with hot coals. The more he became aware of his body, the more intensely he felt the pain.

It was humiliating to be so profoundly helpless.

Wait—the excruciating pain must have caused his muscles to jerk, his hands to move over his belly, maybe even a distressed moan, for now the voices were nearer. Sadie's sounded panicked. Dr. Shurtleff said something in a more measured tone, and then Wyatt felt a hand gripping his arm, the sharp prick of a needle on the inside of his elbow, a warming sensation flowing through his body, and....

...and....

...all

...went

blank.

~ • ~

Rain fell.

Wyatt slowly woke.

He was lying on his side in the bed as his eyes blinked open. He raised up on one elbow and, when his eyes adjusted to the dim candlelight, he saw Sadie, Stuart Lake, and Dr. Shurtleff surrounding him, all dozing in their chairs, and Earpie asleep at the foot of the bed. Quietly, without disturbing them, he pulled the covers away and rose up.

He spoke Sadie's name, but she didn't respond. So he shouted it. Still nothing. It was as if she and Shurtleff and Lake were drugged, unable to hear him, unable to feel his touch. He became aware of a light on the dining table, as the flame of the candles in the Menorah grew in intensity. He sensed it was a beacon, beckoning him to approach.

Trudging slowly to the table, he saw the picture-puzzle there, almost completed. He sat down, and scanned the pieces scattered about, looking for particular colors and shapes to go in specific areas. He picked a couple of them up, and snapped them into place. Then tried another. It didn't quite fit where he thought it would, so he kept looking.

After a few minutes, he heard a rustle in the darkness. Craning his head toward the noise, he saw Doc Holliday moving forward from the shadows. Doc approached the table on weak, spindly legs. He was thin, sallow-faced, with a long, neatly-clipped mustache, and wore a black 1880s suit. "Evening, Mr. Earp," intoned Doc in his disarming Southern drawl.

"Wondered when you'd show up," said Wyatt. "Seems like everywhere I go, you turn up sooner or later."

"Like a bad penny," said Doc, putting his fingers out to touch the Menorah on the table. That simple gesture reminded Wyatt of the falling out he'd had with Doc, sitting in a restaurant in Albuquerque, New Mexico, where they'd fled to avoid the arrest warrants for the murder of Frank Stilwell. At that time, Wyatt was just becoming more deeply involved with Sadie, who'd gone back to her family in San Francisco while Wyatt and his posse went after his brother's killers. When they reached Albuquerque, Wyatt elected to stay with a prominent Jewish businessman. Weeks of riding all over the Southwest had both Wyatt and Doc on edge, and while they were dining at Fat Charlie's The Retreat Restaurant, Doc casually mentioned that "that Hebe bitch" was turning Wyatt into a "damn Jew-boy." Wyatt told Doc to go to Hell and stormed out.

Doc apparently recalled it as well; now, as he ran his fingers along the branches of the Menorah, he looked at Wyatt with a quizzical smile and an upraised eyebrow. Wyatt pointed at the seat across from him, and said, "Pull up a chair."

Holliday settled into the seat and leaned back. "Missed you at my funeral," he said.

Wyatt concentrated on the puzzle. "I'd 'a come if you'd told me you were dead. By the time I found out, you'd done been two months in the ground."

"Still could 'a come."

"If I'd known you'd be chewing fire about it after all this time, I would've. I just never understood this whole idea of paying respects to people after they're gone. If you've got any strong feelings, or anything to say about 'em, tell 'em while they're still kicking. Don't wait till they're dead and buried."

"I don't mean to be pissy, Wyatt. I'm just a mite peeved that none of my obituary writers had the wit or audacity to write the headline, 'Death Takes a Holliday.'"

Wyatt laughed.

Doc picked up one of the puzzle pieces and examined it, saying, "Figured an old card shark like you would be playing solitaire."

Wyatt scanned the board, and found a place for a piece he'd been holding. "I like puzzles," he said. "Like how the odds keep tipping in your favor with every piece you put in. A thousand pieces to put together, a thousand to one. Put one in, 999 to one."

Doc took a long look at the puzzle in the dim light, three-quarters completed. It was a painting of gunfighters shooting it out on a Western street.

Wyatt put another piece in its place, adding, "And the more it comes together, the faster the pieces fall into place. Until finally, you know where that last piece fits, and then you see the whole picture."

THE LAST STAGE

Doc cocked his head, looking at the faces of the men in the painting. "That s'posed to be us?" he asked.

"Think it's from the cover of one of them dime books."

"Hear they pretty much boiled me down to a quick draw and a cough."

"Pretty much."

"What do they say 'bout you? Lawman? Villain? Killer?"

Wyatt smirked. "Depends on who's writing."

"And that's why you're writing your own."

"That's more Sadie's doing."

"Good old Sadie," said Doc. "Never thought you two would last, but here you are..." He picked up one of the puzzle pieces and began rolling it back and forth between the phalanxes of his fingers like a coin. "Time's running out, Wyatt. Why don't you just die gracefully?"

"How's that possible when I've done so many disgraceful things?"

Doc chuckled. "Surely you don't let all that prairie justice we meted out bother you?"

"Don't you?"

"Whatever conscience I had got coughed up with my lungs."

Wyatt sighed. "Well, I reckon it irks me 'cause I've been around a bit longer than I had any right to be. Had more time to think on my sins."

"I reckon you have," said Doc. "Time moves on. And the farther down the line you get, the more burdens you carry. How much more of a load do you think you can bear?"

"Not much. But I'm not going without a fight."

"Didn't expect you would. Your trouble is you've never been defeated. You don't know how to lose."

Wyatt took a long look at Doc. In the glow of the candlelight, he looked healthier than he did in the lobby of Denver's Windsor Hotel in the winter of 1886, when he and Sadie were staying there on a business trip. Hearing that Wyatt was there, Doc came to see his old friend. It was four years after their heated parting in Albuquerque, and the Doc who walked across the lobby on wobbly legs looked gray and emaciated. After exchanging pleasantries with Josephine, Doc stepped away with Wyatt to speak quietly, reminiscing about their past adventures—though Doc's tales were interrupted by frequent coughing. Wyatt thanked Doc again for saving his life in Dodge City, and said, "Isn't it strange that if it weren't for you, I wouldn't be alive today—yet you're gonna go first."

As they parted, Doc put his frail arms around Wyatt's strong shoulders and said, "Goodbye, old friend. It'll be a long time before we meet again."

How was it that he could see Doc so clearly now? Was he truly here, or was this a Doc conjured from his memories, an apparition of his own creation?

"Doc...?"

"Yes?"

"Are you real?"

"Just as real as you are, Wyatt."

Wyatt scanned all the puzzle pieces looking for a particular one to fit a space he hadn't filled. "Then tell me this—is it true that if you die in your dream, you die in real life?"

"Couldn't say," Doc said with a grin. "I wasn't dreaming much at the end." Leaning forward, he said, "You know, after all the men you've sent to their Maker, I never thought you'd be so scared of crossing over yourself. Or is it just that you're worried about who'll be waiting on the other side?"

Why indeed, wondered Wyatt, was he clinging on to his own diminishing life so stubbornly? Was it simply fear of passing into what Hamlet called "the undiscovered country from which no traveler returns?" No, that wasn't it. His reason for hanging on was dozing in a chair behind him. "More worried about who I'm leaving on this side," he said.

"Hardest part of loving is leaving," said Doc. "But we all do, eventually." Glancing over the puzzle pieces, he put his finger on one. "I think this here's the one you're looking for."

Wyatt picked up the puzzle piece and fit it into the empty space. And when he looked back up, Doc was gone.

Wyatt rose, turned, and saw his own weak, diseased body lying in the bed, silent and still in the candlelight, with Sadie, Lake, and Dr. Shurtleff surrounding it, all of them still sleeping. He walked slowly to Sadie's chair and knelt beside her. Sliding one arm over her shoulder, he wrapped his other around her waist, and tenderly kissed her cheek.

Chapter 24

A GLOW IN THE NIGHT

Wyatt was comfortably in bed with Sadie, side-by-side and spooning, with one arm under her head and the other across her midriff. He kissed her cheek. She smiled, and snuggled closer against him. "Uhmmm," she purred, "a woman likes to be held and loved up on a little."

"Snug as a bug in a rug," said Wyatt.

They remained silent for a while, simply enjoying the quiet of the moment and the warmth of each other's caress. Rolling onto her side towards him, she touched his face and said, quietly and with grave concern, "Hon... now that we got all this money, why don't you go see a specialist?"

Wyatt grumbled, "Oh, I don't need..."

"No, you're going," she interrupted sternly. "I'm not gonna let you die of mule-headedness."

Wyatt rolled onto his side, turning his back to her. He felt her body press against his, and her fingertips glide over his forehead and cheek. She kissed the bald spot on the back of his head. And he felt her hand glide across his back and over his hip, coming to rest on his genitals, gently fondling him. In the past, this would have been a signal that she was ready for him to make love to her. But now, her touching and caressing generated flares of pain, not passion. He shuddered and grunted as her fingers landed on a particularly tender area. Reluctantly, he brushed her hand away. She leaned over him to look into his sad blue eyes, and he could see in hers a yearning for the way it used to be, and regret that it would never be that way again.

Rolling onto his back, he felt her fingers now interlace with his, at his side. The infirmities that he tried so hard to hide had, some time ago, robbed him of the benefits of physical affection. He recalled how amorous he had been as a young man; when he was first married, he enjoyed spending mornings in bed with Aurilla, exploring each other's bodies and pleasuring each other with abandon. After she passed, he left Missouri under a cloud and stopped running in Peoria, Illinois. There, he worked as an enforcer in a brothel, which gave him ample opportunity to bust heads and ball women. He knew he was headed down a dangerously destructive spiral when he realized he enjoyed the former more than the latter; his short fuse and inclination to violence had already landed him in jail three times in an eight-month period. So, he lit out again, this time for the Kansas prairie.

For a while, he made money as a government surveyor and buffalo hunter, an occupation that afforded him much time alone. After months of self-examination and self-reflection, he concluded that he'd rather be a law enforcer than a law breaker. He served briefly as a peace officer in Wichita, and then moved on to Dodge City, where he became Assistant Marshal. Dodge City was the nexus of the cattle trade, a magnet of mayhem and men with dubious morals. It was the perfect place to romance a quiet, unassuming prostitute named Celia Ann Blaylock, who went by the name of Mattie. When the cattle business slowed and Wyatt's salary was cut, he took Mattie with him to join his brothers in Tombstone, the next thriving boom town, where he intended to start a stage line.

He left twenty-eight months later, after his family's clashes with the Clantons and McLaurys led to the infamous gunfight at the O.K. Corral and, eventually, to the wounding of his older brother, Virgil, and the death of his younger brother, Morgan.

Wyatt's subsequent actions caused considerable controversy in the Territory, so he once again decided it would be best to leave his troubles behind. Among those troubles was Mattie. Abandoning her, he reunited with Sadie in San Francisco, and the two of them had been inseparable ever since.

No one was more surprised than Wyatt that he'd managed to stay with Sadie for so long, or that she'd managed to abide by him. In his youth, Wyatt had been an earnest, outgoing man, but circumstances drove him to be distrustful of others, and turn inward. He was most often described as stoic, or taciturn—not warm-hearted and easy to know. Opening his heart to another person, revealing himself, giving his absolute trust to another—that took real courage. Compared to that, shooting it out with the McLaurys and Clantons was a piece of cake.

Although he was low-key and she was high-strung, deep down, he and Sadie were doppelgangers. Both were risk-takers yearning for the big break, the easy haul, that would set them up for life, so they'd spent most of their lives going from boom town to boom town, betting their futures on mining claims and stock investments and land deals that all tended to go bust, usually because Wyatt had to sell short to cover Sadie's gambling debts. Frustrating as it could be, he understood her intentions and her inability to say no to overwhelming temptation, so he always forgave her. At their core, they were both gamblers. And they'd bet on each other. And they were both all in.

His reverie was interrupted by Sadie touching his shoulder. Having gotten his attention, she pointed to the window. "Look," she said, "it's snowing."

Wyatt had never seen snow in the lowlands of the Mojave Desert, but he turned his head to the window and, after a moment, he did, indeed, see a white flake drift by. It was soon followed by a couple more. Curious, he climbed out of bed to investigate. Going to the window, he raised it up, and as soon as he did, he caught the whiff of smoke in the air. He leaned his head out. Looking southeastward, he saw an orange glow on the distant horizon, toward Vidal. It appeared to be about the center of town… where the Leung's store was located.

His heart sank.

Snatching his pants off the back of a chair, he said brusquely, "Get dressed."

Minutes later, he and Sadie were in their car, Wyatt at the wheel, Sadie in the passenger seat. Wyatt drove fast towards town, the red glow growing larger before them. A fire engine, siren blaring, came up behind them and whizzed past.

Soon, they came down the main street to Leung's General Store. It was an inferno, with rolling black smoke belching white-hot cinders into the sky. The fire attracted what seemed to be the whole town, who thronged around, staring blankly, with some moving aside so the fire engine could pull through.

Wyatt's car rolled to a stop behind the crowd. He and Sadie hopped out and pushed forward, shocked by the blaze. Wyatt eventually made his way through the onlookers to Mary, who was being held back by Javier and Sheriff Ledbetter. Tears poured down her cheeks as she fought against their restraint and screamed, "HENRY! HENREEEEEEEE!!"

Just as Wyatt managed to get to her, she broke free. He grabbed for her, but she was beyond his reach, running into the blazing building. He and Javier trotted after her, but as they neared the door they stopped and recoiled from the heat and smoke.

Ledbetter yelled, "Get back!" Wyatt ignored the warning, and—gathering up his courage—ran into the store after Mary, just as the firemen turned on their hoses and trained them on the blazing roof.

The inside of the store was a cauldron of flame and cinders. Wyatt, hand over his mouth, took a few steps inside, his eyes watering from the acrid smoke. He called out to her—"Mary! MARY!!!"

He caught a glimpse of her pushing open the door that led to Henry's room. The hallway beyond was a tunnel of flame. But she dashed into it.

Wyatt was about to run after her, but at that moment, the roof collapsed in front of him, a burning beam barely missing him, sending up even greater flames and sparks and hopelessly blocking his way. He might still have fought his way through, but he felt arms circle around his torso and pull him back.

Outside, Sadie screamed, hysterical, tears pouring—until she saw Javier pulling Wyatt out of the inferno. Wyatt was coughing, blackened with smoke, wiping his eyes. She limped forward as Javier pulled him back towards the crowd, Ledbetter rushing to help. Wyatt fell onto all fours, gasping for breath and coughing. Sadie hugged him tightly.

All the other bystanders stood shocked, murmuring. They were silenced by the sound of Mary's screams. She was trapped, and screeching in agony. Wyatt shoved Ledbetter, saying, "For God's sake, help her!"

The lawman said grimly, "No helping her now."

Mary's screams continued for seconds that seemed like eons…

…then abruptly stopped.

And now there was just fire, and smoke, and the sound of timbers popping in the heat.

Wyatt wiped his eyes. With a look of utter defeat and desolation, he rose slowly to his feet. As he did so, Javier, agitated and wailing nearby, dropped to his knees, his face wet with tears, praying fervently and crossing himself.

"Let's go home," said Sadie. Leaning on her for support, Wyatt went back to their car. They climbed in, Wyatt shocked and silent. For a moment, he just sat there, staring out the windshield at the onlookers as a handful remained to watch the building burn.

Finally, reflecting on what he'd just witnessed, he spoke, saying, "Don't make sense, her running in there like that."

"Makes perfect sense," said Sadie. "She'd rather die with her husband than go on without him." She and Wyatt exchanged a look. And then he gazed out again at the slowly dispersing crowd. As the townspeople trudged away, he noticed, far off to one side, Hayden, Hightower, and Jenkins, looking on without emotion.

Wyatt set his jaw grimly. Starting the car, he backed it onto the road. And, as firemen fought the blaze and the townspeople headed to their cars and trucks and horses, Wyatt's Packard proceeded up the road, until it was swallowed by the darkness.

Chapter 25

THEIR CLAIM

By morning, the Leung's store was just a smoldering heap. Wyatt took his car into town and found a handful of other looky-loos milling around the periphery, staring at the smoking and, in some spots, still burning ruins. Prominent among the remains was the scorched, steel frame of a wheelchair. Beyond it, upwind and far away from the devastation, Javier stood, guitar slung over his back, hands hanging loosely at his sides, head bowed, and tears streaming.

Wyatt walked around the smoking ashes to Javier and simply stood next to him for a while, offering comfort just by his presence. Javier, being polite, tried his best to compose himself. Wyatt offered his handkerchief. Javier took it and wiped his eyes.

In a calm, even tone, Wyatt asked, "Javier, last night… did you see anything?" Javier shook his head. "Hear anything?" Javier shook his head again.

"What happened?" asked Wyatt.

Javier stammered, "Sleeping. Smelled smoke. Got up. Opened door. Fire." His voice cracked as he repeated, "Fire. Everywhere. Grabbed clothes. Guitar. Ran out."

Wyatt and Javier watched as firemen carefully removed the bodies of Mary and Henry—charred beyond recognition—out of the ashes.

"I seen 'em," said Javier, his voice cracking as he wiped away tears. "Seen 'em go."

"Seen who go?" asked Wyatt.

"Henry. Mary. Walked out. Got on." Javier made a swooping motion with his arm and hand, tilting up at the end. "Went away."

THE LAST STAGE

Wyatt looked at him skeptically. "You know Henry can't walk."

"Seen it," said Javier. "Got in. Off it went." He made the swooping motion with his arm again.

"Off what went?"

"The stage." He held the handkerchief back out to Wyatt.

"Keep it," said Wyatt. Javier stuffed it into his pocket.

The firemen placed Mary and Henry's bodies on stretchers, threw sheets over them, and carried them to an ambulance. When the ambulance doors closed, Javier turned and trudged away. Wyatt wondered what he would do now without the beneficence of Henry and Mary, and without a place to stay—the fire had consumed not only the store but also the shed where Javier slept.

Then Wyatt stepped into the ruins. The acrid smell of scorched wood and burnt flesh hung in the air, and he could feel the heat of the smoldering ashes through the soles of his boots. A fireman still looking through the rubble said to him, "Can I help you?"

Wyatt pulled out his wallet and flashed a badge. The fireman went back to his work. Nodding toward the ambulance, Wyatt asked, "Any signs of violence?"

"Hard to say," said the fireman. "But we found 'em side by side, holding each other. If it's any consolation, they probably suffocated before…"

Wyatt cut him off. "That's enough," he said brusquely. Stepping away from the fireman, he walked slowly to an area of the ruins that used to be Henry's quarters. Kicking away some ashes with the toe of his boot, he uncovered the fire-blistered Wells Fargo strongbox, yawning open. Empty.

He looked up to see Sheriff Ledbetter stepping across the rubble, approaching him. "Wyatt," said Ledbetter. "I know what you're thinking."

"Do you?"

Matter-of-factly, Ledbetter said, "Hayden and his friends were all playing cards at the cafe last night right up until after the fire started. Thought I'd better tell you, lest you go gettin' any ideas."

"Well—you've told me." Wyatt moved carefully through the ashes and debris, heading back to the street.

Ledbetter, at his side, continued, "I hope I don't have to remind you that this is the twentieth century. And violence just isn't a very evolved way for a civilized man to deal with his problems."

Wyatt drawled, "Who said I was civilized?"

"I'm warning you—that vigilante stuff you used to get up to, it's liable to get you arrested now—if'n it don't get you killed."

Wyatt raised his head and gave the Sheriff an icy look, saying, "Longevity's overrated."

Wyatt left Ledbetter and loped on down the street to the cafe. As he entered, he saw it was doing a much more brisk business than usual. The tragedy nearby was good for their business, the cafe being the focal point for people of the community to socialize and theorize about the devastation down the block. Was it an electrical fire? Was it just that strange old recluse, Henry, committing suicide? Or did the Leungs borrow from the Chinese Tongs and couldn't pay up, and this was their revenge? The rumor mill was heading into overdrive.

Wyatt strolled through the entirety of the cafe, looking for Hayden and his men. They weren't there. He went to the counter in front of the kitchen and waved Sam, the proprietor, over.

"Wyatt," said Sam, "can I get you anything?"

"Just want to ask you something," said Wyatt, casually. "Was Gib Hayden around here last night?"

"Yeah, he was here."

"He have a little fellow and an Indian with him?"

"Don't he always?" chuckled Sam. "They all sauntered in here around sundown. Sat over yonder." He nodded towards the back of the cafe. "They ordered up some sandwiches and played poker until after dark."

"How long after dark?"

Sam shrugged. "A few hours. They didn't stop until ol' Rand Douglas ran in here shoutin' about the store being on fire." Sam said it all with a straight face, but Wyatt knew he was a good liar. And that he could be bought.

"Any idea where they're staying?" he asked.

"Nope," said Sam. And then he excused himself to help a customer with a lunch order.

As Wyatt headed for the door, Tom Wendler came wobbling up behind him, a little tipsy—despite Prohibition, the cafe was pretty liberal about serving liquor. Fiddling with a toothpick between his teeth, Tom said, "Say, Wyatt, congratulations on your gold strike."

Wyatt stopped in tracks and spun around. "Word gets around fast," he said.

"Got anyone watching it for you? 'Cause if you wanna hire my boys…"

"Tom, this ain't the time," said Wyatt, his eyes narrowing.

"Claim like that, you gotta protect it."

Wyatt turned his back on Tom and again started for the door.

"Oh, and Wyatt…" called Tom, "sorry about Henry and Mary. Pitiful. Just pitiful."

Wyatt paused in his tracks. "Pitiful? That's all you've got to say?"

Tom could sense that Wyatt was on a short fuse. Twiddling the toothpick between his lips, he tried to lighten the mood, chuckling nervously and saying, in a low voice, "Well, come on. I mean, what's a couple less Chinamen?"

In a flash, Wyatt reeled on Tom. With his left hand, he grabbed Tom's hair and yanked his head back, while simultaneously snatching the toothpick out of his mouth with his right hand. He held the toothpick in front of Tom's bulging, frightened right eye. Boiling inside, he wanted to blind the man, whom he'd called a friend for years. And if Tom had said one more word, any word, he might've. Instead, Tom just quaked, scared by the ferocity and suddenness of Wyatt's attack. And seeing him quivering, Wyatt realized that Tom would never have responded with such fear to the Wyatt he knew. But this wasn't that Wyatt. This was the Lion of Tombstone.

Releasing Tom, Wyatt flicked the toothpick at him. Tom flinched, still shaking in his shoes. And without another word, Wyatt turned around and stalked out the door, the adrenaline coursing through his veins making him stand tall and straight.

He went to his Packard and climbed in. Then slammed his palm against the dashboard. Then banged it with his fist. And then hit it three more times in rapid succession. He knew he needed to cool down before he got on the road, so he sat there, simmering. "A couple less Chinamen." Tom had been shopping at the Leung's store for years. If you'd asked him a week ago, he'd have said they were friends. But now that they were gone, he dismissed them as though he were talking about cattle, like they were less than human. How could he be so heartless?

But Tom was right about Wyatt's mine. He did need to put at least some kind of nominal deterrence around his claim. Why make it easy for claim jumpers and thieves to clean him out before he'd even got started?

He fished the key out of his pocket and started the car's engine. Driving to the hardware store at the end of the street, he kept his head facing forward as he passed the smoking ashes that had been Henry and Mary's store.

Their home.

Their claim.

Chapter 26

GUNFIGHT AT THE O.K. CORRAL

Wyatt returned to the mining camp with his horse pulling a small cart laden down with rolls of barbed wire, a bundle of narrow signposts and a couple of painted signs saying 'KEEP OUT—PRIVATE PROPERTY.' He dismounted and called, "Jack!"

He heard the hammering down in the tunnel stop, and soon Jack appeared, climbing up the ladder out of the pit. Jack helped Wyatt unload the supplies. Over the next few hours, they dug holes and planted signposts around the perimeter of the mine. Wyatt tacked one of the 'Keep Out' signs on a post near the entrance, and put another on the opposite side. Putting on thick leather gloves, he and Jack spooled the barbed wire along the signposts, one strand along the bottom, another along the top.

Around noontime, with the sun high up in the sky, they took a break under the shade of the tent. Standing in the door flap, staring out at the desert, Wyatt said, "Jack, I want you to do something for me."

"Yessir?" said Jack, sitting in one of the canvas chairs, chomping on an apple.

"I want you to go into town and ask around about Gib Hayden. See if you can find out where he's staying."

"Who's he?"

"You prob'ly seen him 'round. Big fella. Usually has two others with him—an Indian about the size of a grizzly and another one about your age—a little fellow with a big mouth." He looked back at Jack. "I figure they're in the hotel down the road, or maybe renting one of those old ranch hand's shacks the other side of Fernando Armendariz's place."

"And what do you want me to do if I find 'em?"

"Just come tell me."

There was an icy finality in Wyatt's voice. Jack took a final bite of the apple and stood up. He stepped up beside Wyatt, tossed the apple core out into the sand, and asked, "You going after 'em?"

"I might."

"What for? What'd they do?"

Wyatt looked down at the ground. "I'd bet my life they're the ones who killed Henry and Mary."

"The storekeepers?" After a moment's heavy silence, Jack asked, "If you find them fellers, then what?"

"I'm gonna bring 'em in."

"What if they ain't inclined to come along peaceful?"

"They're either goin' before a county judge or a heavenly judge. Up to them."

Jack was taken aback with how casually Wyatt spoke of murder. "Wait a minute, now," he said. "This ain't like when you was a Sheriff."

"I'm still a Sheriff," said Wyatt. Jack looked at him with consternation. Wyatt pulled out his wallet, flashed a badge to Jack, and said, "Honorary Deputy Sheriff of San Bernardino County."

Jack squirmed. "What I mean is, we ain't in the 1800s anymore."

Wyatt's eyes narrowed. "Justice never goes out of fashion."

"Is that what this is? Justice? Or revenge?"

"Either way, killing the men who killed my friends satisfies both."

Jack may not have fully agreed with what Wyatt had in mind to do, but a little while later, he hopped on his horse and rode towards town.

Wyatt went into the desert, beside the big rock, to relieve himself. He stood there for a long time while he waited to urinate. Finally, he let go with a dribbling puddle on the weeds, and felt a bit less pain in his gut. As he buttoned up his jeans, he looked out at the expanse of sand and was surprised to see a dust cloud moving across the desert, just as he had a few days before. Ahead of it was the same white stagecoach pulled by white stallions. Wait—was he dreaming, or was a dark-haired woman waving to him from inside? Just like before, the coach disappeared behind a rise, and the white cloud of dust trailing it dissipated in the arid breeze.

It was hot standing there with the sun bearing down on him. Best get to work, he thought, before he fell over with heat stroke. He strode back to camp, picked up his pick hammer and bucket, and returned to the pit. As he descended into the cool darkness of the tunnel, his mind descended into the past, reviving memories of the events that lifted him from lawman into legend.

If people really knew the true facts behind the gunfight at the O.K. Corral, Wyatt mused, they'd either be astounded or confounded; probably the latter. The origins of the gunfight were complicated. It happened for a confluence of reasons, the least of which was two lawmen in their mid-30s fighting over the affections of a 20-something chanteuse.

As best as Wyatt could remember, it all started with a stagecoach robbery on March 15, 1881—the Ides of March—and ended seven months later on October 26 with a shootout on a city street that left three men dead.

On that March evening, a Wells Fargo stagecoach with Bud Philpott as the driver and Bob Paul as the shotgun messenger left Tombstone heading up the road to Benson. Inside the stage was a strongbox full of gold coins and a few passengers. Along the way, near Contention, a group of armed outlaws stepped into the road and shouted for the coach to stop. Since the desperadoes were blocking the road, Philpott had little choice but to comply. But rather than give up their cargo, Bob Paul emptied both barrels of his shotgun at the men. Naturally, they fired back. Philpott was killed and a passenger inside the coach was mortally wounded. Bob Paul took the reins of the stagecoach and sped away under a hail of bullets. Against all odds, he managed to get the stagecoach, the dead driver, the dying passenger, and the gold to Benson.

News of the event soon reached Tombstone. Everyone in town believed the culprits were members of an outlaw gang called the Cowboys—a group mostly known for cattle rustling who were becoming increasingly violent as tensions rose between the ranchers whose lands surrounded Tombstone and the bankers and businessmen inhabiting the fast-growing town.

Sheriff Johnny Behan immediately formed a posse to ride out after the outlaws. Though several men volunteered their services, Behan only wanted Bob Paul and the Earp brothers—Deputy U.S. Marshal Virgil Earp, sometime stage driver Morgan Earp, and Wyatt, who had previously been a deputy in Dodge City. Virgil asked Bat Masterson—a former Dodge City Sheriff—to join the group, along with a Wells Fargo agent named Marshall Williams.

Wyatt spent three long days with the posse tracking the outlaws, ending up at a ranch owned by Len Redfield, whom the Earps believed to be an ally of the Cowboys. While Wyatt went up on the porch of the ranch house to speak to Redfield, Morgan noticed a man trying to sneak away and grabbed him. He brought the man to Wyatt, and they soon found out his name was Luther King. Wyatt told Morgan to take King into the house, and then he asked Sheriff Behan not to let King speak to anyone. He then he went over to the posse's horses to figure out a game plan with Bob Paul. The Earp brothers had dealt with members of the Cowboys before, and Wyatt knew that in the backcountry, the threat came not only from them but also from the ranchers who protected them.

As he spoke to Paul, Wyatt saw Behan lead Redfield into the ranch house. Were they just getting out of the heat, or was something else afoot? He strode across the dusty ground, bounded up the steps, and came inside to find King talking to Redfield and Redfield's brother, Hank. Something wasn't right; either Behan was powerful forgetful, or he had ignored Wyatt's orders to keep the Redfields and King separated.

Taking charge, Wyatt asked Luther King to step aside so he could ask him a few questions. As they talked, Hank Redfield said he needed to drain his snake and went out the back, presumably going to the outhouse. Wyatt should have had Morgan follow him, but he didn't, and a few minutes later he heard hoofbeats. He looked out a window to see Hank riding away at full gallop. Now Wyatt was angry not only at Behan but at himself, for being so careless. He returned to his interrogation of King, his questions now sharp and heated. Under Wyatt's relentless verbal assault, King eventually confessed that he was in on the robbery and named three others who were involved, telling Wyatt where he could find their camp.

As the lawmen left the ranch house, Behan said he would take King to Tombstone and put him in jail while Wyatt and the rest of the posse continued after the other outlaws. Since Wyatt had his doubts about Behan, he was glad to be rid of him. But he suspected, even before they started, that the posse would never catch up to the Cowboys, because he was sure that while he was questioning King, Hank Redfield had ridden lickety-split out to the stagecoach robbers to warn them that the lawdogs were coming.

Thus began several days of the posse chasing false leads and arriving at locations where the outlaws were supposed to have been only to find that either they'd never been there, or they'd already come and gone. As the days wore on, Wyatt became more and more discouraged. It was as if they were being taunted, made fools of. Plus their horses were wearing out, after days of carrying their riders over rough ground and rocks and shifting, sandy dunes. At every town they came to, Virgil Earp sent telegrams to Behan pleading for him to send fresh mounts. Behan kept wiring back that he'd take care of it, but the horses never came.

The older horses were having a particularly hard time of it. Nine days into the search, as the posse led their steeds through a barren, scorching desert, they paused to rest in the shade of a rocky outcrop. Bob Paul's horse was breathing rapidly, more than a normal twenty to forty breaths per minute. Wyatt took a look at the distressed animal, opening its mouth and pressing on its gums with his fingers. Instead of feeling slimy, they were dry as dust, and where he pressed, they blanched white and stayed that way. He then rubbed his hand along the horse's flank and pressed his ear against it, just behind its ribs. He should have heard gurgling sounds from the beast's belly, but there was only silence.

Wyatt told Paul the horse was heat exhausted, and wouldn't last much longer out in the sun. Paul just hoped it would carry on long enough for them to make the next town, or ranch, or creek, where it could get some much-needed water. They waited a couple of hours for the sun to go down before setting off again. About a half-mile into their trek, Paul's horse began to slow down and falter, until it eventually wobbled, fell over, and died. If it had been able to hold on just an hour longer, it would have made it to the ranch where the posse spent the night.

That evening, as they ate the meager dinner the rancher's wife provided, Wyatt and Bat Masterson debated whether they should continue on with what seemed to be a hopeless task or return to Tombstone. Come morning, they presented their decision to Virgil Earp—they were going back. Virgil wanted to stay on the trail of the outlaws, but he let the other men decide whether they would remain or go. Morgan Earp, Bob Paul, and Marshall Williams decided to stick with Virgil. Wyatt left his horse behind for Paul to ride, and Bat left his, which was too spent to go any farther, at the ranch. Then, saying their goodbyes to the rest of the posse, Wyatt and Bat walked the eighteen long, hot miles back to Tombstone.

Wyatt already had reason to distrust Sheriff Johnny Behan. For starters, even before he encountered the man, he'd heard that Behan was an unrepentant ladies' man, the kind who'd buy you a drink one minute and sleep with your wife the next. In addition, the two men were political rivals. In July of 1880, Wyatt was appointed Undersheriff for the eastern section of Pima County by Sheriff Charles Shibell, who had his eyes set on being reelected in November. Shibell was a Democrat with the support of the Cowboys, who were mostly ex-Southerners. Wyatt, like most of Tombstone's businessmen, was a Republican, and as such he supported Bob Paul's candidacy. Everyone expected that Paul would win, but when November rolled around and ballots were counted, Shibell emerged the victor by a 46-vote margin.

Seventeen days after the election, Paul filed suit, accusing his opponent of ballot-stuffing; the San Simon Cienega precinct delivered 103 votes to Shibell and 1 to Paul, even though the total number of voters in the precinct was estimated to be about 15. During the subsequent hearing, James Johnson testified that ballots were left under the supervision of Fin Clanton, brother of Ike Clanton and a known associate of the Cowboys.

Unable to stomach working for a corrupt sheriff, Wyatt resigned. With the Undersheriff position now open, Shibell filled it with Johnny Behan, a Democrat, who'd arrived in Tombstone just a couple of months earlier and was soon managing the bar of the Grand Hotel, a favorite watering hole of the Cowboys. Behan also partnered with John Dunbar in the Dexter Livery Stable, renting horses to local businessmen. Between his jobs at the hotel and the livery stable, Behan, always gregarious and outgoing, was able to hobnob with the movers and shakers of Tombstone. The following February, the controversial election results of the previous November were thrown out by the election commissioners, and in April, Shibell was removed from office.

During this time, there was talk of splitting Pima County in two. At the beginning of February, while the vote counting incident was still being investigated, the split happened with the creation of Cochise County, whose county seat would be Tombstone. Both Wyatt and Behan aspired to become the new region's Sheriff, a position that would bring with it lucrative revenue from the mines and railroads, since the Sheriff would also be the tax collector and could keep a portion of the revenues collected. Behan approached Wyatt with a deal—if Wyatt would step aside, Behan would name Wyatt Undersheriff and split the tax collecting profits with him. Wyatt knew the charming Behan, whose Dexter Livery partner Dunbar had family connections to a prominent U.S. Senator, stood a better chance of being selected for the position than he did, so he went along with the deal, shaking hands on it.

On February 10, 1881, Behan was appointed Sheriff, as expected. But unexpectedly, he appointed the man who had pushed through the bill to form the new county, Harry Woods, as Undersheriff, despite having promised the job to Wyatt. Wyatt understood why Behan made the politically expedient choice, but nonetheless, he felt betrayed. After all, when you shake hands on a deal, that's a compact, a sacred trust not to be ignored. From that time on, Wyatt always thought of Behan as little more than a glad-handing, self-serving, backstabbing liar.

~ • ~

After arriving back in Tombstone, Wyatt went to tell the wives of Morgan and Virgil that their husbands were still scouring the desert for the outlaw desperadoes, and assure them they were doing fine. But his own wife was doing poorly; during his absence, missing her man and fearing the worst, Mattie leaned even more heavily than usual on laudanum, which only exacerbated her worries. Wyatt tried his best to soothe her, and when she'd exhausted her tears upon his tired shoulder, he put her to bed and let her lull off to sleep.

After getting some rest himself, Wyatt learned that Marshall Williams had also given up the fruitless search. He met Williams at his Wells Fargo office. The company had now agreed to offer a reward of $300 each for the stage robbers. Wyatt told the detective that it was very likely there were already Cowboys in town seeking to break Luther King out of jail, and no sooner had the words left his lips than they received word that King was gone. The rumor mill whispered that Undersheriff Harry Woods—the man who'd been given the post promised to Wyatt—had simply let King go out the jail's back door to a waiting horse.

Meanwhile, Virgil, Morgan, and Bob Paul were becoming increasingly worn down by their vain search for the stagecoach robbers. They continued the hunt into Mexico, at one point going two days without food or water. Starving and unable to secure fresh horses, they finally gave up the manhunt and made their way back to Tombstone.

Behan's incompetence in leading the posse, his abandonment of it half-way to escort King back to Tombstone and what appeared to be a pre-arranged freedom, and his ignoring of the posse's requests for fresh horses, gnawed at the Earp brothers. Adding insult to injury, once they had all returned home, Behan refused to pay the posse for their services, instead keeping for himself all the money he received from billing the city supervisors for the posse's expenses.

Wyatt was particularly rankled that Behan seemed to be in cahoots with the Cowboys. He determined that if he were Sheriff, the lawless element would be driven out. The next election was just nine months away, and if Wyatt was going to stand a chance of winning, he'd have to boost his popularity among the townspeople, especially the ones who were blinded to Behan's grafting by his friendly, glad-handing persona. One sure way he could raise himself up in the community's eyes would be to bring stagecoach driver Bud Philpott's killers to justice, and he devised a foolproof plan to do just that.

Wyatt knew that Ike Clanton had become a de-facto leader of the Cowboys, who often stayed either at Clanton's ranch or at the McLaury ranch. He arranged to meet secretly behind the Oriental Saloon with Clanton, McLaury, and another Cowboy, promising them that if they would tell him where the three accused murderers were hiding, he'd give them all of the reward money—which by that point Wells Fargo had quadrupled to $1,200 each for the three wanted men. Furthermore, Wyatt promised he'd never divulge who had given him the information. Ike was interested in the deal, but only if Wyatt could assure him the reward would be paid whether the men were dead or alive. Wyatt wasn't certain, so he went to Williams and asked him to send a telegram to his Wells Fargo supervisor in San Francisco to verify that the reward would be honored if the men were brought in sans breathing. The reply came quickly: Yes, it would.

But fate, or just plain bad luck, intervened. Not long after Ike accepted Wyatt's offer, two of the men who held up the stagecoach and killed Philpott were themselves cut down by a couple of ranchers. It was said the outlaws coveted the ranchers' property and had threatened to kill them if they didn't hand the ranch over to them. Not long afterwards, the ranchers ambushed the thieves. But before the ranchers could collect the reward, they were themselves shot down by the third member of the stagecoach-robbing gang.

Sometime after that, Marshall Williams wondered about that telegram Wyatt had asked him to send clarifying if the reward would be paid regardless of whether the men were dead or alive. He figured something was afoot, and assumed that Wyatt had cut a deal with the Cowboys. During an evening at the Crystal Palace, where he indulged in a few drinks too many at the bar, he approached Ike Clanton and hinted that he knew Wyatt had cut a deal with him. Clanton was mortified. He assumed that Wyatt had spilled the beans to Williams about their secret pact. And if Wyatt had mentioned it to Williams, who else had he confessed it to? He confronted Wyatt, who denied he'd ever spoken a word of it to anyone. But the damage was done—Ike felt betrayed and no longer trusted Wyatt.

In October of 1881, the fifth stage robbery since February occurred in Cochise County. Frank Stilwell and Pete Spence, friends of Ike Clanton and Frank McLaury, were arrested for the crime by Virgil and Wyatt Earp. Shortly thereafter, Clanton, McLaury, Johnny Ringo, and two other Cowboys confronted Morgan Earp on the street and threatened his life.

Meanwhile, Ike Clanton's paranoia had grown to become all-consuming. For months he'd feared that one of the Earps would slip up and reveal that he'd ratted out the stage robbers who killed Philpott, and that Ringo or some of the other Cowboys would then kill him for selling out one of their own. The only way he could assure his own survival would be to silence the Earps. All of them.

On Tuesday, October 25th, Wyatt saw Ike quarreling with Doc Holliday in the lunchroom of the Alhambra Saloon. Wyatt told Morgan he ought to break it up. Morgan did so by grabbing Doc by the arm and pulling him out into the street. But Ike soon followed, continuing to mouth off at Doc until Virgil arrived and threatened to arrest both of them if they didn't split up and go their separate ways. Doc went to the Oriental Saloon. Ike went to the Grand Hotel. Wyatt, meanwhile, moseyed over to the Eagle Brewery for a game of faro. A short while later, he stepped into the street and had only taken a few steps before a drunken Ike confronted him, saying, "All this fighting talk between us has gone on too long. I reckon it's time to fetch it to a close."

"I don't want to fight anyone," said Wyatt.

Ike stomped away, declaring, "I'll be ready for all y'all in the morning."

Wyatt continued on over to the Oriental Saloon, where Ike—who somehow had now procured a pistol, which was stuffed into his pants—followed him, again repeating that he would be after all the Earps come morning. Wyatt did his best to avoid the ranting drunk and eventually went home. Ike, however, stayed in town.

As the clock edged past midnight, Ike became engaged in an all-night poker game at the Occidental Saloon with Frank McLaury, Sheriff Behan, and—of all people—Wyatt's brother, Virgil. Apparently, Ike figured he could make a killing off Virgil before killing all the Earps in the morning. When Virgil finally got up to go home at 7 A.M., Ike said he had a message for Virgil to deliver to Doc Holliday: "Tell that damned son of a bitch he's got to fight."

"I'm going to bed," said Virgil, "and I'd rather you didn't raise any disturbances while I'm sleeping."

But Ike didn't listen. He kept drinking and railing against the Earps and Doc Holliday throughout the morning, claiming that as soon as they showed themselves in the street, they'd have to fight. He moved from saloon to saloon, drinking and cursing his enemies, creating a growing anticipation in the town that a showdown was inevitable. Carrying a Winchester rifle, he even showed up at the boarding house where Doc Holliday was staying with Big Nose Kate. When Kate woke Doc to tell him Ike Clanton was armed and looking for him, Doc drawled, "If God will let me live to get my clothes on, he shall see me."

A little before mid-day, Wyatt awoke, put on his coat, and headed to the Oriental Saloon, where a friend told him Ike was armed with both a pistol and a rifle and was hunting the Earps. A little after noon, Ike found an Earp, or rather, one found him. Virgil, having awakened to learn that Ike hadn't heeded his warning against raising disturbances, saw Ike carrying the rifle with the pistol still stuffed in his trousers. Virgil walked up behind him, grabbed the rifle with one hand and, as Ike was reaching for his six-shooter, buffaloed him with the other. Virgil then arrested Ike for carrying firearms within the city limits.

By now, Wyatt was getting damn tired of Ike's constant threats. After all of Clanton's tough talk, he felt it was just a matter of time before the Cowboys felt compelled to assassinate him and his brothers. And if a fight was inevitable, he wanted it to be on his terms—standing toe to toe with the Cowboys and shooting it out face to face. That way, they'd get it over with all at once instead of being picked off one by one over time in a series of ambushes.

While Virgil went looking for the judge, Wyatt burst into the recorder's court to find Morgan leaning against the wall, holding Clanton's weapons. Nearby was Ike, patting his bleeding head—where Virgil had buffaloed him with his pistol—with a handkerchief. Wyatt confronted Ike, saying, "You damn dirty cow thief, going all over town threatening our lives! I think I'd be justified shooting you down anywhere! So if you're so anxious to make a fight, you just tell me where and when!"

Clanton spat back, "All I need is four feet of ground and I'll be glad to make a fight with you!"

Morgan joked, "Hell, Ike, I'll pay your fine just to see you follow through on those words."

"I'll fight you anywhere or any way!" snarled Ike. Morgan held Ike's confiscated pistol out to him, but Ike, surrounded by Earp brothers, didn't take it. With a scowl, he muttered, "I don't like the odds."

The judge finally arrived and fined Ike $25 plus court costs of $2.50 for carrying guns in town. Virgil left Ike's weapons at the Grand Hotel, and around 1 P.M., the men filed out of the courtroom. Ike, his head still bleeding and feeling queasy from drinking, was taken to a doctor's office by another of the Cowboys, a young drover named Billy Claiborne.

As Wyatt was heading out of the courtroom, he saw Tom McLaury, younger brother of rancher Frank McLaury, and asked him, "Are you heeled?"

"Wyatt," said McLaury, "you're my friend, and I've never done anything against you Earps. But if you want to make a fight, I'll fight with you anywhere."

Wyatt had had enough of the Cowboys' threats. "Alright," he exploded, "make a fight." He slapped McLaury, then slammed his pistol against McLaury's head. McLaury stood wide-eyed and trembling, blood trickling down his face. Leaving the rancher dazed and dumbfounded, Wyatt stalked out.

Meanwhile, Frank McLaury and Billy Clanton rode into town and settled in at the Grand Hotel. As they were having drinks, Doc Holliday, having roused himself and now dressed in a long gray coat, entered and greeted them with a polite, "How are you?" All he got in response were glares.

Shortly after, a friend of Frank McLaury's came into the bar and called him aside. He told McLaury that his little brother Tom had been pistol-whipped by Wyatt Earp over at the courthouse. Hearing this, McLaury and Billy Clanton decided it was time to get Ike and all the other Cowboys in town back home, before things spiraled out of control.

But it was too late. All of Ike's threats had gotten under Wyatt's skin. As he went to the tobacconist to buy a cigar, he was alert to every Cowboy he saw in town, half expecting to be shot any minute. Then, confirming his suspicions, he passed by Spangenberg's Gun Shop and, through the window, saw Billy Clanton, Frank McLaury, and Tom McLaury loading bullets into their gun belts. As he watched, Frank McLaury's horse became untethered from the hitching post and wandered up onto the sidewalk, popping its head through the gun shop's doorway.

Wyatt stepped into the gun shop. A hush fell over it as every head turned his way. Getting a good look at the men loading up on ammo, he grabbed the bit of McLaury's horse and led it back out. Billy Clanton and the McLaury's rushed outside, the young Clanton with his hand on his pistol. McLaury took the bit of his horse from Wyatt's hand. Wyatt looked at him and said, as though nothing were amiss, "You'll have to get this horse off the sidewalk."

As McLaury walked the horse into the street, Ike Clanton appeared. He stepped into Spangenberg's, where some of the other Cowboys were still gathered, and tried to buy a pistol, but since he still had a fresh wound on his forehead, Spangenberg refused to sell him one.

Knowing that trouble was brewing, Virgil Earp went to the Wells Fargo office, where he retrieved a shotgun he kept there in case he needed a little extra persuasion to handle disturbances. As he was leaving, a man ran up to him, saying, "Wyatt's down at the gun shop all alone, and the Cowboys are there, and they're liable to kill him."

By then, the Cowboys were on the move. They began gathering at Dexter's Livery and Feed Stables, the establishment owned by Johnny Behan and John Dunbar. After retrieving Billy Clanton's horse, they then ambled across the street to the O.K. Corral.

After downing several shots of courage, Doc Holliday left the Grand Hotel and caught up with the Earps at the corner of Allen and Fourth Streets. Just then, one of the townspeople wandered by and told Virgil that the Cowboys meant trouble, and they were all gathering at the O.K. Corral. "I think you'd better go disarm them," the man said.

Sheriff Behan, having slept late, was enjoying a shave at Barron's Barber Shop when a man came in saying there looked to be trouble between the Clantons and the Earps. Behan asked the barber to hurry and finish, and then went to talk some sense into the Earps. As soon as he caught up with them, Virgil pulled him into Hafford's Corner

THE LAST STAGE

Saloon for a more private parley, away from the foot traffic of the street corner. Virgil asked Behan to come with him to disarm the Cowboys. Behan responded, "If you go down there, there'll be a fight for sure. Let me go alone and disarm them. They won't hurt me." Virgil agreed; all he wanted was for the Cowboys to give up their arms while they were on the streets of Tombstone.

As Virgil made his way back to his brothers, a local businessman passing by asked him what he was going to do about the Cowboys, who were clearly looking to stir up trouble. "Nothing, I hope," said Virgil. "I won't have to bother 'em at all if they just stay in the corral. But if they go out into the street, then I'll be duty-bound to uphold the city ordinance and take away their weapons."

The businessman chortled, saying, "Why, they're all down on Fremont Street now."

Goddammit, thought Virgil, that's the last thing he wanted to hear. He walked on to Wyatt and Morgan, who were now standing chatting with Doc Holliday. Virgil told them the Cowboys were armed and gathering, and there might be a fight. Wyatt told Doc he didn't need to get involved, but Doc wasn't about to let Wyatt go it alone. He insisted on coming with them, so Virgil handed him his shotgun in exchange for Doc's ebony walking cane. He asked Doc to hide the weapon underneath the long coat he was wearing, and then the four men began marching toward the O.K. Corral.

Sheriff Behan, meanwhile, encountered the McLaurys and Ike Clanton at Fourth and Fremont Streets and told them to give up their guns. Frank McLaury, fearing the Earps would shoot him down if he was unarmed, said he had no intention to do so unless the Earps gave up theirs first. Frustrated, Behan quickly patted down Ike Clanton, finding no weapon. Tom McLaury opened his coat to show he didn't have one, either. Behan neglected to search Billy Clanton and Billy Claiborne, both of whom had wandered into a vacant lot nearby, next to Fly's Photo Gallery.

Then Behan caught sight of the Earps coming down the street. In a panic, he rushed to them and reminded them that he was the County Sheriff and he wasn't going to allow any trouble. Virgil proclaimed that they were just going to disarm the Cowboys. Behan insisted he'd already disarmed them, and that if the Earps went down there, they'd be killed. Wyatt had to wonder just how exactly they'd be killed if Behan had, in fact, taken away their guns. But then again, he knew Behan was a no-account, backstabbing liar…

Ignoring Behan, the Earps continued their march forward, approaching the Clantons, the McLaurys, and Billy Claiborne, all gathered in the vacant lot. Wyatt's biographers always wanted to know what he was thinking as he made that fateful walk toward the O.K. Corral. Honestly, he couldn't rightly remember; it was all a jumble. His focus was on the men they were going to face. How many would there be? Were they armed? Were any of them in hiding, ready to ambush Wyatt and his brothers? And most importantly, were any of them good shots?

Ideally, in those situations, you didn't want to think, you just wanted to react. You were acting on instinct and emotion. So, these biographers would ask, what emotions were you feeling? He'd shrug, because he knew they wouldn't like the truth.

Fear.

He felt fear.

As they came within spitting distance, the Earps could plainly see that, despite Behan's assurances, Billy Clanton and Frank McLaury were armed with pistols, and Tom McLaury was reaching for a rifle in his horse's scabbard.

"Boys, throw up your hands," yelled Virgil. "I want your guns." As he said it, Virgil raised Doc's ebony walking stick with his right hand. Maybe the nervous Cowboys mistook it for a rifle. Or maybe they were just as eager as Wyatt to put an end to all the ill feelings between themselves and the Earps. All Wyatt knew is that he instantly heard the clicks of weapons being cocked as Frank McLaury and Billy Clanton drew their pistols.

Virgil threw up both his hands, saying, "Hold! I don't want that!" And now Wyatt saw Billy Clanton lifting his pistol.

And then all hell broke loose.

Wyatt yanked his gun up and fired at the same time as Billy Clanton, but instead of firing at Billy, he shot the man standing next to him, Frank McLaury—the best marksman among the Cowboys. McLaury dropped, wounded in the stomach.

Then hot lead flew in fits and starts. Tom McLaury's horse reared when the shooting started, so the younger McLaury wasn't able to free his rifle from its scabbard. Doc Holliday, raising the shotgun Virgil had

THE LAST STAGE

given him, closed in on Tom and shot him under the armpit. McLaury staggered into the street.

Ike Clanton—the man who'd stirred up this mess—rushed to Wyatt and grabbed his arm. Wyatt should have shot him then and there, but he had no legal cause to do so; he could see that Ike wasn't armed, so killing him would be murder. He shoved Ike aside, snarling, "The fight's commenced! Get to fighting or get away!" So Ike—seeing the fire in Wyatt's eyes—got away, running through photographer Camillus Fly's house and Kellogg's Saloon before being arrested two blocks away on Toughnut Street for being drunk and disorderly.

Though he was wounded, Frank McLaury got off a shot that pierced Virgil's calf. Morgan put three rounds into Billy Clanton, hitting his chest, his wrist, and his stomach. But Billy kept firing, even as he leaned back against the wall of a house and, dying, slid to the ground. One of his rounds caught Morgan in one shoulder and passed out the other. Morgan yelled, "I'm hit."

Holliday tossed away the shotgun and drew his six-shooter. Frank McLaury, his stomach bleeding, attempted to hide behind a horse, and shot at Morgan. The horse broke free, leaving him exposed. Holliday found him squatting in the street. McLaury stood, took aim at Holliday, and said, "I've got you now."

"You're a daisy if you have," replied Doc. McLaury pulled the trigger, grazing Doc's hip. "I'm shot right through," shouted Doc.

McLaury kept coming, staggering across the street despite his stomach wound. Both Doc and Morgan Earp fired at him, Morgan's bullet catching him in the head, Doc's hitting him in the chest. McLaury fell, but still tried to move. Doc ran up to him shouting, "The son of a bitch has shot me, and I mean to kill him!" And so he did.

Less than thirty seconds had passed, but they were the longest thirty seconds of Wyatt's life. When they were over, Frank and Tom McLaury and Billy Clanton lay bleeding in the dirt, having sacrificed themselves for… what? Ike's honor? Such a waste, thought Wyatt, but he knew damn well that if you went looking for trouble, you were apt to find it, and it was liable to lead to a bad end.

For himself, he felt fortunate not to have been hit, especially considering that Doc, Virgil, and Morgan were all wounded. Now, he focused on getting them to safety, thankful they hadn't been killed—though he sensed this wouldn't be the end of his troubles with the Cowboys. Like as not, they'd seek retribution for their fallen martyrs.

~ • ~

Billy Clanton was carried into a nearby house, where he writhed and shouted, "They've murdered me! I've been murdered!" After being injected with morphine to dull the pain, he objected to all the curious onlookers crowding into the house to gawk at him. He couldn't breathe, he said; his last words were, "Drive the crowd away."

Tom McLaury was also brought into the house and put on the carpeted floor near Billy Clanton, with a pillow shoved under his head. He soon died from his shotgun wound, without having said a word.

His older brother, Frank McLaury, bled to death in the street.

Meanwhile, Wyatt arranged for Virgil and Morgan to be taken to their homes. After ensuring that they were comfortable, he went back into town with his friend, Fred Dodge, a Wells Fargo agent. As they approached the Sheriff's office, Johnny Behan marched out into the street.

"Wyatt," said Behan, "I'm gonna have to arrest you."

Eyes narrowing, Wyatt searched for a response more gentlemanly than the obscenities he felt like hurling at Behan, and said tersely, "A decent officer can arrest me, but that doesn't include you or any of your kind!" Behan started to protest, but Wyatt cut him off, saying, "You deceived me, Johnny. You told me they weren't armed. I won't be arrested, but I'm here to answer for what I've done. And I'm not leaving town."

Two other men, a theater manager and a city official, joined the fray, telling Behan, "There's no hurry in arresting Wyatt. He did right killing those men. The people will stand by him." For the time being, Wyatt felt like the citizenry were on his side. It wouldn't last.

Ike Clanton was already locked up in the city jail. As nighttime fell, his older brother Fin came into town. Fin went first to the morgue to see the body of his little brother, Billy, then to the jail where, fearing for his own life, he placed himself under Sheriff's guard. He spent the rest of the night in a cell with Ike, the two of them surrounded by ten deputies.

That same evening, Sheriff Behan went out to the Earp cabin to speak to the brothers. Besides the injured Virgil and Morgan, he found Wyatt, James and most of the Earp wives there, along with their friend Sherman McMasters. Behan told them he didn't want to argue, and questioned them about the shootout. He initially assured them that he was their friend, but as he set about establishing the sequence of events, the Earps felt like he was measuring them for a hangman's noose and ran him off.

The next day, while the local newspaper saluted the Earps' actions, the bodies of Billy Clanton and Frank and Tom McLaury were placed upright in their coffins in the local undertaker's window, beneath a sign that read, 'Murdered in the Streets of Tombstone.' The following day, the funeral procession escorting them to the graveyard consisted of roughly three hundred followers on foot and dozens more in carriages and buggies, all falling in line behind the wagon conveying the coffins. The deaths of the three men divided the community, as now even some of the wealthier townspeople began to wonder if the killing of these ranch dwellers was justified.

A coroner's inquest followed, at which Sheriff Behan claimed that before the shooting started, Billy Clanton had yelled out, "Don't shoot me! I don't want to fight," and Tom McLaury had opened his coat to show he had no weapons and screamed, "I have nothing."

Miserable, backstabbing liar, thought Wyatt.

Ike Clanton was questioned next, and said the Cowboys had only been stopping in town to buy a few essentials, and that when the gunfight began, it was the Earps who opened fire while the Cowboys were standing there with their hands in the air. Another witness claimed that he'd heard Virgil Earp say to Behan, "Those men have made their threats. I won't arrest them but I'll kill them on sight." With other witnesses testifying that Wyatt had pistol-whipped Ike Clanton and Tom McLaury, it seemed the inquest was heading for a verdict that would paint the Cowboys as innocents and place all the blame on the Earps and Doc Holliday. When the coroner made his report, he stated only the facts, saying that Billy Clanton and the McLaurys had died from pistol and shotgun wounds. He made no determination about whether the Earps had acted in the line of duty, or whether Wyatt and Doc Holliday should be charged.

Soon after, the city council suspended Virgil as Police Chief, pending further investigation. It seemed like that would be the end of the affair, until Ike Clanton brought murder charges against Wyatt and Doc Holliday, who were then hauled off to jail. There they remained while a preliminary trial was convened, where Behan doubled down on his particular version of events, painting the Cowboys as innocents gunned down by the Earps. As the trial dragged on, public sympathy began to turn against Wyatt and his brothers; apparently, thought Wyatt, if you repeat a lie, even an outrageous one, enough times, people begin to believe it. Where at first the Earps were hailed as heroes, they were now seen as murderers.

It began to seem inevitable that Wyatt and Doc would be bound over for trial, and probably be convicted, until Ike Clanton took the stand. His recital of events was so full of holes, exaggerations, and outright lies that it collapsed under cross-examination by the Earps' defense lawyer. By the time Clanton stepped down from the stand, the prosecution's case was decimated.

And now the tide of opinion began to shift again. Wyatt took the stand in defense of his family's honor, telling his recollection of events, refuting the misrepresentations of Behan and Clanton, and presenting statements of support from Dodge City and Wichita praising his honesty and integrity. Virgil also gave testimony, with the court convening in his room at the Cosmopolitan Hotel, where he was still recovering from his wounds. He told of the threats against the Earps and Holliday from the Cowboys, and said the fight was one he'd tried to avoid.

At the end of November, Judge Wells Spicer delivered his verdict, saying that while he couldn't condone all of Marshal Virgil Earp's decisions on that fateful day, he believed that Virgil and Wyatt's version of events was corroborated by subsequent witnesses, and that the Earps had the right to repel force by force. He concluded that no trial jury in the Territory would, on the basis of the evidence submitted, find the Earps and Holliday guilty of any offense.

The trial was finished.

Wyatt and Doc were released from jail. Neither would be tried for murder. And Virgil was allowed to retain his commission as U.S. Marshal. But their reputations had taken a hell of a beating, and many townspeople believed there was more to the story than had come out at trial, especially since the one-time friends, Johnny Behan and Wyatt Earp, had reasons other than Behan's broken promises and affiliations with the Cowboys to stir up animosity between them.

After all, Wyatt was consorting with the Sheriff's former lover.

~ • ~

Throughout the preliminary trial and beyond, the two leading newspapers of Tombstone—the pro-Earp *Epitaph* and the pro-Cow-

THE LAST STAGE

boy *Nugget*—engaged in a war of editorials that further inflamed opinions and elevated emotions to a boiling point. Tombstone had become a powder keg, waiting to explode.

It didn't take long before rumors were circulating that the Cowboys had a 'death list' that included the Earps, Doc, Judge Spicer, and the Earp defense attorneys. One day, Wyatt returned to the Earp cabin to find his older brother James distraught. James said there'd been a knock at the door, and when he opened it, he saw a man dressed as a woman who quickly hightailed it away. Wyatt believed it might have been one of the Cowboys in disguise come to shoot him, and figured they would have if he'd been the one opening the door.

Soon after that, the family packed up and moved into town, settling into the Cosmopolitan Hotel with armed guards protecting them. Across the street was the Grand, a hotel favored by the Cowboys. Virgil, despite being crippled from the leg wound he sustained in the O.K. Corral shootout, was back on duty, with Wyatt as his Deputy, though Wyatt also continued dealing faro games.

One afternoon, Jack Altman, a clerk at the Grand, came to give the Earps a warning. He'd noticed a great deal of activity surrounding a particular room at the Grand which was being rented by members of the Cowboys, including Pony Deal, Curley Bill Brocius, Johnny Ringo, and Ike Clanton. Suspicious, Altman had gone into the room when the occupants were out, and he noticed a slat missing from one of the window shutters. Looking through the opening, he clearly saw the Earps' room at the Cosmopolitan across the way. But Wyatt and his brothers didn't seem too concerned by the news; ever since Morgan and Virgil had recovered, they'd been receiving daily tips that they were going to be assassinated. It had become so commonplace they stopped giving the rumors much credence.

But they should have.

On December 28, three nights after the Christmas holiday, around 11:30 at night, Virgil left the Oriental Saloon to go back to the Cosmopolitan. As he crossed the street, there were three shotgun blasts coming from a burned-out building nearby. Virgil fell, just as several men dashed out of the decrepit building and disappeared down a dark street.

Remarkably, Virgil staggered to his feet and returned to the Oriental Saloon. Wyatt was shocked when he saw his brother enter, with bleeding arm hanging limply at his side. He hurried Virgil back to his room at the Cosmopolitan and summoned two doctors. Not long after, the doctors arrived and examined Virgil, determining that his left arm had taken the brunt of the attack; it was fractured between his shoulder and elbow. He'd also been hit in the back, just left of his spinal column, but thankfully that blast had missed his vital organs.

As they patched him up, one of the doctors told Virgil he was sorry for him. Virgil said, "It's hell, isn't it?" Virgil remained nonchalant even as his wife, Allie, cried over him. He tried to soothe her, saying, "Never mind. I've got one arm left to hug you with." But Virgil was far from being out of the woods; he would spend the next three months recuperating.

Virgil told Wyatt that, as he was leaving the Oriental Saloon, he'd seen Frank Stilwell entering the burned-out building across the street. When Wyatt went there to have a look around, he found Ike Clanton's hat at the rear, apparently dropped as he was running away. In Wyatt's mind, that plus Virgil's sighting of Stilwell was pretty conclusive proof of the identity of the assassins.

The next afternoon, Wyatt sent a telegraph to the U.S. Marshal in Phoenix, telling him Virgil had been shot and asking him for an appointment that would give him the power to enlist deputies. "Local authorities are doing nothing," wired Wyatt. "The lives of other citizens are threatened." The U.S. Marshal responded immediately, appointing Wyatt a Deputy U.S. Marshal, with the ability to appoint deputies of his choosing. Wyatt could now go after the Cowboys with the authority of the federal government behind him.

At the end of January, Ike Clanton and his brother Fin were brought to trial on suspicion of the assassination attempt on Virgil Earp. But as February began, Ike's attorney brought forth seven witnesses who testified that Ike had been in nearby Charleston at the time the shooting occurred. Given that alibi, the judge released both Clantons.

In mid-March, Morgan was killed while playing pool at the Campbell & Hatch Billiards Parlor. The following Sunday was Wyatt's 34th birthday. He spent it making arrangements to send Morgan's coffin to the Earp homestead in Colton, California, where Morgan's wife, Louisa, had already gone for a visit. Older brother James Earp would escort Morgan's body.

THE LAST STAGE

With that task completed, Wyatt next went to Virgil's bedside and told him it was time for him to go home, as well. "I'm going to try to get those men who killed Morgan," said Wyatt, "and I can't look after you and them, too." With his deputies—Warren Earp, Doc Holliday, Turkey Creek Johnson, and Sherman McMasters—Wyatt escorted Virgil and Allie to the train station. They were tipped off that Ike Clanton and Frank Stilwell were in Tucson, watching every train that came in, looking for Virgil so they could finish the job they'd started months earlier.

Wyatt wasn't about to let that happen.

Wyatt caught sight of Stilwell at the Tucson train station, and left him there, with a belly full of buckshot. That was the beginning of the vendetta ride, and Wyatt's fulfillment of his promises to Morgan and Virgil to put an end to those who wished to put an end to them.

When it was all over, Wyatt knew he wouldn't be able to return to Tombstone. But there was nothing for him there, anyway. Not anymore. His family had now moved on to California.

And so had she.

Chapter 27

BOOM AND BUST

Lake and Dr. Shurtleff tried valiantly to stay awake, but after a taste of whiskey and coffee, they were napping in their chairs, both snoring contentedly. It was annoying, but Sadie was glad for the racket—it drowned out the sound of the clock, whose every tick sounded like the click of a gear's notch, lowering her soul into oblivion.

There was a rumble of thunder as the storm rolled in again. The rain outside began pounding harder, blown against the windows by a powerful gust. The room felt colder. Frightened by the thunder, Earpie leapt off the bed and into Sadie's lap. His furry little body warmed and soothed her.

There in the dim candlelight, Sadie's thoughts drifted back to happier times with Wyatt. It was in the waning months of 1882 when Wyatt, with his brother Warren, arrived in San Francisco, leaving the ugliness of the Tombstone vendetta and the cold of laying low in Colorado behind. Virgil had already moved to the city, where'd he been briefly arrested for running an illegal faro game until he found the right officials to bribe, promising them a cut of future proceeds. But reuniting with his brother was not the only reason Wyatt had gone west.

He came looking for her.

Wyatt enjoyed Sadie's company. Like his brothers, he was a Midwesterner at heart, and Midwesterners tended to be very matter-of-fact; they felt embarrassed expressing their feelings, if they had them at all. The Midwest way was to shut up, keep your head down, do your job quietly and keep your belly-aching to yourself, so Wyatt was re-

served, stern, seldom spoke, and disliked crowds, unless he was sizing them up to see whom he could corral into a game of poker or faro.

Sadie wasn't wired that way. She'd come from a loud, boisterous, Jewish clan who not only wore their emotions on their sleeves but wiped them on everyone else's sleeves, too. She was gregarious, full of life, loved to be the center of attention, and thrived on drama; if all was well in her orbit, she would find some way to create chaos and focus all the attention on herself. And while Wyatt rarely so much as chuckled, Sadie had a laugh that was as pleasing as the tinkling of a champagne glass, and she employed it often. She brought light to the dark recesses of his life.

Once they were reunited, she and Wyatt settled for a time in Gunnison, Colorado, where Wyatt ran a faro bank until he was summoned to Dodge City, Kansas to help settle a dispute between two old friends. From Kansas, they embarked on a five-year odyssey of running saloons in the boomtowns of Colorado and Idaho. In Eagle City, a snow-covered wide-spot-in-the-road that became the epicenter of Idaho's Coeur d'Alene gold rush, they purchased a round circus tent, raised it, and turned it into a dance hall.

Next came brief stints in El Paso, Texas and Aspen, Colorado, always chasing a dollar, sometimes catching it, then losing it and starting over again. In those early years, it was all a grand adventure. Wyatt was her man, she was his girl, the world was their oyster, and thus it would ever be.

In 1886, they settled in for a nearly four-year sojourn in San Diego, during a land boom. Wyatt leased concessions for three gambling halls and became a sporting man, judging horse races and refereeing fights. Once in a blue moon, he engaged in sport of a more dangerous sort — bounty hunting.

In the 1890s, they returned to San Francisco as a couple of swells, hanging about with a much more sophisticated crowd of bankers, businessmen, and captains of industry. Wyatt listed his occupation in the San Francisco City Directory as capitalist and horseman, having secured a position managing horses for a stable in Santa Rosa, north of the city. He and Sadie ate in fine restaurants and spent much of their time socializing at the racetrack.

Whenever they had a win, Wyatt would buy her a piece of jewelry. Sadie amassed a pretty impressive collection in her jewelry box until she began laying bets of her own. Unlike Wyatt, she lost more often than she won—much more often. This put Wyatt in the embarrassing position of having to pay off her debts. Eventually, he became so frustrated with her that he refused to bail her out again. But that didn't deter Sadie—she simply borrowed money from their friend, "Lucky" Baldwin, a millionaire real estate developer who bred Thoroughbred racehorses. She always expected she'd be able to pay Baldwin back from her winnings. When Lady Luck spurned her, as happened more often than not, she'd make good on her debt by handing over to Baldwin some of the jewelry her man had gifted to her. Wyatt was mortified when he found out about the arrangement. He admonished her and bought back the jewelry, a scene that repeated itself more than a few times before Wyatt told Baldwin to stop bailing Sadie out.

And then Wyatt was corralled into refereeing the Sharkey-Fitzsimmons fight, was accused of throwing it, and suffered the slings and arrows of outrageous accusations from the city newspapers. His reputation in tatters, and their wealth steadily decreasing with Sadie's continuing bad luck at the track, they left San Francisco society behind and returned to the desert, settling in Yuma, Arizona.

There they might have remained, but in the fall of 1897, the city was buzzing with news of the latest gold strike, this time in the Alaskan Klondike. With the thrill of new adventures stirring his blood, Wyatt took Sadie back to San Francisco to gather the provisions they'd need for a prolonged stay in another distant, barren frontier.

Their plans were hampered by Wyatt's accident—hopping off a streetcar onto a rain-slick street to get a better look at the first automobile he'd ever seen, Wyatt slipped and injured his hip. But despite the mishap, three weeks later, anxious to get on their way, they boarded a boat for Alaska, eventually settling in Nome.

Wyatt fell back into mining the miners, managing saloons and gambling concessions until he became a partner in the Dexter Saloon. There was a brothel above the establishment, and in the cold Alaskan nights, Wyatt sometimes found warmth in the arms of the saloon's wanton women. Sadie could smell their perfume on his clothes, and it repulsed her, bringing back memories of Johnny Behan's philandering. When she confronted him, Wyatt would either be sullen and silent or try to shrug it off with a casual "it don't mean nothing." But it did mean something to her. It signaled a rejection by the man in whom she'd invested so much of her life. And as her patience with his extracurricular dalliances wore thin, she began drinking and gambling more, which angered him and further deepened the growing chasm between them.

This was the unhappiest time of their years together, made all the more stark in comparison to the happy years they'd just spent in San Francisco. Several times, Sadie left Wyatt and returned to California to stay with family members. But despite their grievances, they always returned to each other's arms. Their relationship was no longer the fairy tale it had seemed in the beginning, but after so many years together, it was simply easier to stick it out with someone familiar than to face the uncertainty of perhaps never finding compatible mates and spending the rest of their lives alone. Sometimes still, the familiarity bred contempt, but the contempt would eventually give way to comfort and routine, and their shared history with each other once again bred companionship. They were, in many ways, polar opposites, but her strengths were his weaknesses, and vice versa, so together they were a formidable couple. Without her Wyatt, she would simply be incomplete.

Such was her life with Wyatt—boom and bust. It was sometimes nerve-wracking, but never dull. When the Klondike boom petered out and they returned to California with money to invest in diggings not only in the Golden State but also in Nevada, they were able to leave their marital miseries, for the most part, in the cold Alaskan snow. The sunshine of California and the western territories burned away their blues and renewed their affections. With him by her side, she felt secure, content that she could weather any storm. At his best, Wyatt had a way of making even the down times seem like boom times.

But now, it seemed, their journey had reached its end.

Wyatt was dying.

How could he do this to her? How could he abandon her and leave her all alone? Didn't he realize how much she needed him? Why hadn't he listened to her, and gone to the doctor when his abdominal pains first began? If he had, he might've been cured. She reckoned that after surviving so many close calls, so many gunfights where the bullets simply seemed to deflect away from him, he'd come to believe he was invincible. Looking now at his frail body, and hearing his increasingly labored breathing, she was so frustrated with him that if he weren't already dying, she'd kill him.

It was stubborn. It was stupid. This was a bullet he could have easily dodged, but his ego told him he was too much man for this disease—he'd weather it and be back to his old self in no time. And in no time it had broken him down until he was too weak to fight back. Wyatt survived a lot of close calls and gunfights in his time, but he couldn't survive his own stubborn, stupid ego.

She knew in her heart that their time together was ebbing away. It would just be a matter of hours before her boom times would end forever. And after Wyatt cashed in his chips, the remainder of her life would be one prolonged, empty bust.

Wyatt moved ever so slightly upon the bed, shifting his weight, and let out a faint whimper. She wondered if her man was dreaming.

And if he was, was he dreaming of her?

Chapter 28

PRACTICE

A couple of hours passed before Jack came clambering down the ladder with nervous excitement. He rushed to Wyatt, who was bathed in sweat from laboring in the mine. "You were right," gushed Jack. "They're all bunking together in a shack over by the stables."

"Good work," said Wyatt, wiping his brow with his forearm. "Just one more thing…"

"What's that?"

"You want to stay here, or come with me?"

Jack looked at his feet. "Sounds like it could be a mite reckless."

"Nothing to worry about," said Wyatt. "Hayden may be a murderer, but he's no Curly Bill Brocius."

Jack looked up at him. "And you're no Wyatt Earp. Not anymore. You're older, slower…"

"Wiser."

"Are you?" After a quiet moment, Jack continued, "What if your luck runs out this time?"

"That's why I want you there—to make sure it don't," said Wyatt. He took in a deep breath, and stood straight and tall. With a half-smile, he said, "Don't worry. You'll be fine."

"You certain of that?"

Wyatt nodded. "You'll be with me."

Wyatt decided that if Jack was going to come with him, it might be a good time to bring his gun slinging skills up to snuff. They climbed back up the ladder to the campsite and Jack followed Wyatt out a ways into the desert, far enough that their gunfire wouldn't be in danger of spooking the horses. Or, in Jack's case, killing them.

"First things first," said Wyatt. "Let me teach you how to draw." He put his hand on his pistol. "Make sure you've pulled it up far enough to clear the holster before you point and fire." He demonstrated, whipping his gun up and out in an instant, but not firing it. He reholstered it. Jack mimicked his movements, but couldn't resist twirling the gun a couple of times before plopping it back into his holster.

"All right, Tom Mix," said Wyatt. "Let's see if you can do it at speed, under pressure."

Wyatt raised his right arm straight up, shoulder high, hand flat and level to the ground. With his left hand, he pulled a nickel out of his pocket and set it on the back of his right hand.

Jack watched with curiosity. "What's the nickel for?" he asked.

"When I tilt my hand, it'll fall, and they say it takes about half a second before it hits the ground."

"What's that got to do with shooting?"

"The trick is to clear your holster and shoot before the nickel hits the dirt."

Wyatt took a deep breath, concentrating on his hand, the nickel, the heavy gun on his slightly aching hip. It had been a while, and he wasn't entirely sure he could still pull this off, but he was counting on instinct. He tilted his hand. The nickel began its descent. Quick as lightning, Wyatt snatched the six-gun from his holster and fired, just before the nickel hit the sand. With a self-satisfied smile, he picked up the nickel and tossed it to Jack. "Your turn."

Jack shook his right hand to loosen up. Standing with his legs apart, he put his right arm straight out in front of him, and placed the nickel on the back of his hand.

"Just concentrate," said Wyatt, "and go when you're ready."

Jack tilted his hand. The coin fell. Jack went to snatch the gun out of his holster, but he didn't clear it fully. The tip of the barrel caught on the holster's lip. Jack fumbled and lost his grip. The nickel hit the ground. And the gun tumbled down beside it a split second afterward. Jack blushed with embarrassment.

Wyatt calmly picked up the pistol and handed it back to Jack. "Maybe we need to work on the draw first, and worry about the fast part later."

And maybe, thought Wyatt, he should leave the kid behind, so the damn clumsy fool wouldn't end up shooting him by mistake.

Chapter 29

HIDEOUT

Wyatt, behind the wheel of his Packard, drove down the dusty road that led to Armendariz's stables, with Jack in the passenger seat. As they neared the stables, Jack said, "It's down this trail here." Wyatt slowed and turned the steering wheel, veering to the right. The path was uneven and full of potholes, so Wyatt had to drive at a crawl. After going a few hundred feet, he decided they'd be better off walking, so he turned the car around and parked just off the side of the trail. And now, if he needed to make a speedy getaway, at least the car would be pointed in the right direction.

He and Jack got out, their gun holsters almost hidden by the coats they wore despite the heat. They trudged along the trail, heading for the lodgings up ahead. These ranged from a bunkhouse for Armendariz's ranch hands to a half-dozen decrepit shacks—some looking like they might have been constructed by pushing two chicken houses together—that Armendariz rented out to the seasonal workers who drifted through the area.

There were a few people out—tanned ranch workers in their cowboy hats, and one old, grizzled cowboy with a chinful of white stubble walking bow-legged in his boots and jeans—but these men minded their own business and, save for occasional suspicious glances, ignored Wyatt and Jack. As they marched along, Jack said, "If I'd'a known that striking it rich was gonna cause all this trouble, I don't know… I might'a just turned around and gone the other way."

"That's life, Jack," said Wyatt. "You can't have a horse without horse shit."

Jack shook his head. "You and your sayings…"

"You still could, you know."

"What?"

"You still could turn around and walk way."

"And give up my cut? I reckon I'll take my chances." Casting a wary glance at the ranch hands, he added, "Even if it kills me."

There was a shack at the end of the street notable for the rusty steel 55-gallon drum sitting outside it, with empty liquor bottles scattered around it. Ratty curtains covered the windows, and a house number was crudely painted beside the primitive-looking door. There was nothing behind the house but a great expanse of desert. "That's the one," said Jack.

"You sure?" asked Wyatt.

"That's the house number I was given by the feller I spoke to in Vidal."

"Well... one way to find out."

Jack was hesitant. He asked, "So how do we do this?"

"Same way I always have," said Wyatt. "Just walk forward and talk in as pleasant a voice as I can. If they start chatting with me, then I know I've got 'em. But if they keep quiet... well then, grab your hog leg, 'cause I reckon we're about to commence shooting."

"That's the plan?" Jack asked incredulously. "The whole plan?"

"That's it." Wyatt said. "Just don't lose your courage. That's one of the most dangerous things you can do. As long as you keep your fighting spirit, you've got a chance."

"Uh-huh."

"I mean it, Jack. Your courage might be enough to cause the other feller to weaken. But if your courage goes, you're beaten—your enemy'll know it, and your fear'll give him courage." He cast a glance at Jack. The closer they got to their destination, the more Jack looked like a scared rabbit. "Jack," asked Wyatt, "I don't suppose you ever shot a man?"

"Nossir," said Jack. His eyes were wide, betraying his fear. "What's it like?"

"Not as hard as you think," said Wyatt. "The hard part is not making a habit of it." He noticed Jack's hand had a slight tremor. "Tell you what—you stay here. Any of these sons of bitches 'round here shoot me—plug 'em."

Jack nodded.

Wyatt walked towards the shack, as calmly as if he were dropping off an invite to the church's pancake social, speaking loudly enough

THE LAST STAGE

for anyone inside to hear. "Hayden! Jenkins! Chief! Any of you men in there? If you are, say something now, before I reach the door. Because if I get there and you ain't made yourself known… I'm gonna kick the door in and shoot anything that moves." Nearing the door, he drew his gun, pointed it forward. Reaching the door, he gave it a good, hard kick. It flew open.

Beyond was a dim, disheveled interior. Wyatt thought he caught a glimpse of something in the shadows. Without breaking stride, he kept moving, until he was in the center of the room. Pistol still at the ready, he pivoted from side to side, and turned to look behind him. Then he focused his attention on a room in the back of the shack. "Last chance!" he said. "Anyone here?" He heard a floorboard creak. If there was someone there, he needed to flush them out. He fired a shot at the top of the wall; inside the confines of the shack, the pistol blast was deafening. "That's my last warning," he shouted. "You can either walk out or be carried out. Your choice."

A bronze hand appeared from behind the wall, waving a white flag of surrender. Except it wasn't a flag—it was a handkerchief, one that looked familiar to Wyatt. He recalled who he'd given it to.

"Javier? Is that you?"

Javier slowly stepped out from behind the wall, shaking with fear.

Wyatt holstered his pistol. "Come on out. I won't hurt you."

As Javier stepped into the room, Wyatt went to the door and waved Jack forward. Then he yanked open the threadbare curtains to let the sunlight in. Looking about, he saw two stained pallets on the floor, and another area cleared out that Wyatt surmised was where Hightower, or maybe Jenkins, had slept on a blanket. In the corner was a table and three chairs; a fourth chair was overturned on the other side of the room.

Jack stepped inside, cautiously, pistol ready. "What was that shooting?"

"Heard a noise," said Wyatt. "Turned out it was just Javier." Jack slipped his pistol into its holster. Wyatt kept looking around, and noticed a burlap bag on the floor of the kitchen, with a few cans of food and some fruit inside. Above it was an open cabinet. Wyatt turned to Javier. "You in here lookin' for food?"

Javier nodded sheepishly.

Helping Wyatt with his inspection, Jack went to the table. On top of it were dirty dishes, some scattered playing cards, and a pamphlet folded into four narrow sections. Jack picked up the pamphlet – it was a train schedule. "Wyatt," he said, "look at this." Wyatt stepped over to him. Jack pointed out one place name on the list of outbound cities that was circled in ink: Prescott. "Looks like they've moved on down the line," said Jack.

"What time's that train leave?"

Jack ran his finger across the timetable. "'Bout an hour ago."

Disappointed, Wyatt walked outside, Jack and Javier following. Wyatt saw glowing embers inside the barrel, among the ash and remnants of papers and trash. He put his palm against the side of the barrel. It was still hot to the touch. Hayden and his friends hadn't been gone long—but it was long enough. "Looks like they made a little bonfire on the way out," said Wyatt.

Jack nodded. "I expect they knew you'd come after 'em, and got scared."

"Or somebody tipped 'em off."

"Probably somebody in town who overheard me askin' about 'em," said Jack.

"Probably," Wyatt agreed. He reached into his pants pocket to see how much cash he had on him. Fourteen dollars. He handed it to Javier, who gave him a grateful nod. Wyatt thought maybe he should make Javier one of the beneficiaries of the mine profits, to make sure he'd be taken care of throughout his remaining days. Henry and Mary would appreciate that. "Careful where you hole up, Javier," he said. Javier again nodded.

Wyatt started back for the car. Jack, at his heels, said, "I expect they've crossed the line into Arizona by now."

"Says it all, don't it?" Wyatt grumbled.

"What do you mean?"

"Innocent men don't run."

"They might," said Jack. "I mean, if they didn't do it, but figured that you thought they did, they might run just 'cause they're scared of what you'd do to 'em."

Wyatt opened the car door. "They ought 'a be."

Chapter 30

TABLES TURNED

Wyatt was in a sour mood when he returned to the house. It worried him that he'd missed his quarry. Maybe Jack was right—maybe Hayden and his men had moved on. But what if it was a ruse? What if they returned to the shack? He could lie in wait there for them to come back, but that would just make them out to be stupid and himself out to be a cold-blooded murderer.

And now he had other concerns. Even before he entered the house, he heard Earpie's incessant barking, almost completely drowned out by the radio playing loudly—Ruth Etting singing "Lonesome and Sorry".

The jauntiness of the piano and cheeriness of Etting's voice belied the melancholy lyrics of the song, playing loud enough to run the rattlesnakes out from underneath the house. Wyatt entered, went to the radio and turned the knob to click it off. Earpie was at his heels, panting. He looked down at the dog and said, "Where's your ma?"

As Wyatt looked about the house, he saw dishes from a couple days' meals on the table, with more stacked in the kitchen sink, which was half-filled with murky water. Earpie's water bowl, however, was empty. Wyatt picked it up, filled it with water from the tap, and set it down.

"Here you go, boy," he said. Earpie eagerly lapped it up.

Sadie, looking like she'd just awakened, limped in from the bedroom. She was in a sorry state—barefoot, hair straggling loose and disheveled, dress half-buttoned.

"Hey, shug," she said, eyes half-mast, slurring her words, giving Wyatt a dopey smile.

Wyatt, feeling angry and disappointed at the same time, said, "You're looking mighty unlimbered."

"Um jesh—Um jesh tired, is all. You leaf Jack ut da mine?""

"You're drunk. I can smell it on your breath. And hear it in the way you're slurring your words."

"No, uh… uh took shum med—medicine."

"80 proof?"

"You leaf Jack ut da mine?"

"You already asked me that!" There was a sharp edge to his voice.

"Did I? Don't have tuh be sooo cranky…"

"Where is it?"

"Wheresh whut?"

"The bottle. Where is it?"

"I dunno whatcher talkin' 'bout…"

He stomped into the kitchen and began opening cabinets and drawers, searching. Sadie hobbled over to him and tried to pull him away, saying, "Stop it! STOP IT!"

Under the kitchen sink, in a cleaning bucket with a rag tossed over it, Wyatt found what he was looking for—a bottle of whiskey. Nearly empty. Holding it up, he just glared at Sadie. Caught, she lowered her chin to her chest, sullen.

"Where'd you get this?" Wyatt asked tersely.

"Mary," murmured Sadie. "When we whur at duh store… lasht time."

"Damn that woman! I told her never to sell you any liquor!"

He moved to pour the remaining whiskey down the sink. Despite her sprained ankle, Sadie let out a shriek and shoved herself into him. Grabbed for the bottle. They wrestled over it, until she snatched it out of his hands—but she didn't have a firm grip on it. It dropped and shattered, covering the floor with whiskey and broken glass. Sadie, shocked, cried, "Damn you! Damn you!"

Wyatt grabbed her shoulders and pulled her away from the sink, afraid that she'd step on the broken glass and cut her bare feet. He pushed her down into a chair at the table. She struggled to hold back tears, as Wyatt reached for the broom beside the stove and swept the glass pieces into a neat pile. He took the dustpan from the cabinet under the sink, swept the glass onto it, and dumped it into the trash can. Then he dampened a dish towel and wiped it over the floor, sopping up the whiskey, but also clearing out the tiniest slivers of glass that the broom missed. It was the tiny slivers you couldn't see that cut the deepest.

As he worked, Sadie sobbed loudly. Secretly, she wanted Wyatt to forget about the floor and comfort her. And he knew that. But he ignored her to punish her. The altercation appeared to have sobered her up, a little. When she stopped crying, she said, with noticeably less slurring, "How can you say 'that woman'? How can you damn Mary when she's just died?"

"Thought you didn't like her much."

"We got on okay," she said, sadly.

Finishing with his work, Wyatt threw the dish towel into the trash can. He stepped in front of her, hands on his hips, head hung in defeat, and asked, "When are you ever gonna quit?"

She wiped her runny nose and said, "I can't."

"You said…"

"I know what I said," she said curtly. She didn't like the superior tone in his voice. Hated being accused. Hated being caught. So she lashed out. "Look at you!" she said. "One wife addicted to opium, another can't stay away from the bottle… Let me ask you something… you ever stop and think that maybe it's not us that's to blame? You ever think maybe you being so hard and distant and… and… empty drove me to drink, or drove Mattie to kill herself?"

"Hush!"

"You say you love me, but do you? Do you even know how? The only love you ever had died with Aurilla! You've been a walking dead man ever since!"

Wyatt put his hand under Sadie's face, jerked her head up to look into her tear-wet eyes. "You bet I loved Aurilla!" he barked. "She was a saint! If she'd lived… everything would 'a been different. Everything!"

Sadie, her feelings hurt, slapped his hand away and let the tears roll, not even bothering to wipe them away. "Oh, hell, Wyatt! Everyone feels like that! If I'd gone this way instead of that, made this choice instead of that one… I might just as well say if only I'd stayed with Johnny Behan."

"Behan didn't give a damn about you!" snapped Wyatt. "All you were to him was a whore."

Eyes blazing in anger, she hoisted herself up and slapped him.

Fuming, feeling the hot sting on his cheek, he instantly raised his hand to slap her back, but caught himself. He stood stock-still for a moment, eyes narrowing, hand raised. There was a look of defiance in her eyes, daring him to hit her.

If he'd seen fear, he might've.

And that scared him.

So instead, he slapped the empty vase next to her on the table so hard it flew across the room and smashed against the wall.

All the commotion agitated Earpie, who scampered in half-circles first around Sadie, then Wyatt, barking loudly.

Shaking with rage like a volcano about to erupt, Wyatt stormed out the door.

Sadie went limping after him, Earpie at her heels.

As she reached the door, she saw Wyatt climb up into his saddle. Ignoring the stabbing pain in her ankle, she hobbled onto the porch and down the steps, trying to catch up to him. He cast a steely glance at her and muttered, "Trouble. Everywhere I go." Then he nudged the horse's ribs and snapped the reins. The horse bolted off, kicking up dust. Earpie, still barking, chased them until they were past the road.

Taking futile, painful steps toward him, Sadie shouted to be heard over the hoofbeats of Wyatt's horse. "I give and I give and I give… for NOTHING! You're just a big empty hole with nothing inside! That's what you are, Wyatt Earp—NOTHING!"

Her voice receded as Wyatt charged the horse northward, toward the mountain. Toward quiet. Toward peace. The dust he left in his wake scattered in the wind blowing across the desert, carrying with it the quiet words Sadie sobbed as he became ever smaller on the horizon—

"Please… Don't go…"

~ • ~

Wyatt rode hard to get away from Sadie, away from the house, away from his troubles. But there was no escaping them. Sheriff Ledbetter was right—he did attract trouble. It wouldn't matter how fast he rode, or how far, or for how long—there'd still be trouble along the way, and trouble waiting for him at the end, not because trouble followed him, but because he was trouble.

He reined the horse in, slowed its pace. No need to punish this animal as well as himself. The short burst of hard riding had been painful; his once-broken hip ached, and his side flared like he was trying to pass a boulder through his kidneys.

THE LAST STAGE

Arriving at the mine site, he dismounted in agony and tied off the horse. Jack's horse wasn't there. Thinking he might be just over the ridge of the mining pit, Wyatt called for him—"Jack? JACK!" No response.

Wyatt checked to make sure there was clean water in the horse trough; there was a bit more than enough. Trudging into the stuffy tent, he laid down on a cot and rubbed his abdomen, which was on fire after being bounced around on the galloping horse.

He thought about what Sadie had said. Maybe she was right. Maybe he was empty inside, a void, a blank slate. Or maybe he was a mirror, one that allowed others to see what they wanted to see him in him. Optimists saw a fine, upstanding crusader for law and order; cynics saw a charlatan profiteering off the system, or worse—a murdering, card-creasing horse thief.

Wyatt never killed near as many men as Billy the Kid, Jesse James, or John Wesley Hardin, who were all bona-fide outlaws. Those men were real villains, who had been elevated by those damn dime magazines and picture-show movies into folk heroes, maybe because they had the good fortune to die young. For some perverse reason, that fact alone appealed to the general public—they loved the tragedy of youth cut down in its prime in a quick burst of violence, and apparently accepted their deaths as a form of combined retribution and absolution. Wyatt, on the other hand… he'd just lived too damn long, long enough to become obsolete, remembered—when he was remembered at all— mostly by those who wanted to denigrate him. That was his fate, and his tragedy.

His temper had cooled now, and with it the pain in his gut. He rose up off the cot, took a swig of water from his canteen, and prepared to climb down into the coolness of the mine.

~ • ~

Wyatt stood before the quartz slab, chopping out bits of the gold vein with the pick hammer, letting the chips and nuggets and slivers drop into the bucket underneath. Here was all the wealth he'd ever dreamt of right in front of him, there for the taking. So why wasn't he satisfied?

Again, he felt rage bubbling inside, and as it rose to the surface, he let it out with a forceful swing against the rock. It was a glancing blow - the hammer twisted to the side, his hand rammed into the hard rock. He scraped his knuckles on the sharp edges of the broken quartz and dropped both the hammer and the bucket. The bits of rock and gold scattered. Enraged, he snatched the hammer back up and attacked the wall again with raw ferocity, striking blow after blow with such force that it reverberated through the bones of his arm up to his shoulder. He let out an animal roar that became an anguished scream. And when his energy was almost spent, he gave the bucket at his feet a savage kick, sending it skittering. Its contents spilled over the ground.

Exhausted, he slumped to the ground and leaned back against the wall. His eyes suddenly felt puffy, his cheeks warm. And then tears rolled in torrents. He tried to suppress them, hold them back, but he couldn't. So he stopped fighting, gave in to his sorrow, and wept freely.

It was as if a dam had burst deep within him, flooding his heart with a lifetime of grief and regret and longing—feelings he'd always fought to keep at bay, now escaping. Grief for Aurilla, taken before their life together had barely begun. Grief for Morgan, whom Wyatt had convinced to come to Tombstone only to watch him die on a poolroom floor. Grief for older brother Virgil, who survived an assassination attempt in Tombstone only to be caught in a mine cave-in in Cripple Creek, Colorado fifteen years later that crushed his feet and ankles and dislocated his hip. He survived, but never fully recovered; he and his wife Allie ended up living in Goldfield, Nevada, where Wyatt and Sadie also settled for a time. It was while they were there that Wyatt saw Virgil for the last time, before he passed away at St. Mary's Hospital after saying to Allie, "Light my cigar, and stay here and hold my hand."

Wyatt pulled a handkerchief from his pocket. Wiped his face. Blew his nose. Inhaled a big gulp of air into his lungs. And then he studied his battered knuckles, skin scraped, drying blood mixed with dust and grime. With his other hand, he tied the handkerchief over his sore knuckles.

He got down on all fours and began picking up the little granules of gold, depositing them back into the bucket. But the more he collected, the emptier he felt. This had been his goal his entire life—a fortune so vast even Sadie couldn't spend it all in their remaining years. The search had taken him all the way to Alaska, a lifelong quest that separated and isolated him from friends and family, all sacrificed for the sake of these little yellow nuggets. And now he'd found them. He'd fulfilled his quest, yet the fulfilling of it left him feeling profoundly unfulfilled. So he stopped collecting them. Let them be. And leaned back against the cave wall.

THE LAST STAGE

With Virgil's passing, Wyatt was the last living participant of the gunfight at the O.K. Corral. And his abdominal pains were a constant reminder that his own time was winding down. When his end came, would Sadie be there to light his pipe and hold his hand?

Sadie.

What would become of her? How would she manage without him there to restrain her from her own worst impulses? She would soon and forever be alone, adrift, abandoned. And no amount of gold would change that.

When they first met, she was the ace up his sleeve, hidden from others—particularly Mattie – but giving him great comfort and strength in a trying time. And from the time they reunited in San Francisco, she was sometimes a joker—particularly when drink altered her personality into a vicious, spiteful Sadie he couldn't stomach—and sometimes his trump card, the ally who would show up unexpectedly to help him through a rough patch. Even though his macho manliness rarely allowed him to speak the words, he loved her, through and through. And he would love her to his dying breath and through all the eternities beyond.

After a quiet moment, immersed in the silence and solitude of the tomb-like pit, he heard Jack calling from up above—"Wyatt!" His name echoed through the tunnel.

Wyatt stood up and, leaving the bucket behind, trudged toward the entrance. He yelled back, "Jack! Where the Sam Hill have you been?"

"Come quick!"

On the one hand, Wyatt was peeved that Jack had shirked his duties for nearly the whole damn day. But on the other hand, he was thankful the younger man hadn't been there to witness him weeping like some damned woman.

He emerged from the tunnel just in time to see the ladder being pulled up out of the pit. He rushed forward, yelling, "Jack!" But before he get to the ladder, the bottom rungs and legs swung up and went flat on the rim above, so high it was out of reach of even Wyatt's long arms.

For a moment, there was just silence, as though no one was there. And then came the sound of bootsteps in the sand, as Jack ambled forward and peered over the edge, pistol dangling from one hand and a coiled lasso in the other.

Regarding Jack warily, Wyatt said, "What's going on, son?"

"Toss me your pistol," Jack said calmly. He pointed his Colt directly at Wyatt, who suddenly felt a deep sting of betrayal. "Carefully."

Wyatt's handkerchief-wrapped hand slowly went to the gun holstered on his hip. "You know," he said, "I could just shoot you."

"You wanna slap that leather, you go right ahead," smirked Jack. "But if you kill me, then you're stuck in that hole forever. And besides, if me and you ain't both back down to your house by sunset, Sadie's a goner."

Wyatt suddenly felt a tinge of fear course down his spine.

"So, old man," Jack continued, "you think you can get out of that hole without your ladder?" He cocked his pistol. "Now toss your gun up."

Wyatt knew he didn't have any viable options, so he did the only thing he could do, and relented. He tossed his pistol up onto the rim. Jack picked it up and slid it into his coat pocket. Then he stepped away, out of Wyatt's view. After a moment, the legs of the ladder began tilting down, as Jack lowered it back into the pit. When it touched ground in front of him, Wyatt moved to it and began climbing up. As he came over the rim, he saw that Jack, standing several feet back, still held him at gunpoint.

Eyes simmering with ferocity, Wyatt asked, "Hayden put you up to this?"

Jack laughed. "Hayden?" he asked incredulously, nudging a small rock out of the way with his toe. He looked coolly into Wyatt's piercing eyes.

"Hayden works for me."

Chapter 31

SHOWDOWN

Wyatt was shocked by Jack's revelation. But as soon as he heard it, the final piece of the puzzle fell into place, and now he saw the big picture—from the very beginning, this damned little wet-nose had planned to rob him, squirreling his way into Wyatt's good graces, observing from the inside, while Hayden and his accomplices kept him off-balance by harassing him from the outside.

Jack tossed the business end of the lasso at Wyatt's feet. "Loop that around you," he said. Wyatt picked it up and lowered it over his body, to his waist. "Not like that," said Jack. "Put it over your arms, not under. And cinch it at your elbows." Wyatt did as he was told. The kid was smart, restricting Wyatt's mobility. When he'd finished, Jack commanded, "Get over to the horses."

As Wyatt walked toward the horses, Jack picked up the other end of the lasso and followed him. Keeping the gun trained on Wyatt, Jack unhitched his horse and hopped up in the saddle. Then he tied his end of the lasso around his saddle horn. He backed his horse up, leaving little slack in the rope between him and Wyatt.

"Now untie your horse and get on," he said.

Wyatt loosened his horse's reins from the hitching rope and climbed up into the saddle. "You mind your manners, now," chided Jack. "Start ginnin' about and you'll be chewing gravel."

Wyatt looked back at Jack. "Now what?"

"Now you're going home."

~ • ~

Sitting astride his horse, upper arms cinched tightly against his body, Wyatt felt hopeless. If he tried to gallop away, he'd be pulled off his horse. And if he made any suspicious moves, Jack could yank him off the horse and drag him over the sand and through the cacti. For now, Wyatt decided it was best to just play along, until some kind of opportunity for escape presented itself. But he also had to make sure Sadie was safe, so any action he took would have to wait until he arrived back at the house.

They were traveling slowly, the horses at a steady walk, so—as Jack put it—there wouldn't be any surprises. And every time his horse got a little too far ahead, Wyatt could feel the rope biting deeper into his arms, so he'd get his steed to ease up.

"Gotta hand it to you, Jack," he said, "when we were out at that shack, I thought you really were scared to death. Bill Hart's got nothing on you. You missed your calling. Should 'a been a picture star."

"Might be yet," said Jack. "Bet I could act rings around ol' William S. Hart."

The kid certainly had the cockiness to be a film star, thought Wyatt. He'd probably fit right in with all those robber barons in the picture business. Wyatt reconsidered the events of the past several days, and had a few questions to clear up. "So, when I sent you into town to find out where Hayden was staying—you already knew where he was, didn't you?"

"'Course I did. Where do you think I been staying?"

"So you never went to town at all. You just rode straight out to the shack to warn them."

"Uh-hm."

"And then you staged that little scene with the train schedule to make me believe they'd left town, but… what? You got them hotel rooms with the money I gave you?"

"Hotel rooms? Hell, nah.," said Jack. "They just stayed in town playing cards till I let 'em know the coast was clear. We was all right back there in the shack that night."

"Was Javier still there?"

"He was," said Jack with a chuckle. "Gonna be there a real long time, now, feedin' the worms 'neath the floorboards."

Wyatt felt the blood rushing to his cheeks. Why did these animals have to kill Javier, who never hurt a soul in his life?

"And by the way," continued Jack, "you didn't just give me that money. I earned it, breaking my back down there in that stinking hole…"

"But—how did you know we were gonna strike gold?"

"I didn't. I just heard them rumors in town about you hiding money around your house, and thought maybe if I spent some time around you, you'd let slip where it was. But you're a tight-lipped old cuss, Earp. To tell you the truth, if it hadn't been for that strike, I'd'a prob'ly killed you days ago."

Wyatt was angry with himself. He'd stepped right in it. Hayden, Jenkins, Hightower—they were the big pieces of broken glass; it was easy to spot their sharp, dangerous edges. But Jack… Jack was the tiny sliver you overlooked and couldn't see, the one that cut the deepest. Wyatt felt he'd gone soft with age; the younger Wyatt wouldn't have been duped so easily.

After they rode on a little farther, Wyatt asked, "So how do you see this going?"

Jack explained, "The other fellas are all waitin' back at your place with Sadie. Maybe she's already showed 'em where you hide your goods. But if she ain't, then you're gonna show us."

They were getting closer to Wyatt's house, there ahead on the flats, with the town of Vidal visible far beyond.

"Just one thing," said Wyatt gravely, "you didn't have to kill Mary and Henry."

After a pause, Jack said, "What makes you think it was me?"

"'Cause Hayden, Hightower, and Jenkins had an alibi, playing cards at the cafe. But where were you that night?"

"Well," said Jack, "you can blame yourself for that."

"How so?"

"You're the one who cut 'em in for a third. I just didn't see any reason to be sharing any of my money with a couple of yellow-skinned coolies."

Wyatt burned with suppressed rage. Jack was right. It was his fault. If he'd never come back to Vidal, his friends and Javier would still be alive.

They continued on across the hard desert, which appeared crimson now as the sun sank lower, turning the sky a deep blood red. Wyatt called back to Jack, "You do know I'm dying?"

"Dying?" scoffed Jack. "You stupid old coot! You're dead! All this time, you been running away from death, and death's been right here alongside you."

"Well, a dying man's got nothing to lose," said Wyatt, "so when I go, I promise I'll take you sons-a-bitches with me."

"Keep dreaming, old man."

As the sun went lower and the air turned cooler, Wyatt arrived at his home with Jack. Wyatt saw three other horses there, tethered to the porch rail. And at the opposite end of the porch, Earpie's leash was tied, the small dog leaping and squirming to get loose, barking in a frenzy.

Jack dismounted from his horse and pointed his pistol at Wyatt's head. "Get down," he ordered Wyatt. "Untie yourself."

Wyatt slid carefully off his horse. He loosened the lasso around his chest and let it fall. Earpie continued barking wildly. Wyatt shouted, "Earpie! Hush!" But the border collie kept yapping, and now that Jack was there, added some growling, as well.

Wyatt worried that Jack might plug Earpie, but the young turncoat was unperturbed by the racket. Waving his pistol at Wyatt, Jack commanded him, "Tie up the horses." Wyatt looped the horses' reins over the porch rail. Then Jack nodded at the door. "Now get inside."

Wyatt entered, Jack following behind. Hayden, Hightower, and Jenkins were in the dining area near the door. He immediately noticed that Jenkins had traded in his sombrero for a battered fedora, and recognized the hat as Javier's. Seeing it atop Jenkins's stupidly grinning face turned Wyatt's stomach.

Hightower stood immediately behind Sadie, keeping the end of a shotgun barrel just inches from her head. She looked worse for wear, her face bruised from being slapped around, the left sleeve of her blouse partially ripped at the shoulder, where she'd no doubt been grabbed as she tried to escape.

Hayden, holding his Browning pistol casually, pointed it at Wyatt. "Well, well, well!" he said in mock cordiality, a smug grin on his face. "Wyatt High and Mighty Earp. Come on in and sit a spell, why don't you?"

Wyatt saw that the cottage was in shambles—tables overturned, chair cushions ripped, cupboards emptied. The men had made a mess of it looking for his secret hiding place. With the sunlight fading, Jenkins struck a match and lit a kerosene lantern on the dining table.

"Power out?" asked Jack.

"Is now," said Hayden. "Some idiot took a warning shot at the missus and hit the fuse box." Jack cast a glance at Hightower, who shrugged sheepishly.

"Find anything?" asked Jack.

Hayden shook his head. "Whatever's here is hid real good. And this sage hen ain't talking." He gestured at Sadie, who kept her head low.

Jack sidled next to Wyatt and said, "So this is real simple, see. We know you've got a lot of cash and gold and Lord knows what else stashed 'round here. Show us where, and she gets to live."

Wyatt and Sadie locked eyes. Though she was trying to be strong, there was fear in her eyes, especially since the man she expected to rescue her was now equally helpless. But Wyatt just glared at the men, unwilling to show any sign that they had the upper hand. He had to keep his courage up to have a fighting chance.

He watched as Hightower rubbed his fingertips across the back of Sadie's neck. She shuddered, and a whimper escaped her lips.

"You mind taking your hands off my wife?" Wyatt asked in a steady, but commanding, tone.

Hightower snorted, "Or what?"

"Or you get might get into some trouble."

"Really? What kind of trouble would that be?"

"Considerable."

Hightower swept his hand over Sadie's back and then rubbed and squeezed her buttocks, deliberately provoking Wyatt. She closed her eyes tight, but her body trembled with fright.

"Where is it?" asked Jack. Wyatt kept quiet.

Hayden moved up behind Wyatt and hissed in his ear, "Listen here, you old coot—tell us what we want to know, or we'll take you out back and bury you up to your chin and let the ants feast on your head."

"Oh, naw," said Jenkins. "I ain't diggin' no damn deep hole. I say we just sling him up by his thumbs and watch 'em stretch out till they pop off."

"Sadists," scoffed Jack. "Why go to all that trouble when just a plain, old-fashioned hanging will do?" He pointed at Wyatt. "Except, not him..."—he pointed at Sadie—"...her." He saw Wyatt's face turn red with suppressed fury. "Think we touched a nerve," he said. Then he commanded, "Jenkins, go bring that lasso in out of the yard."

Jenkins took a few steps towards the door. Wyatt called out, "Wait!" Jenkins paused. Wyatt looked at all the men, one after the other, and then, with a resigned sigh, he walked over to the window and removed the board underneath. Reaching inside, he found the lockbox, pulled it out, and set it on the table.

Jack motioned for Hayden to keep Wyatt covered. Then he raised the lid of the lockbox. There was cash inside, and a couple of small pull-string bags. Jack took them out, laying the stacks of cash atop the table. Then he opened one of the bags and poured the contents into his palm—gold nuggets. "Holding out on me?" he asked.

"I expect you snuck out a fair amount when I wasn't looking," answered Wyatt.

Jack gave Wyatt a little grin. He carefully dropped the nuggets back into the bag, cinched it closed, and plopped it in the middle of the table. The other men were fixated on the paper money spread over the table as well as the bags of gold, but Jack reached into the inner pocket of his coat and pulled out a document folded in threes. Smiling, he said, "See this, boys? This right here's worth way more than anything in this lockbox you've all been so anxious to get your hands on."

"What's that?" asked Jenkins, craning his neck for a better look.

"Freedom," said Jack. "Freedom from ever having to work another job, freedom to travel and see the world, freedom to have the life of a king." He smoothed the document out with his palms and pushed it in front of Wyatt.

Wyatt quickly glanced it over. "A quitclaim?"

"What's that mean?" asked Hightower.

Jack said, "Means if anything happens to Mr. Earp, ownership of the Happy Days mines reverts to his partner, which would be me."

Wyatt just glared at him.

Jack said, "You were right about seeing a lawyer. I went out and found me a shyster this mornin' and waited while he drew up this here. All I need now is your John Henry." Pulling a pen from inside his coat, he held it out to Wyatt, saying, "Now sign it."

Wyatt crossed his arms. Jack nodded at Jenkins, who pulled his switchblade from his pants pocket, clicked it open, and held the blade at Sadie's throat.

Looking at Jenkins on one side of Sadie and Hightower on the other, Wyatt said coolly, "So what are you gonna do first? Cut her throat or blow her brains out?"

Jack looked at Jenkins and glanced down to Sadie's hand. Jenkins nodded, grabbed Sadie's hand, and flattened it on the table, splaying the fingers out, keeping a tight grip on her wrist. Then he jammed the knife into the table, between the two middle fingers. Sadie screamed, shuddering in fear. Gripping the knife's handle, Jenkins began bringing it down slowly to cut off her ring finger.

"Stop!" shouted Wyatt. Jenkins paused. Wyatt's eyes went from one man to the next, assessing the situation. "How about we make a deal?" he asked.

"A deal?" said Jack, incredulous. "We're ready to cut her damn fingers off, and you wanna make a deal?"

"I'll sign it, but only if you put away that knife and let her go."

Jack admired the old's man audacity. "Alright. Fine. You sign and we'll release her."

The tone in Jack's voice was hardly convincing. Wyatt said, "Put away the knife."

Jack nodded to Jenkins. Jenkins pulled the knife out of the table and let go of Sadie's wrist.

"I said put it away," Wyatt reiterated.

Jenkins scoffed. "You don't get to tell me what—"

"Just do what he says," said Jack. Jenkins, glaring at Wyatt, retracted the blade and put the knife back into his pocket. Jack then looked at Wyatt. "Your turn."

Reluctantly, Wyatt picked up the pen and signed the document.

"Smart man," said Jack. He pulled the quitclaim away from Wyatt and set it next to the lockbox.

Hayden, Hightower and Jenkins grinned gleefully at each other, all with eager expressions that said, "We're rich!"

Jack smirked at Wyatt, "Remember how you said it's all about the searching, not the finding? Well, the way I see it, it's a lot easier when somebody else does all the searching, and you just do the finding part." He chuckled, and added, "Guess you're not the only one who knows how to mine the miners."

"Alright," said Wyatt. "You got what you wanted. Now let her go."

"We'll let her go, all right," said Jack. "We'll let her go running out that door and see how far she gets 'fore we fill her full of holes."

Wyatt's eyes narrowed. "That wasn't the deal."

"C'mon, Wyatt," said Jack, mocking him. "You seem to know all those old sayings. Ain't you ever heard the one that says there's no honor among thieves?"

"I think it means something different than what you believe it does."

"Oh yeah? What's that?"

Wyatt looked at Hayden, Jenkins, and Hightower. "You fellas do realize that those papers mean when I'm gone, it all belongs to Jack? Your names aren't in there anywhere, so no matter what he promised, he doesn't have to give you squat."

"He ain't gonna cross us," said Hayden.

"Oh, no?" said Wyatt. "He's already incinerated two people just so he'd get a bigger cut. So what makes you so sure he won't get rid of you?"

Hightower grunted, saying, "Man's got a point."

"And that," said Wyatt, "is what they mean by no honor among thieves."

"Enough of this," said Jack. "Let's get to work."

As Hightower began to push Sadie towards the door, Wyatt grimaced, his hands clawing at his gut. He let out an anguished moan.

"What's got into him?" squawked Jenkins.

"Look at 'im squirm!," said Hayden. "Like a snail in a salt pit."

"The man's sick," Jack explained. "Got some kinda problem with his spindle."

"How 'bout we just put 'im out of his misery?" said Hayden, adding, with a glance at Sadie, "Both of 'em."

There was a noise from Wyatt's gut, a sound that was like a combination of water gurgling and a frog croaking. Oh no, he thought. Not now. Not when he needed to be stern and intimidating. Not n—

…and then he saw how he might possibly throw the men off-guard. He gritted his teeth, contracted his stomach muscles to put pressure on his abdomen. Beads of sweat formed on his forehead and dripped down his face. Then a wet stain spread over the front of his pants, and down his leg. He let out a long, relieved breath.

The men all looked at Wyatt, astounded.

"What in the good goddamn…" muttered Hayden.

"He pissed his pants!" exclaimed Jenkins. "Sumbitch pissed his pants!"

Jenkins laughed, and Hightower and Hayden joined in. "He's scared!" guffawed Hayden. He laughed so hard he couldn't help but double over, hands on his thighs. "We scared 'im!"

Wyatt and Sadie exchanged a quick knowing glance. Then, with lightning speed, Wyatt grabbed the back of Hayden's collar with one hand and his belt with the other and, with blazing fury, slammed Hayden's head into the edge of the table so hard that the table jolted. When he let go, Hayden, stunned and semi-conscious, immediately dropped to the floor, teeth gritting, both hands pressing on what felt like a skull split in two.

In that same instant, Sadie shoved the men next to her aside and pushed the table. The kerosene lantern was already teetering from Hayden's head being rammed into the table; now it toppled over, the glass well and globe shattering. The burning wick inside landed in the kerosene oil spreading over the table and instantly ignited it—it erupted in a big whoosh of flame.

Jack and Hightower instinctively reached through the flames to retrieve the gold and cash. The paper money caught fire, along with the quitclaim and Hightower's sleeve. Hightower slapped at it, as their jackpot went up in smoke.

Jack yanked down a curtain and flung it over the table to snuff out the blaze. When he looked up, Wyatt and Sadie were dashing out of the room, toward the back door. Jenkins got off a couple of wild shots—one chipping a door frame, the other smashing a window.

Jack yelled, "GET 'EM!"

Wyatt and Sadie rushed outside. Holding her hand, he started toward his car, but saw that there was a bullet hole in the fender, and the front tires were flat. Immediately changing course, he headed for the barn. Sadie moved as fast she could, limping on her injured foot, while Wyatt stayed behind her, shielding her and urging her forward. If Jack and his men began shooting, he wanted to be first in the line of fire.

They trotted inside the barn and went to an empty horse stall in the back, kneeling down. Sadie hugged Wyatt tightly. "Damn fool thing to do, puttin' yourself at risk like that."

"Just trying to save your life."

"For what? If I lose you, my life ain't worth living."

Wyatt put his hands on her shoulders, and nodded towards the desert in back of the barn, saying, "Run out there and hide."

"I ain't leaving you!"

Wyatt looked around, desperate. "Sadie, they're gonna kill us both!"

"I don't care." Wyatt looked in her eyes. He saw her fear, and her determination to stay by him to the bitter end. She asked, "Why'd you do that back there?"

"Do what?"

"Sign those papers! You gave 'em everything we've got!"

He cupped her face in his hands, and said, "You're everything I've got." He gave her a deep, forceful kiss. Then he said, "You stay here. I'll go up front and see what they're doing."

He trotted to the front of the barn and crouched down beside the door, behind a barrel, against which rested an axe. Wyatt pressed his face against the wall to get a better look through a space between the boards.

He saw Jack, Hayden, Jenkins, and Hightower come out of the house. Smoke trailed out the door after them, but it appeared the fire inside was out. Agitated, the men looked around, apparently trying to determine in which direction Wyatt and Sadie had fled. Jack gestured towards the barn, but Hayden pointed in the opposite direction, toward the desert.

"What're they doing?" asked Sadie, in a low voice.

"Trying to figure out where we went."

Wyatt kept watching as Jack and the other men conferred for a moment, and then Jack disappeared around the corner of the house. Hayden, Jenkins, and Hightower waited, Hightower rubbing his sore arm, Jenkins loading a gun.

"Let's run for the horses," said Sadie.

"Too late," said Wyatt. "They'll cut us down before we get ten feet." And then he saw something that made his heart sink. "Shit!" he said.

"What is it?"

Through the crack in the wall, Wyatt saw Jack come back around the corner to the men, holding Earpie. The dog squirmed, so Jack set it down—and it took off like a bullet for the barn. "Get ready!" warned Wyatt.

All the men except Jack ran toward the barn. Hightower followed in Earpie's path, while Hayden and Jenkins veered off to opposite sides, making flanking maneuvers.

Wyatt reached for the axe and snatched it up, crouching behind the barrel. Sadie, in the back, hid in the stall. As Earpie got closer to the barn, Wyatt said to her, "Call him!"

Sadie let out a short, sharp whistle.

Earpie dashed inside, pausing momentarily as he passed Wyatt. Sadie snapped her fingers, whistling again. Alert, Earpie ran to her.

Hightower jogged into the barn behind Earpie, raising his shotgun, and aimed for the stall where he assumed both Wyatt and Sadie were hiding. But before he could pull the trigger, Wyatt leapt up behind him and swung the axe with enough force to embed the blade in Hightower's back, between his shoulder blades, severing his spine. The big man pitched forward, bleeding profusely. As he fell, his arms went limp and let go of the shotgun. It bounced toward Sadie, who swiped it up and ran back for the cover of the stall, Earpie at her heels. Wyatt returned to the front and crouched behind the barrel, listening for any movement.

In the stall, Sadie held the shotgun close, trying to be as silent as possible. She heard footsteps outside, and saw a fleeting shadow pass by the open cracks between the wall boards. Someone was approaching Sadie's end of the barn.

Earpie barked.

There was a gunshot. A neat round hole appeared above Sadie's head, a shaft of sunlight catching the dust and shining through it. Then another gunshot, lower, closer to her, with another shaft of light beaming through.

There was the sound of footsteps crunching on the ground outside. Through the small spaces between the boards of the barn, she could see someone moving forward, the sound of his stalking footsteps coming ever closer.

And then he was right there, on the other side of the wall. It was Hayden. He leaned forward to spy through the higher bullet hole, his head momentarily blocking out the shaft of light. And in that instant, Sadie quickly stood, pressed the barrel of the shotgun against the hole and pulled the trigger. The blast blew out a chunk of the dried-out boards. And through the gaping hole, she could now see Hayden, sprawled face down, blood pooling around what was left of his head.

Jenkins, coming around the opposite corner, saw Hayden's body and panicked. Though he talked a good game, he was a coward at heart. He backpedaled away, exclaiming, "Oh, hell, naw! Hell, naw!" He dashed back toward the house.

Watching from his hiding place near the barn door, Wyatt saw Jenkins rush towards Jack. Wyatt took the opportunity to scurry over to Hightower's unconscious body. He patted it down, checking for any weapons, but found nothing. Looking up at Sadie, he could see that she was shaken by having killed Hayden and then having seen his dead, mutilated body. Quietly, he spoke her name—"Sadie?"

Terror in her eyes, lip trembling, she said, "One thing to think about killing a man. Something else to do it."

"He needed killing."

She saw Hightower, splayed out face-down on the barn floor, and asked. "Is he…"

Still speaking quietly, Wyatt asked, "How's that shotgun?"

"Empty," she said. That wasn't what Wyatt wanted to hear. Best as he could tell, Hightower didn't have any extra shells. "Stay there," he said to Sadie, and went back to his place at the front of the barn. He saw and heard Jack and Jenkins arguing.

"Where're you goin'?" Jack shouted as Jenkins approached.

"I ain't gonna stay here and get slaughtered!" yelled Jenkins.

"You will if you want your cut."

"Keep your goddamn gold! Ain't worth dyin' for!" Jenkins started for the front of the house, where the horses were tethered. Jack drew his pistol and fired. A puff of dirt kicked up near Jenkins' feet. Jenkins stopped, and looked at Jack with consternation.

"Draw," said Jack.

Jenkins knew he didn't have a chance, so he carefully pulled his gun from his holster and tossed it on the ground. Then he shifted his stance so that Jack couldn't get a good view of his right hand, which slid into his pocket.

Jack looked at Jenkins with disdain, saying, "Should 'a known you're a yellow-belly!"

Jenkins stealthily removed the switchblade from his pocket. Clicked it open. He spit in the dirt, hoping to create a distraction. Sure enough, Jack's eyes followed the spit. And quick as a flash, Jenkins flung the knife at him. It made a nasty arc and stuck at a slight angle in the dirt, a good foot away from Jack. Jack chuckled. And now Jenkins began to quake in his boots.

Jack raised his arm, twirling his gun, stopped it in his palm, and put a bullet into Jenkins' right eye. Jenkins crumpled like a marionette with its strings cut.

Seeing this, a chill went down Wyatt's spine. Jack didn't learn to shoot like that in a day. He was a seasoned gunslinger. He'd only been acting clumsy to fool Wyatt, and he'd succeeded. Wyatt had been hustled. He remembered his admonition to Sadie: stay at the table too long and you lose everything.

Jack spun his pistol around a few times and holstered it. There was an eerie quiet as he strode confidently toward the barn. He stopped

THE LAST STAGE

about twenty feet from the entrance. "Wyatt—enough of this foolishness," he yelled. "Come on out here and let's settle this like men."

Wyatt, crouching for cover at the barn entrance, yelled back, "Take the gold, Jack. Take the whole damn mine." Sadie came up behind him, holding Earpie.

"And have you huntin' me down? I don't think so." Jack paused, waiting to see if Wyatt would take the bait. When he didn't, he continued, saying, "You got any guns in there?"

"Why don't you come in and find out?"

"Don't feel much in the mood to be bushwhacked. I'd rather you come outside, where I can see you."

"Might have a long wait."

"Come on, now," said Jack. "Me and you both know there's only one way this ends. So, are we gonna do it the old-fashioned way, or do I have to burn your barn down to get you out here?" When Wyatt didn't answer, he tried a different tactic. "You know, I've heard a lot about Wyatt Earp over the years. Heard people call you a hero, and heard people call you a villain. But one thing I ain't never heard anybody call you is a damned lily-livered coward."

The words stung Wyatt. Sadie could see the anger flash in his eyes, the flinch in his jaw. "Wyatt, don't," she said plaintively, grabbing his bicep with her hand to hold him back. "Don't listen to him."

Jack kept up his verbal attack. "I 'bout decided you ain't got nothin' in that barn but an empty shotgun. And I'm fixin' to walk in there and empty my pistol in both of you. What do you say to that, coward?"

Wyatt wrapped his hand around Sadie's, and lowered his head. And she knew he'd made his decision. He yelled back, "Still got my pistol?"

Jack removed Wyatt's pistol from his coat pocket and tossed it forward. It landed a few feet from the barn entrance. Sadie tightened her grip on Wyatt's hand, saying, "Please, Wyatt. Don't. For God's sake, if you love me, don't go."

Wyatt's piercing blue eyes looked deep into hers. "It's time to end this." He gently kissed the back of Sadie's hand. "I love you," he said, and kissed her lips. Her lips pushed forcefully against his, and he could feel her hot tears as their cheeks pressed together.

He gently pushed her away and stood up. Taking a deep breath, and with a last look at Sadie, he walked out through the opening of the barn. Just a few steps over the threshold, he paused, standing erect with shoulders back, eyeing Jack across the open space.

"You know," said Jack, "I could just shoot you down right now and be done with it."

"You could," said Wyatt. "But then you'd spend the rest of your life wondering."

"Wondering what?"

"If you were faster'n me."

Jack nodded at Wyatt's pistol. "Pick it up," he said.

Wyatt went to his Colt, crouched down, and retrieved it. Rising back up, he inspected it, half-cocked it, clicked the loading gate back, and turned the revolving drum with his thumb. There was only one bullet in the cylinder. One single .45 caliber black-powder round.

Jack asked, "You need bullets?"

"I got one."

"Just one?"

Wyatt nodded. "It'll do."

Wyatt forced himself to focus on his surroundings. There was a breeze blowing from the north. He could feel it rustling his shirt and cooling the sweat on his back. Jack was standing downwind. That would work to Wyatt's advantage. Providing Jack didn't get him with the first shot, every time Jack pulled the trigger, there would be a hot cloud of black powder smoke blowing in his face and stinging his eyes.

Wyatt sheathed the pistol in his holster. Jack held his arms to his sides, giving his right hand a shake to limber up his wrist. He's nervous, thought Wyatt. Maybe scared. But nonetheless, Jack—whether out of courage or out of a foolish pride that wouldn't allow him to back down—said, "Now, let's see who's best."

Wyatt made one final plea. "I'm begging you, Jack—don't do this." Before he'd finished speaking, Jack's hand moved to whip the pistol from his holster.

For Wyatt, time seemed to slow down. Here it was again—the familiar dance with death. He dropped to his knee, snapping his own pistol up from its holster, fast as lightning, as Jack fired. There was a burst of flame and a great cloud of smoke from the barrel of Jack's gun, and a boom that echoed off the distant hills. The bullet passed through the space Wyatt's head had occupied mere micro-seconds before, slamming into the barn wall behind him. Still crouching, Wyatt raised his

THE LAST STAGE

gun, taking his time to look down the ten-inch barrel to the sight on its tip and take aim.

Meanwhile, Jack lowered his gun, and got off another shot. Another burst of flame, another puff of black powder smoke, another supersonic boom as the projectile left the barrel. The bullet whizzed past Wyatt's ear, kicking up dirt behind him. And now, with his elbow half bent and his eyes narrowed, Wyatt had Jack focused in his sights.

And Jack lowered his aim to get Wyatt in his. He fired.

In that same instant, Wyatt's thumb pulled back the hammer of his Colt, cocking it, then he pulled the trigger with his index finger. The cocked hammer snapped forward. The firing pin hit the primer, igniting the black powder in the cartridge and propelling the bullet out of the barrel with a belch of flame and acrid smoke. The kick of the pistol jolted Wyatt's arm upward, as the projectile sped out at 970 feet per second with a loud, sharp boom, and spanned the distance between Wyatt and Jack almost instantaneously. There was a brief burst of red mist just off-center of Jack's chest as the 230-grain lead bullet pierced a neat hole through his heart, followed by a dark crimson blossom spreading over his shirt.

Stunned, Jack dropped to his knees. "You cheated," he said, unbelieving. "You moved."

"No honor among thieves…" said Wyatt, "or gunslingers."

Jack grinned, then laughed. And then his face went slack, his eyes rolled back, and he pitched face forward.

It was over. Wyatt had done his duty. Sadie was safe. Jack was dead. And Mary and Henry and Javier were avenged. Still crouching, Wyatt tossed his pistol away.

He felt sick. There was a searing pain in his lower abdomen, a burning sensation from inside his body far worse than any he'd felt up to now. As he rose from his crouching position, Sadie—rushing toward him—stopped in her tracks and let out a gasp, eyes wide in shock as she saw the blood spreading from his punctured belly.

"Oh, god! Oh, god!" said Sadie, stunned. She threw her arms around him and sobbed. Then, getting her emotions in check, she took charge. "We gotta get you to a doctor."

She put Wyatt's arm over her shoulder and walked him as quickly as she could on her sprained ankle around to the front of the house, where the horses were tethered. She unhitched Wyatt's horse from the porch rail, got up in the saddle, and grabbed his arm to help him climb up after her. Once seated behind her, he leaned against her, arms tight around her waist, and they took off across the desert, making a bee-line for Vidal.

Earpie scampered after them.

Chapter 32

THE LAST STAGE

Wyatt and Sadie rode at a good clip, but not a full gallop. Earpie kept up with them, running beside the horse to stay out of the wake of the dust it kicked up. Wyatt slumped, leaning his cheek against Sadie's shoulder. He could feel himself growing weaker by the minute. Before they were halfway to Vidal, he began to loosen his grip around Sadie's waist. Sadie called back to him, "Hang on, hun."

In the bungalow, Wyatt writhed in pain, his hands clutching his gut. He gritted his teeth, grimacing and whimpering. A tear escaped the corner of his eye. Seeing him in agony, Sadie became frantic. She clutched Dr. Shurtleff's arm, pleading, "He's in pain! Can't you do something?"
"Anything I give him now'll just hurry the inevitable," the doctor said.
"Please…!" Sadie pleaded.
Dr. Shurtleff shook his head, and said adamantly, "I can't. I took an oath…"
Tears streamed down Sadie's cheeks. She wiped them away, took a deep, staggered breath, and released a long exhale. Wyatt—her man, her love, her world—lay before her, groaning in pain, his eyes clinched in agony. Imagining the torment he was feeling, she finally accepted what she had never wanted to face—that it would be selfish to prolong his agony. Even if he miraculously pulled through, he would be diminished, devoid of all the spirit and grit and fire that made Wyatt… Wyatt. She couldn't let him die like this. Not if she truly loved him. He deserved a peaceful end, and it was up to her to make sure he had one,

even though it meant she'd no longer have his security and protection, and would forever after be totally and irrevocably alone.

Her heart aching, she glanced at Dr. Shurtleff's medical bag, then looked up to him with wet, pleading eyes, and said, almost in a whisper, "If you can't do it, then... show me."

Sadie and Wyatt continued riding towards the town, visible on the horizon. The horse was slowed by the soft desert sand and the uneven terrain. She could feel the mass of Wyatt's body leaning against hers. His arm dropped away from her waist. The horse's hooves mired in the deeper sand of a slight incline, and the animal slowed almost to a stop. Sadie snapped the reins, trying to urge it forward. The horse took a lunge forward, and Sadie could feel Wyatt behind her sliding off the saddle. She reached back to grip his sleeve, but it didn't help; he eased off the mount and onto the ground. She pulled on the reins for the horse to stop.

Lake stood away from Wyatt's bed, watching Dr. Shurtleff and Sadie at the bedside table, their backs to him. The doctor's bag was open. Dr. Shurtleff handed something small to Sadie, then stepped over to stand beside Lake—but unlike Lake, Dr. Shurtleff stood with his back to Wyatt, staring at the floor.

As Sadie turned around, Lake saw that both her hands were at her bosom, and in them was a hypodermic needle and a ligature. She knelt beside Wyatt's bed, stared at him through tear-stained eyes for a long moment, then bowed her head, saying a silent prayer as he continued to writhe in pain.

Then, raising her head and summoning every ounce of her resolve, she tied the ligature tightly below his bicep, and rubbed his inner elbow. A vein was barely discernible. She took a deep breath, steadying her hands long enough to inject him with the fluid from the hypodermic needle.

The deed done, she dropped the needle onto the floor and loosened the ligature. Scrunching her eyes tight, she vainly tried to hold back the tears, her hands shaking, and finally let out a howl of soul-searing pain. Then she lowered her head to the pillow, resting it against Wyatt's.

THE LAST STAGE

Wyatt felt Sadie pull him tighter into her embrace, her forehead against his, repeating, "No!.... No!" He was losing sensation in his legs, feeling a chill.

Sadie wrapped her hand around his wrist, felt his weak pulse.

His skin was clammy.

Sadie wrapped her hand around Wyatt's wrist, trying, and failing, to hold back her tears. "He's cold," she said in a quavering voice. "He's cold!"

Dr. Shurtleff pressed his stethoscope to Wyatt's heart. The beats were irregular, increasingly faint. "His body's shutting down," he said quietly.

The desert sands grew colder as the sun descended behind the distant mountains. Sadie cradled Wyatt in her arms, saying, "Hold on, Shug! Hold on."

Wyatt looked up into her eyes, and said, in a weak voice, "Tell me you'll be all right."

"How am I gonna live without you?" she said, sniffling.

Wyatt rested his head on her shoulder, and through half-closed eyes, he saw a faint cloud of dust on the horizon. It was the white stagecoach, drawn by four stallions at a gallop, getting closer.

Earpie circled Wyatt and Sadie, whimpering, as Sadie tenderly stroked Wyatt's face.

"Time for me to step away from the table," said Wyatt, his voice weak.

"No! You can't! You're my whole world!"

"You have to... let me..."

Sadie tried to hold back her tears, but her grief overwhelmed her. She saw the pain he was in, and she wanted it to end. Accepting the unthinkable, she held him tightly, tears raining down her cheeks.

"Alright, dear," she whispered. "Alright..."

Sadie hugged Wyatt close to her, tears streaming. She kissed his forehead and stroked his face, which was now peaceful, showing no pain.

She whispered, "Let go, hon."

Wyatt's breathing became raspy, labored. Knowing this was the end, Sadie held his hand in a tight grip.

Earpie was suddenly on alert as the stagecoach rolled up close to them and stopped. Through half-closed eyes, tightly gripping Sadie's hand, Wyatt looked up at it. The stagecoach seemed almost to glow in the fading sunlight.

Wyatt gasped for air.
Sadie slowly climbed atop the bed, lying beside him. She pulled him onto his side, his head against her bosom. Cradling him in her arms, she stroked her fingers through his soft, silky hair. Through tears, she said, "Go on, Shug. Let go."
He curled his fingers into a fist, held close to his face. She wrapped her own fingers over his, and could feel his breaths on the back of her hand.
Erratic.
Staccato.
Long pauses between.
And she was terrified.

Sadie kissed Wyatt tenderly, her tears dripping onto his face. His eyes batted open. In a weak voice, he asked, "Remember what Hamlet said before he died?" Sadie shook her head. Simply and clearly, Wyatt answered, "Tell my story."

Wyatt concentrated on the sensations of this moment, staring up at the twilight sky, with its streaks of crimson and blue fighting vainly against the encroaching blanket of darkness. The more he did so, the more he felt the searing pain in his torso. Was it the pain of the bullet wound, or the excruciating pain of his heart ceasing to function?

The stagecoach door opened. Aurilla, Morgan, and Doc Holliday stepped out. Morgan and Doc removed their hats, as Aurilla stepped forward to Sadie and Wyatt.

Wyatt sat up straighter. Sadie hugged him tightly, her head against his chest, close enough to hear his heart beat. Except, chillingly, there wasn't one.

She remained sitting in the sand as Wyatt stood, and she held onto his hand for as long as possible, kissing his fingers. But Aurilla now had his other hand in hers, and gently guided Wyatt away from Sadie's arms. His fingers slipped from her touch.

THE LAST STAGE

Looking up at Aurilla, Sadie said, "Where are you taking him?"
Aurilla smiled at her and said simply, "Home."

Earpie crawled up the bed to Wyatt and Sadie, snuggling against them. He lowered his chin onto Wyatt's side as Sadie continued to cradle her husband, sobbing, feeling the cold creep up his arms and legs as his heart weakened and his blood stopped circulating.

Sadie remained crouched in the desert sand, tears streaming, watching as Doc Holliday, Morgan, and Aurilla climbed back into the coach. They all reached out to help Wyatt join them inside. As he took his place among them, sitting next to the window, Wyatt leaned forward to the open door and said to Sadie, "Say you'll be fine."

With her lips close to Wyatt's ear, Sadie whispered through her tears, "I... I'll be fine."
Wyatt took a long, deep breath. And then his breathing stopped. The room was heavy with the weight of acute silence. And after an unbearable wait, Wyatt exhaled a death rattle, his final breath escaping his lungs. Sadie sobbed so hard she shook, so intensely that she made no noise.

Wyatt kept his eyes on Sadie. He gave her a reassuring smile, and quietly closed the stagecoach door.
And the stagecoach rolled away.

Dr. Shurtleff and Lake watched as Sadie, tearful but mindful of her duties, straightened Wyatt's arms, closed his mouth, closed his eyes, kissed his forehead, and pulled the sheet over his head. She lit a fresh candle at the head of his bed.
Feeling he was intruding on an intensely private scene, Lake turned away and stepped toward the dining table. There, atop the completed puzzle, he saw the envelope with his name scrawled across it. It had been opened, the pages laying atop it. He picked them up.

Sadie collapsed in the sand, crying from a hole in her heart so deep nothing would ever fill it again. The stagecoach glided away into the crimson-gold sunset, across the white sands, kicking up dust.

Earpie chased after it.

Lake's heart leapt to his throat as he scanned the pages. It was the questions he'd typed out for Wyatt and given him some time ago at the beach, except now they bore Wyatt's distinctive handwriting in his responses beneath the questions, in the margins, and sometimes continuing on the back of the page. Lake put the papers back into the envelope, and slid it into his inner coat pocket.

Sadie walked past him, to a window. The rain had stopped but the panes were still wet, and as she looked outside, the dim sunlight coming through the glass cast shadows of rain streaks onto her stoic face, like tears falling, though she had no tears left.

In the fading light, Sadie watched as the stagecoach, with Earpie chasing it, receded into the distance, toward the brilliant ruby-red streak at the edge of the onyx-black sky. A wake of white dust powdered up into the air behind the stagecoach, obscuring it. And when the dust drifted away in the desert breeze, the coach had disappeared.

Earpie stopped, and sat.

And stared at... something?

Nothing?

Sadie raised the window. And now the tears came again, escaping from the corners of her eyes, rolling down her warm, flushed cheeks. Her lip trembled as she looked up into the pale blue-gray sky, where the storm clouds, pink from the rising sun, rolled back in.

The rest, she thought, is silence.

A cold breeze caressed her.

Her heart was numb.

Her Wyatt was gone.

Rain fell.

EPILOGUE

Wyatt Earp died January 13, 1929, at age 80.

After Wyatt's death, Sadie wrote to family friend John Flood, "I am sick grieving over my husband… I really don't care what happens to me as I have lost my best friend."

Josephine "Sadie" Earp died December 20, 1944, at the age of 83, still living in the same Los Angeles bungalow she had shared with her husband.

Wyatt and Sadie now rest together at the Hills of Eternity Memorial Park in Colma, California, a Jewish cemetery near San Francisco.

Stuart N. Lake's biography, *Frontier Marshal*, was published in 1931.

The book inspired several movies, including John Ford's *My Darling Clementine* (1946), and John Sturges' *Gunfight at the O.K. Corral* (1957).

On September 6, 1955, the weekly TV series *The Life and Legend of Wyatt Earp* premiered, starring Hugh O'Brien. Stuart Lake acted as consultant for the series, which ran for 229 episodes over 6 years.

By the end of the 1950s, the movies and TV program had cemented the mythic image of Wyatt Earp in popular culture.

Stuart N. Lake passed away in San Diego on January 27, 1964, at age 74.

And the legend of Wyatt Earp lives on...

ABOUT THE AUTHOR

Bruce Scivally is a lifelong lover of tales of the Old West, both on film and in print. Born in Plevna, Alabama, he moved to Los Angeles to attend the University of Southern California, and then worked in numerous positions in the film industry before becoming a teacher of scriptwriting and video production in Chicago. Since returning to Los Angeles in 2017, he has written several award-winning screenplays.

The Last Stage is his first novel.

ABOUT
HENRY GRAY PUBLISHING

"Select books for selective readers"

Henry Gray (1893-1960) was our grandfather. He lived his life as a farmer and carpenter in rural Tennessee, raising a family of seven children.

We've honored his memory by naming our publishing company after him, for like our grandfather, we strive to provide quality works at a reasonabl price.

fun and games from Henry Gray Publishing!

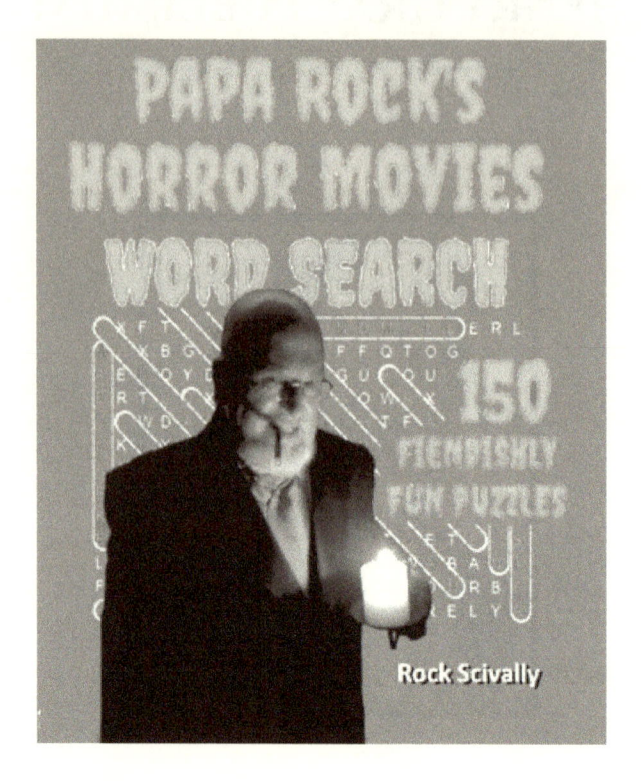

PAPA ROCK'S HORROR MOVIES WORD SEARCH
by Rock Scivally

"Enter... if you dare!"

Sharpen your stakes - er, pencils - to solve these unique puzzles designed for anyone who loves classic horror movies from the first Frankenstein film in 1910 to the giant bug movies of the 1950s. Remember Frankenstein? Dracula? How about King Kong? Godzilla? The Amazing Colossal Man? The Incredible Shrinking Man?

Here are 150 puzzles, each one pertaining to a specific film, where you can search for characters, actors, locations, props, memorable lines of dialogue, etc. If you love streaming iconic horror films, or grew up watching scary movies presented by a local horror host, or collected plastic model kits of monsters or read monster magazines, then this is the Word Search book for you!

for more information or to join our mailing list, go to www.HenryGrayPublishing.com

from Henry Gray Publishing
**the mesmerizing debut novel by
Emily Dinova**

Morning Falls Asylum.
Many women have been sent there.
None have returned.
Until now.

1922. Lorelei Alba, a fiercely independent and ambitious woman, is determined to break into the male-dominated world of investigative journalism by doing the unimaginable—infiltrating the gothic hospital to which "troublesome" women are dispatched, never to be seen again.

Once there, she meets the darkly handsome and enigmatic Doctor Roman Dreugue, who claims to have found the cure for insanity. But Lorelei's instincts tell her something is very wrong, even as her curiosity pulls her deeper into Roman's intimate and isolated world of intrigue...

for more information, visit HenryGrayPublishing.com

If you enjoyed this book and think others would, too, please kindly leave a review on your bookseller's website page for **The Last Stage.**